When I was a kid, my parents took me to all sorts of specialists to find out what was wrong with me. I wasn't afraid of anything, not spiders, snakes, heights, wild animals—nothing. That's when they figured out that if there was a fear gene, I was missing it. So I guess you could say I'm fearless. Like if I see some big guy beating up a little guy I just dive in and finish off the big one—and I can, because my dad trained me to. He figured if I was going to keep getting myself into trouble I might as well have the skills to protect myself. And my dad knows trouble—he's in the CIA. At least I think he is. I haven't seen or heard from him since, well, since something happened that changed our lives forever.

Anyway, you'd think that because I'm fearless my life would be pretty great, right? Wrong. In fact, if I had three wishes, one of them would be to know fear. Because without fear, I'll never know if I'm truly brave. That wouldn't be my first wish, though—my first wish would be to have my dad back. For obvious reasons. My last wish . . . well that's kind of embarrassing. I'd like to end my unlucky seventeen-year stint as Gaia-the-Unkissed. Do I have anyone in mind? Yeah. But I'm beginning to think it'll never happen. . . .

Don't miss any books in this thrilling series:

FEARLESS™

Available from SIMON PULSE

FEARLESS™

Double Edition #3
Run (#3) & Shock (#27)

FRANCINE PASCAL

SIMON PULSE

New York   London   Toronto   Sydney   Singapore

First Simon Pulse edition May 2003
Run text copyright © 1999 by Francine Pascal
Shock text copyright © 2003 by Francine Pascal

Cover copyright © 2003 by 17th Street Productions, an Alloy, Inc. company.

SIMON PULSE
An imprint of Simon & Schuster
Children's Publishing Division
1230 Avenue of the Americas
New York, NY 10020

 Produced by 17th Street Productions,
an Alloy, Inc. company
151 West 26th Street
New York, NY 10001

Fearless™ is a trademark of Francine Pascal.

Printed in the United States of America
10 9 8 7 6 5 4 3 2 1

ISBN 0-689-85926-0

Run and *Shock* are also published individually.

RUN

To Mia Pascal Johannson

Do you know what hell is?

I do.

It's not fire and brimstone. Not for me, anyway.

It's watching your hopes die.

It's watching the guy you love—the guy who makes you understand why that poor sucker built the Taj Mahal, why Juliet buried a dagger in her chest, why that Trojan king destroyed his entire fleet—making love to another girl. A girl you despise.

It's seeing your father—a man you believed was a superhero—for the first time after five long years only to discover he was a dishonorable creep show all along.

Hell is experiencing both of those things in one night. Hell is the way the ceiling looks above your bed when you open your eyes the next morning. Hell is the morning after that, when the ceiling looks just as hopeless, and you realize the pain

hasn't begun to fade and that
maybe it never will.
    That is hell.
    What is heaven?
    I don't know.
    I had an idea about it a cou-
ple of days ago, but that was before hope died.
    If you happen to find out,
will you let me know?

One of his
eyes was
black-and-
blue,
swollen
shut, and he
looked
frighteningly
pale. Weak.

save

sam

"HELLO? ANYBODY UP THERE?"

Gaia had just stepped out of the shower when she heard the voice floating up the stairs to greet her. She wrapped a too-small towel around herself, went to the landing, and leaned into the stairwell. It was a familiar voice, but not one she expected to hear before eight o'clock in the morning.

You've Got Mail

"Ed?"

"Yeah."

"Um . . . what the hell are you doing here?"

She heard him laugh under his breath. "Just fine, thanks, and you?"

At the sound of his voice, a minute ray of happiness filtered down into the blackness of her mood. She hadn't spoken a word out loud since Saturday night, since everything . . . happened. Now it was Monday morning, and her words were so far back in her brain she had to hunt around for them. "N-Not that fine," she responded hoarsely. "I had . . ." How could she begin to convey the true horror that was her life? "Sort of a rough weekend."

"What else is new?"

She heard both affection and wariness in Ed's voice. He knew a "rough weekend" for Gaia meant more than teenage angst—that it would involve things like firearms and kickboxing.

4

"Tell me about it over breakfast," he called. "I brought bagels."

Her stomach grumbled loudly. One thing this city had going for it—authentic, fresh-out-of-the-oven bagels. They almost made up for the high price of Apple Jacks. She glanced down at herself and the small puddle forming under her feet. "I'm wearing a hand towel and a few cups of water," Gaia said, wishing Ella hadn't left early this morning, so that she could be disturbed by this exchange. At least Ella had taken George with her wherever she'd gone. Gaia disliked offending George as much as she enjoyed offending Ella.

"I repeat," said Ed, laughing again. "C'mon down!"

Gaia rolled her eyes, trying to ignore the undertones of the remark. Two minutes later, she'd slipped into her most-worn cargo pants and a gray T-shirt and was on her way downstairs, her hair dripping water over her shoulders. On the landing, she paused to study the familiar snapshot that hung in a frame there on the wall—the photograph George had taken so long ago of Gaia and her parents. Gaia had tried to get rid of it, but Ella insisted it remain. She squinted at it, looking hard at her father.

Her father. She'd seen him two nights ago. Actually seen him and spoken to him. *And decked him,* she reminded herself bitterly.

After that he'd disappeared—again.

Her stomach churned, both with confusion and

with sadness. Why had he shown up here after all this time? What could it mean?

Was it some paternal sixth sense that had dragged him back into her life? Did he somehow know she'd been on the verge of ditching her virginity, and he'd crawled out from whatever rock he'd been hiding under all these years to give her an old-fashioned heart-to-heart talk on morality, safe sex, and self-control?

Or was it just one more whacked-out coincidence in her life?

She leaned closer to the photo and stared into his eyes.

They appeared to be soft, kind, intelligent eyes—and the smile looked genuine. The man she'd met on Saturday night had not seemed genuine at all. The warmth and gentleness she saw in the picture had been missing from that man. He was different, somehow. Lesser.

Apparently abandoning your kid and living on the run could take a lot out of a person. In the kitchen, Gaia was met by the aroma of fresh bagels and hot coffee. Ed, who had positioned his chair close to the table, looked up from spreading cream cheese on a poppy seed bagel. "You didn't have to get dressed on my account."

She was annoyed at the blush his grin brought to her face. "Shut up." Her eyes narrowed. "How did you get in here, anyway?"

"Door was unlocked," Ed said. "You should really talk to your roomies about that. I mean this is a nice neighborhood, but why court robbery, or worse?"

Gaia collapsed into a chair. That was weird. George never left the door unlocked. Must've been another brilliant Ella maneuver.

"Do you think it's kismet that this place is handicap accessible?" Ed asked suddenly.

Gaia raised an eyebrow. "It's either kismet . . . or the building code."

"I'm serious," said Ed. "Do you have any idea how many places in this city aren't?"

She felt a pang of pity but squashed it fast. "So what's kismet got to do with it?"

"You happen to live in wheelchair-friendly digs. I happen to be in a wheelchair." Ed shrugged. "It's like the universe is arranging it so that we can hang out."

"The universe clearly has too much time on its hands." She sat down and pulled her knees up, leaning them against the edge of the table.

"Like lox?"

"Hate them."

"Then I'm glad I didn't buy any." Ed pushed a steaming cup of coffee across the table toward her. "Three sugars, no cream, right?"

Gaia nodded, refusing to be charmed by the fact that he remembered, and took a careful sip. She could feel him staring at her.

"You look like hell," he said, shaking a lock of brown hair back off his forehead. Suddenly he appeared to realize this was not a smart thing to say to a girl—any girl. "I mean . . . in a good way," he added lamely.

Gaia gave him a sidelong glance. "That's funny. I feel like hell." She took another, bolder sip of the hot coffee, letting the steamy liquid warm her from the inside.

"Now we're getting to it," Ed said, clasping his hands together and then cracking his knuckles. "You were unsurprisingly unfindable yesterday, Gaia. So let's hear it." He broke off a piece of bagel and pointed it at her. "Who was the lucky guy and how did the ceremonial shedding of the chastity belt go?"

Gaia ignored the bile rising in her throat, picked up a marble bagel, and took a gigantic bite. There was a reason she'd avoided Ed all day yesterday—the need to avoid forced emotional spillage. "Subtlety isn't exactly a talent of yours, is it, Ed?" she said with her mouth full.

"Look who's talking."

He had a point there. She studied Ed for a moment—the just-this-side-of-scruffy hair, the eager yet wary brown eyes, the dot of dried blood on his chin where he'd cut himself shaving. Gaia hated that she had to talk about this, but she did. She'd sucked Ed into the whole sorry situation when she confessed her virginity. Like it or not, over the past few weeks she had made Ed a friend, or something very close. He might as well know the truth.

Gaia closed her eyes. Shook her head. Sighed.

"It didn't happen," she said. And her whole body felt empty.

Ed dropped the knife onto the floor with a clatter. "It didn't?"

"Ed!" She opened her eyes and glared at him. "Think you can sound just a little more amused by that?"

"Sorry it didn't work out for you." Ed cleared his throat, and she could swear he was hiding a grin behind his steaming coffee. Some friend. "So what happened?" he asked.

Gaia took another aggressive bite of bagel. She chewed and swallowed before answering. "Let's just say I was witness to somebody beating me to it."

"Shut up!" Ed's eyes opened wide. "Gaia, tell me who we're talking about here. You can't keep me in this kind of suspense."

Say it, she commanded herself. Just say it. "It was Sam Moon."

A sudden shower of chewed bagel bits pelted Gaia's arms. "God, Ed! Food is to go in the mouth. *In*," Gaia said, brushing off her arms irritably.

"Do you mean you walked in on Sam and . . .

Heather?" Ed choked out while simultaneously attempting to wipe his mouth.

Somehow, saying it out loud gave Gaia a bit of distance. The words were vibrating in the fragrant air of the kitchen. Outside of her instead of inside. "Ironic, isn't it?" Gaia asked, flicking one last bagel wad off her elbow.

Ed looked as if he were watching his life flash before his eyes—backward and in 3-D with surround sound. Gaia had never seen his skin so pale. She'd forgotten for the moment that Heather meant something to Ed as well. A big something.

"Man." Ed let out a long rush of breath. His eyes were unfocused. "That had to suck."

It didn't suck. Sucking was getting busted for going seventy in a thirty-five-mile-an-hour zone. Sucking was losing a dollar in a Coke machine. Sucking didn't *hurt*.

"Could've been worse," she mumbled with a shrug. She wouldn't have believed it, except that it had actually gotten worse. The night had been full of mind-bending surprises. But she didn't need to share them now, if ever. They were highly dysfunctional family matters to be discussing over breakfast.

"What could be worse than walking in on the object of your seduction in bed with your mortal enemy?"

It was a decent question. Gaia was saved from needing to explain by the sound of the phone ringing.

Ed reached behind him, snatched the cordless from

the counter, then slid it across the table to Gaia. She hit the button and held the receiver to her ear. "Hello?"

At first, nothing.

"Hello?"

"Gaia Moore?"

Her eyes narrowed. "Yeah? Who is this?"

The voice was distorted, like something from a horror movie. "Check your e-mail." It was a command. Maybe even a threat.

She felt as if ice were forming in her veins. "Who is this?"

"Check your e-mail," the voice growled.

The line went dead.

Gaia was on her feet, running for George's computer, which, luckily, he always left on. When she reached the den, she flung herself into the chair and punched at the keyboard. Ed, maneuvering his chair through the rooms, appeared soon after.

"What's going on?"

Gaia was too morbidly curious to answer. She clicked the mail icon and stared at the screen as it choked out the early, cryptic shadows of a video image, and she tapped her fingers impatiently on the mouse as the picture emerged . . . slowly . . . slowly . . .

It was someone with his back to her, hunched forward. His surroundings were vague, too much light. Gaia reached for the speaker, in case there was audio. There was. Staticky at first. Distant, fuzzy, then clearing.

Clearing ...

"Maybe it's Heather, playing a joke," offered Ed. "To get even."

Gaia was so intent on the image she barely heard him. "I don't think so."

Over the computer speakers she heard his voice. . . .

"Gaia . . . ?"

Her heart seemed to freeze solid in her chest. No, no, no, no.

But the voice through the speaker repeated itself. "Gaia."

No! "Sam?"

As if he'd heard her, he turned to the camera, and suddenly there was Sam's face on the computer screen. One of his eyes was black-and-blue, swollen shut, and he looked frighteningly pale. Weak.

Ed angled his chair close to the desk. "Oh, shit."

Sam's face vanished, replaced by a blank screen, and then there was a blast of static from the speakers as the same distorted voice addressed her. "Gaia Moore. You can see from this footage that we have a mutual friend. Sadly, he's not feeling well at the moment. Did you know Sam is a diabetic? No, I would imagine you didn't. . . ."

Ed stared at the blank screen. "Who the hell is it?"

Gaia shushed him with a sharp hiss as a graphic began to appear on the screen—a message snaking its way from the right side, one letter at a time:

C . . . A . . N . . . Y . . O . . U . . .

The voice continued as the letters slid into view. "He's well enough for the moment, but around, oh, say, ten o'clock this evening he'll be needing his insulin, quite desperately. And that, my darling Gaia, is where you come in. You must pass a series of tests. You must pass these tests by ten o'clock tonight. If you do not, we will not wait for the diabetes to take over. If you do not pass these tests in the allotted time . . ."

The graphic slithered by: S . . . A . . . V . . . E . . .

". . . we will kill him."

S . . . A . . . M . . . ?

For a moment the question trembled there on the dark screen. CAN YOU SAVE SAM? Then the letters went spinning off into the infinite background, and another message appeared in an eye-searing flash of brightness. It read:

    You will find on your front step a videotape.
    You will play it during your first-period class.
    DO NOT view the tape prior to showing it in school.

Without warning, the e-mail broadcast returned, showing a close-up of Sam's beaten face, his frightened eyes, his mouth forming a word, and the word came screaming through the speaker in Sam's voice.

"Gaia!"

Then nothing. The image and the audio were gone,

and the computer whirred softly until George's sickening screen saver—a scanned-in photo of Ella—returned to the screen.

Gaia sprang up from the chair and flew to the front door, which she flung open. The early October air sparkled, and the neighborhood was just coming alive with people on their way to work and school. Gaia paid no attention. Her eyes searched the front stoop until they found the package.

She lunged for it.

Gaia had no idea who had done this. She had no idea why. But she wasn't about to ask questions.

In that instant, it didn't matter that Sam had had sex with Heather or that he didn't return Gaia's overwhelming love for him and probably never would.

Sam life was in danger. For now, that was all that mattered.

"WHAT ARE YOU DOING?" ED demanded, wheeling himself out from the exit under the stoop, afraid for a moment that the package might explode in her hands.

But Gaia had grabbed her ever-present messenger bag and was down

The Knight

the steps. Ed aimed his chair to the left, toward the sidewalk. He could barely see Gaia over the row of potted shrubs as she sprinted away.

He caught up to her three corners later. One good thing about being in a wheelchair—even New York drivers slowed to let you cross the street.

She was bouncing on the balls of her feet, waiting for the light to change.

"Gaia, hold on. You can't just go to school and put that thing in the VCR!"

She didn't turn to face him. "Watch me."

"What if it . . . I don't know . . . what if it starts spewing out poisonous gas or something?" Ed offered.

"This isn't a *Batman* episode, Ed!" Gaia spat out, glancing over her shoulder. "What do you think, the Penguin sent that e-mail?"

"No, but somebody just as wacko did!"

"Somebody who's got Sam." Her voice was grim. Determined.

"Yeah, I get that. But we need to think about this. You don't know what's on that tape." He shook his head. "Okay, I admit, toxic vapor is a little extreme. But this whole thing is freaky, and I'm just saying we should be careful."

"You be careful," she snapped. "I'll be quick."

"Do you *never* think before you act?"

"Ed! Listen!" She grabbed the armrests of his

15

wheelchair and leaned over to look him directly in the eyes. She was so close he could see the pores in the perfect skin around her nose. Her hair was still wet against her cheeks. "I don't know who is doing this or why," she said. "But I have to help Sam."

In the next second he watched, helpless, as she flung herself out into the middle of traffic. A cab swerved. A UPS truck hit the brakes. A bike messenger careened off a mailbox.

But she made it.

He expected her to go right on running, but when she hit the opposite sidewalk, she turned and looked at him.

It was probably the fastest look in the history of eye contact, but that look was loaded. It was part defiance, part desperation, and part apology.

"Go!" he shouted, his voice raw. "I'll see you there."

She nodded almost imperceptibly, then took off down the street.

He followed as fast as his confinement allowed. Thinking.

She wanted to sleep with Sam. Sam Moon. But she hadn't. It had taken complete self-control to keep from popping a wheelie in his chair when she'd confessed that. Saturday night had been torture—the thought of her in someone else's arms, of someone else kissing her, had kept him awake all night. Awake and angry and sick to his stomach.

Because he loved her desperately. In mind, in spirit, in body. He wanted her.

So what if she wanted Sam? Seeing him with Heather must have cured that, right? The fact that she was rushing off to his rescue, no questions asked, just meant she was noble. One more thing to love about her.

Ed's remark about the universe setting them up came back to him, and he cringed. Stupid. Childish. Pathetic.

Yet on some level he'd meant it. He'd found her, that first day in the hall at school. She'd been so lost, and so not wanting to be lost. Ed knew how lost felt. He'd felt it every day since he'd first sat in this chair. Every day he was set apart.

He approached school and entered the crush of people. He imagined Gaia in her first-period class-room, slamming the mysterious video into the VCR. What the hell is on the tape? he wondered, feeling panic press into him.

And if he had to, could he rescue her from it?

He smiled bitterly at the ridiculous image. Sir Edward of Useless Limbs, the knight in not-so-shining armor, rushing in to rescue the fair Gaia, Lady of Brutal Ass Kickings.

Remember that, pal? Three punks in one shot. And

without even having to touch up her lip gloss afterward. His lady had no need for a knight. And, anyway, knights rode horses, not chairs.

He broke from the pack of students and rolled toward the handicapped entrance.

As he did on every other day of the school year, Ed entered the building alone.

To: ELJ
From: L
Date: October 11
File: 776244
Subject: Gaia Moore

She is even more beautiful up close. And far
more dangerous. For now, we proceed as planned.
The trials have begun. We will test her limits. I
want to see how far she will go for this boy.
What she will risk. How much she is willing to
lose.

The boy suffers, but it is all in the name of
authenticity.

I have no doubt she will succeed on her own;
however, if any complications should arise to
impede her various quests, I will arrange for
assistance. Her safety, as ever, is of utmost
importance. She must not fail—for all roads lead
to me. Tonight I will secure my position in her
life. There is much to alter. Much to gain.

To: L
From: ELJ
Date: October 11
File: 776244
Subject: Gaia Moore

I understand what is expected of me. The note is already written and waiting to be planted. Other objects with regard to this aspect of the plan are also in place.

GN and I will leave the city early. He will not be there to help her or to interfere in any way. He will not suspect a thing.

Tonight I will meet the pawn and see that he is where we need him to be, and when.

Sam's face. Sam's bruised
face. It came out of that computer at me like a kick to the
teeth. And then he had to go and
call my name like that.

I wonder if fear feels anything like desperation. Because
that's what I felt when his voice
came reverberating out of those
speakers.

He called *my* name.

This probably sounds totally
inappropriate, but there was a
moment there . . . There was a
moment there when I was glad
he was calling *me.* And I can
think of only two possible
reasons why.

Reason #1. The kidnapper told
Sam he was zapping his image to
my computer, so who else's name
would he say?

But I doubt the kidnapper is
giving him any information pertaining to his rescue, so the
chances of his knowing he was
even being filmed are pretty

slim. Besides, he doesn't know about my . . . talents, or my weird life, so why would he be calling out to me for help? It's not like he'd expect me to be able to come crashing in and kick his captor's ass—which I would do in a heartbeat, if only I knew where he was. So that brings me to:

Reason #2. He's thinking of me. (Could it be?)

Thinking of me insofar as a guy in hypoglycemic shock (or whatever it's called when diabetics need insulin) who may also be suffering a concussion can think.

Like maybe he screamed "Gaia" because Gaia was the first thing that came to his mind.

Gaia. *Me.* Gaia.

I don't know.

What I do know, though, is this: As long as there's an ounce of strength in my body, I am going to do everything I

possibly can to do what that
son-of-a-bitch kidnapper challenged me to do.

I'm going to save Sam.

And when I find out who did
this to him, I'm going to take
the guy down.

She told
herself the
only thing

independent
film

that
mattered was
that she'd
passed the
first test.

"NO, MAN! NO, MAN, *PLEASE!* DON'T!"

CJ closed his eyes as Tarick lifted one rock-solid fist and slammed it against CJ's skull. His eye felt as if it had been dislodged from its socket, and his mouth instantly filled with blood.

Weird Shit

"You let her go?" Tarick shouted, coming at CJ again. This time he wrenched CJ's arm—the one in the sling. The one with the bullet hole in it. The pain shot through his entire body like an explosion, and everything went blurry. CJ sank to the grimy concrete floor on his knees and then fell forward, savoring the feel of the cold, grainy surface against his cheek. It smelled like burnt cigarettes and blood. CJ knew it was the last smell he'd ever experience if he didn't do something.

"Kill him." Tarick's voice.

"Now."

"No! No! Wait!"

He heard them loading the gun.

"I can still do it!" CJ shouted through the pain.

Suddenly he was being wrenched to his feet, and Tarick used one beefy hand to push CJ up against the wall by his neck. "We should have let you bleed to death in the first place, you useless piece of shit." Tarick spat in CJ's face, but CJ couldn't move a muscle. He just let the gob slide down the side of his nose and onto his chin.

"I can still do it," he repeated pathetically, choking on the words. Joey was hovering behind Tarick, gun clenched in his hand. He didn't even look sad or scared. He just looked ready.

Tarick released him and he fell to the ground, sputtering for breath. He bent over at the waist, thought better of taking his eyes off Joey, and forced himself to straighten up.

"Please, Tarick," CJ said, his eyes stinging. "Weird shit is always happening around this bitch. Guys with guns, like she's got a protector or something."

Tarick laughed, showing his yellowed teeth and flashing the stud that pierced his tongue. "This isn't a storybook, CJ," Tarick said. "She don't have a fairy godmother."

Joey cocked the gun.

"Please, man," CJ said, trying hard not to whimper. "Just give me one more chance. I won't let you down again."

Tarick's eyes roamed over CJ's broken and battered body. He sucked at his teeth, ran a hand over his shaved and tattooed head. He glanced at Joey, then looked back at CJ.

"All right, man," Tarick said with a quick nod. "You get one more chance."

CJ let out a sigh of relief and closed his eyes. Then Tarick's voice cut through the darkness, his breath impossibly close to CJ's ear.

"Screw it up again, and I kill you myself."

HEATHER GANNIS DID NOT WALK SO

much as float. With her delicate chin tipped upward slightly, she moved purposefully but gracefully through the posthomeroom

Floating

throng. The look of disdain on her pretty face was to remind the Gap-clad masses that she was, and would always be, their superior. Even if she didn't necessarily feel like it. They were the ones who'd elevated her to that status. She was the one who had to struggle daily to perpetuate the illusion.

She floated, seemingly high on her own significance, weightless in the knowledge that she, and she alone, had the best hair, the best blouse, the best ass.

She was Heather Gannis, too ethereal to simply walk.

That was how they saw her, anyway, and that was what they expected, maybe even needed. And she was the one they'd elected to provide it for them.

Sometimes she thought she'd be willing to chuck the whole popularity thing in a heartbeat. Other times, having swarms of admirers had its perks.

And so she'd float.

Today, though, she had to work harder than usual to pull it off. Today she was dealing with stuff. Big-time confusion. Insecurity—not about her beauty or her position at school, of course. Insecurity beyond the ordinary is-there-lipstick-on-my-teeth variety.

And Heather's self-doubt came in the form of the same pitiful little mutant who'd put her in the hospital. Gaia Moore.

What kind of name was that, anyway? Guy-uh. Sounded like a Cro-Magnon grunt rather than a name.

And Cro-Magnon girl had ruined everything. Shocker.

Saturday night had started out perfect. Then it had gotten even better.

She'd been in Sam's arms—securing what was hers, giving him what he wanted before Gaia had the chance to make an offer of her own.

Heather's motives for Saturday night had been part romance, part strategy. Sleeping with Sam would cement their relationship—take it to the next level. She was reasonably certain that Sam would forget Gaia completely if he believed Heather was committed enough to make him her first.

Sam wouldn't really be her first, of course—she'd lost her virginity to Ed long ago—but he'd *believe* that he was. She'd (briefly) considered telling him the truth, but decided "first" sounded so much more devoted than "next." Ed was her secret, and she was going to keep it that way.

But Gaia had her grubby little hooks in Ed, too. It made Heather's skin crawl to think about that. Ed followed Gaia around like a damn puppy dog.

She realized she was aching to see Gaia, maybe right now, in the hallway, where she could create some big, ugly scene that would make her look great and Gaia look even more pathetic than before.

She remembered with the small section of her brain in which she stored information about school that Gaia was in her first-period class. Fine. She could destroy her there just as easily. Smaller audience, but better acoustics.

Heather's mind spun (but she kept floating) and images of Sam, catapulting off the bed to chase after Gaia, burned in her mind. The Slim-Fast bar she'd eaten for breakfast threatened to come up. What had he been thinking? What was wrong with him, leaving her for Gaia, and just on the brink of . . . well, of everything?

But that bitch—that disgusting, creepy little bitch had shown up, and Sam had freaked.

On the upside, Gaia had looked absolutely miserable upon catching them in the act. Maybe now she'd get the message and back off. The girl had proof now, proof that Sam and Heather were the real deal. Of course, Sam's running after her might have given Gaia cause to wonder. . . .

Damn him! Why had he left? And why hadn't he called? That had been Saturday. This was Monday! No call, no personal appearance. She could have been home crying all weekend and he didn't even care.

A chill shot through her. What the hell had taken place when Sam caught up to Gaia Saturday? Had she said something, done something, to override Heather's sexual surrender?

Was there anything that *could* override sex for a guy? She doubted it, but still. Evidently Gaia had some weird power over Sam. Had she been able to use that power on Saturday, even as his hair was still tousled from Heather's own fingers?

Heather mentally checked her expression. No creases. No frowning. She had to look distant, aloof, as calm as always or else they might suspect. She lowered her eyelids slightly, pushed out her lower lip—sexy, sullen, unconcerned, and floating. Christ, this was getting old.

31

They called out to her, waved. Occasionally she'd reply, but not often enough to give them any substantial hope. And tomorrow she'd do it again.

And tomorrow. And tomorrow.

Shit! That reminded her. She had a Shakespeare quiz later this morning, and she hadn't even opened her notebook. What was it old Willie had said about the moon? The inconstant moon. Sam Moon. Inconstant, big time. Changeable. Fickle. And in love with Gaia Moore?

Maybe.

Heather entered her first-period class and immediately scanned the room to see if Gaia was there. To her amazement, the loser was actually present, actually had the nerve to show her face! Heather prepared herself to deploy her patented secret weapon—a look of death that could make even the thumb-heads on the wrestling team shiver in their sneakers—but Gaia seemed to be looking right through her.

Oh, this one was good. Most girls who found themselves on Heather's shit list would be groveling already. But this freak of nature had the audacity to diss her. On some level Heather was actually impressed. It was almost a relief to know there was someone who didn't shed all self-respect the minute Heather threw her a look.

Okay, so it was impressive. But it still pissed her off.

Heather slammed her books onto her desk, accepted some hellos from neighboring students, then noticed that the classroom television was on. The screen was blank—the same bright blue Tommy Hilfiger used last spring—and the VCR light was blinking.

Thank God! Heather thought. A video was about all she could handle this morning. Probably something about the Civil War. Wait. This was economics, not history. Okay, something boring about supply and demand, then. Perfect.

She wouldn't even have to watch. She could study for Shakespeare and write vicious things about Gaia on the desktop. And wonder if Sam was out of her life for good now.

And if he was, was he in Gaia's life instead? Losing him would be bad. Losing him to her would be unbearable.

God, did that little witch actually believe she could do battle with her? Did she think she was better than Heather Gannis? And if she thought she was, how long would it be before the rest of the people in this school—flock of sheep that they were—began thinking it, too?

She didn't want to think about this. Not now. She wanted to get her mind off Gaia and Sam. She'd allow herself one nasty piece of desktop graffiti, then maybe she'd watch the stupid video after all.

SITTING THROUGH HOMEROOM WAS

torture. What could the cassette possibly contain? Wicked neo-Nazi propaganda? Gang recruitment information? Or maybe something closer to home—a biographical account of her messed-up life, edited for the sole purpose of humiliating her in public? But since Gaia had no idea who'd kidnapped Sam, she couldn't even begin to pinpoint a motive, and therefore could not even venture a guess as to what purpose this video, this "test," might serve.

An Odd Angle

She was about to find out. First period. The moment of truth.

If anyone was surprised that the video was starting before the teacher was present, they didn't mention it. Someone at the back of the room hit the lights. Gaia glanced over her shoulder and saw it was Ed, who'd just arrived. He was supposed to be in English now, wasn't he? But here he was, for moral support.

First bagels, now this. She felt a small cyclone of warmth in her stomach. So this was what friends did for you, huh? Gaia squelched the warmth. She couldn't risk getting used to it.

Ed shot her a look that was part encouragement, part panic. She turned away fast.

The blue screen gave way to a sudden blast of snowy static, then the scene focused.

It appeared to be a wide-angle shot of the upper half of a bedroom. The room was dimly lit, but Gaia could make out posters on the walls, an NYU pennant, a wide window with the blinds pulled.

And there were noises.

The usual New York background noises, of course—distant sirens, car horns, blaring radios. But over those came the more interesting noises.

Sounds like soft growling and deep sighs, sounds that seemed to caress each other.

Now where had she heard that before?

And then the camera panned down, pulling a form into focus.

It was an odd angle from which to film. Even Gaia, with her lack of experience in both filmmaking and lovemaking, knew that. The subjects were unidentifiable. There was a broad back, encircled from below by svelte, ribbonlike arms that tapered into delicate hands and graceful fingers. But the camera angle was designed to provide no clear view of either face.

The noises deepened, grew urgent, began to resemble words.

"Oh. Oh my—"

All the air seemed to flee Gaia's lungs at once. She knew that voice. And now that she looked closer, the blanket covering the bottom half of the couple looked pretty familiar as well.

They, them, him, her.

Gaia gripped the edges of her desk. Shit! What should she do? Let it run? Or jump up (assuming she could actually get her body to jump, since she seemed to be paralyzed) and turn the thing off? After all, sooner or later she'd be making her own cameo in this film.

The class was catching on now, and the howling began. As far as Gaia could tell, they hadn't recognized the female lead just yet. The star herself, in response to the provocative remarks of her classmates, had only just looked up from something she was scribbling on her desktop.

The graceful fingers were now clawing at the broad back.

Out of the corner of her eye, Gaia could see Heather studying the screen. Heather's first instinct, it appeared, was to smile. Hell, it was funny! Funny, as long as it wasn't your inaugural sexual liaison being screened in first-period advanced-placement economics.

Gaia kept her eyes slanted in Heather's direction and watched as the perfect smile flickered once, then vanished. Realization flared in Heather's eyes just as her video incarnation was uttering her first line of dialogue.

"Oh my God . . . Sam!"

To which oh-my-God-Sam replied, *"Heather!"*

Busted!

Gaia snapped her attention back to the screen. Sundance, eat your heart out. Whoever this independent-film director was, he certainly had a flair for timing, because it was at this point that AP econ was allowed to enjoy the first close-up shot of the movie.

And it featured none other than Heather Gannis, perspiring elegantly, eyelids fluttering, flawless teeth clamped down on her lower lip.

The class exploded in reaction. Some of them shrieked in disbelief. Some laughed, some applauded wildly. Most just gasped. Heather, in a surprising gesture that made Gaia feel almost sorry for her, covered her face with one trembling hand and began to sob.

Gaia wondered absently if anyone had seen her stick the tape in the VCR. If they had, this could get really ugly really fast. As if it weren't ugly enough already.

Two of Heather's girlfriends sprang to her side, ostensibly trying to comfort her.

"Somebody eject it!" one of them demanded.

"No pun intended!" replied someone on a choke of laughter.

Another of Heather's sidekicks—a girl named Megan—got up and moved toward the front of the room to turn off the television. Was it just Gaia's imagination, or did Megan seem to be taking her sweet time getting there?

37

AP econ was treated to a few additional renditions of "Oh my God, Sam!" before the electric-green-painted acrylic nail of Megan's index finger connected with the off button.

Instantly the class shut up, as if some cosmic off button had been punched as well.

The room went completely silent. Silent, except for the muffled gulping of Heather's crying.

Shame washed over Gaia.

Worse than fear, she guessed. It had to be.

Suddenly Gaia found herself silently pleading with Heather to go: Run. Get out. The silence pulsed as she kept her eyes glued to her desktop, willing her sworn enemy to escape. The girl was a bitch, sure, and a monster. But nobody, not even Heather, deserved this.

And then, as if she had sensed Gaia's unspoken plea, Heather catapulted out of her seat and stumbled toward the door. Megan and the other two handmaidens went running after Heather, looking appropriately concerned. But just before Megan disappeared through the door, she turned and fixed Gaia with a glare that Megan probably thought was menacing.

She knew. Which meant that in about 1.5 seconds Heather would know, too.

Ed made his exit as well, and the teacher picked that moment to arrive, stepping through the door but looking over her shoulder into the corridor.

"What's happened to Miss Gannis?" she asked.

"I think she lost something," one of the boys answered, biting back laughter. A giggle rippled through the room.

The shame swelled. Who was the monster now?

"Turn to page thirty-four," the teacher said.

In the wake of the X-rated video they'd just seen, the teacher's lecture on inflation and upward trends incited a few scattered chuckles and snorts. But Gaia was barely aware of them.

Numbly she wondered what Ed would say. He might be furious with her. After all, he and Heather had a history. Or maybe he'd just say, "I told you so," which, of course, would be even worse.

She told herself the only thing that mattered to her was that she'd passed the first test, and that Sam was one step closer to safety.

She hoped.

GAIA HUNG BACK AFTER THE BELL,

High School Drama

until the classroom had emptied. Then she snatched the video and stuffed it into her beat-up messenger bag. She'd destroy it later. Crush it, or burn it, or something equally absolute. The last thing she needed was for it to wind up playing 24/7 on the Internet—the scene of her nightmares playing out for the global community's entertainment.

Ed was waiting for her in the hall.

So were Heather and a sea of salivating spectators.

Gaia took one look into Heather's very wet, very red, very livid eyes and considered walking right past her, rather than enduring the obligatory scene of high school drama that everyone was expecting. But Gaia stayed rooted in place. She'd done what she was about to be accused of. Some remote part of her was eager to clothe herself in blame. Maybe even needed to.

"Where did you get it?" Heather asked, her voice surprisingly even. "Where did you get that tape?"

"I found it," Gaia answered. True. There was the requisite murmur from the crowd at this stunning tidbit of noninformation.

Heather's perfectly lined eyes narrowed. "You're not even going to deny it was you?"

"No." Another murmur, this one louder.

"Are you going to explain?" Heather took a step closer. Megan and the other sidekicks exchanged a look that said things were about to get interesting.

"I didn't know what was on the tape," Gaia said with a shrug. Also true.

Heather let out a noise that was somewhere between a shriek and asphyxiation. "Tell me where you got it," she said. She was right in Gaia's face. The tangy sweetness of her perfume made Gaia's nose itch. The girl was brave. But then, she did have the entire school behind her. And she didn't know what Gaia was capable of. Not that Gaia had any intention of letting Heather find out—let alone the ever-growing crowd.

"I already told you," Gaia said.

And then Heather pushed her. It was the kind of push that normally wouldn't have affected Gaia in the slightest—had she been expecting it. But Heather had caught her off guard, and Gaia stumbled backward until her shoulders pressed into the wall.

The crowd let out a little "ooh." Gaia righted herself, standing up straight for the first time in recent memory.

Heather took the slightest step back, betrayed herself with the smallest flinch. Gaia was sure she was the only one who saw it.

"What kind of psychotic freak are you?" Heather said loudly, shoving Gaia again.

This time Gaia didn't budge. "The kind of psychotic freak you don't want to push again," she said under her breath.

There were a few things Heather could do at this point, and Gaia watched her face with interest as

Heather ran through the possibilities in a fraction of a second. Where would the roulette ball land?

Would Heather:

A) call Gaia's bluff and push her again?

B) lose her shit and run?

Or

C) back off with some catty remark, thereby making herself look like the bigger person and the victor?

"You're not worth it," Heather said.

So it was going to be C.

Good choice.

There was a disappointed muttering from the male contingent, a sigh of relief from the females. Heather backed up, fixing a wry smile on her face. "You do realize that your life at this school is beyond over," she said, then snorted a bitter laugh. "Not that it ever started."

The masses laughed and scoffed and made general noises of agreement.

Gaia said nothing. Moved not an inch.

Heather took this as cause to smile even wider, and turned to her friends. "Show's over."

And with that the crowd dispersed, punctuating Heather's threat with their own disgusted looks and comments.

Gaia didn't bother to look like she cared. She didn't care. Heather's idea of hell was social failure, but Gaia knew better. For Gaia, the ridicule of her fellow high school students was about as distressing as a hair in her spaghetti. Gaia took a deep breath. She'd let Heather have her moment. That was the best she could do in the way of an apology.

Now she could get back to what really mattered. Sam.

ED WAS THE ONLY ONE LEFT. ED

Close to Home

and the few hallway stragglers who'd unluckily been too late to catch the action.

"You were right," Gaia said sharply before he could open his mouth. "I shouldn't have shown it without a preview."

Ed shrugged. "You didn't know. You couldn't have known."

Gaia's shoulders slumped. "Heather ..."

"Good call not pummeling her, by the way," Ed said matter-of-factly.

"Yeah, well, she had enough for one morning."

Ed reached up, took Gaia's hand, and squeezed it. Gaia pulled away instantly, but Ed didn't even blink. "I wouldn't feel too bad about putting Heather in a compromising position if I were you," he

43

said. "I think that was more Sam's responsibility, anyway, if you know what I mean."

"Ed!" Gaia said tersely.

"Sorry." He raised his hands in surrender.

Gaia adjusted her bag on her shoulder. "Forget Heather. Here's what I don't get—the e-mail said that showing the video was a test. So what did it prove? I mean, what could humiliating Heather have possibly gained for the kidnapper? If the video made some kind of demand or threat, that would make sense. But this was just . . . humiliating. And cruel."

Ed nodded. "I know what you mean. It was more like a practical joke. A demonic one."

"Maybe the kidnapper just wanted to see if I'd follow directions," Gaia said, glancing over her shoulder at the rapidly emptying hallway. "Which brings me to—"

"To how the kidnapper is going to know what you do and don't do," said Ed, finishing the thought for her.

Gaia sighed. "I guess we can safely figure that I am under constant surveillance."

"Guess so."

Gaia sighed. "Creepy."

"Very."

"So where's the next test?" Gaia said, glaring at the grate-covered hallway clock. "If I have to jump through a bunch of hoops before ten o'clock tonight, why didn't they just give them all to me at once?" She was bouncing up and down again, raring to go. She didn't like this feeling of being watched, of being manipulated, of being out of control.

Sam was out there somewhere, suffering, and there was nothing she could do about it until these assholes decided to contact her. How was she supposed to handle this?

"I could be *done* by now," she said, watching the seconds tick by.

"You know what worries me?" Ed asked, his forehead creased. "Whoever this guy is, he seems to be striking very close to home."

"What do you mean?" Gaia wrapped her arms around herself. The anticipation was making her feel like she was going to explode through her skin.

"I mean you got lucky," Ed said, maneuvering his chair around a line of people waiting for the water fountain. "You went to Sam's room with a mission, remember? It could just as easily have been you on that tape, Gaia."

Gaia tightened her grip on herself. She hadn't thought of that.

"Who knows? Maybe it was *supposed* to be you." Ed lowered his voice as a group of teachers passed. "And that would mean that whoever planted the camera in Sam's room has a serious inside line on you. I mean, even beyond constant surveillance. It's almost like he can read your mind. This can't be just about Sam."

Gaia checked the clock again. "It's not like I know anything about Sam." *Except that I love him . . . and I hate him,* she added silently as the contents of the video burned in her mind.

"But if the kidnapper wanted money or attention or something, why would they contact you?" Ed asked. "Wouldn't they send a ransom note to his parents or something? This whole thing is pretty random."

Gaia stopped walking and stared at a crack in the cinder block wall just above Ed's head. "So you think it's about me." Not a question.

"You're the one with all the secrets, Gaia," Ed said, lifting his chin in an obvious attempt to arrest her line of vision. "Whatever they are."

Gaia scanned the hallway again. No one suspicious. Nothing out of place. "Aren't you glad I won't let you ask questions? You're safer not knowing."

"Somehow I don't feel all that safe." Ed started moving again, narrowly missing the open-toed sandal of an oblivious freshman.

"God! Where are they?" Gaia blurted, covering her watch with her hand as if she could make time stop. "What if they sent another e-mail?" She started bouncing again, as if she were a boxer psyching herself

46

up for a fight. "I can't just stand around like this. I have to find him."

They continued down the hall in silence, Gaia staring every passerby in the eye, glancing over her shoulder every third of a second. When she reached her second-period class, which she had no intention of sitting still through, the teacher met her in the doorway.

"Ms. Moore, I just received a note asking me to send you to the main office to pick up a package," Mrs. Reingold said with a vapid smile.

Gaia's heart gave a leap of actual joy. Good. Let's get on with it.

"Receiving gifts at school, are we?" Mrs. Reingold continued. "Do we find this appropriate?"

Gaia was about to tell the teacher exactly what we could do with our idea of appropriate when Ed pinched her leg.

"You must have left your lunch at home this morning," Ed said.

"Yeah," Gaia snapped, glancing at the withered old teacher. "My parents don't like me to go through the day without three squares."

When Mrs. Reingold closed the classroom door, Gaia spun on her heel and practically flew to the main office. Ed was right behind her.

She burst into the office, told the principal's secretary who she was, and was handed a sealed envelope.

Ed was waiting for her back in the hall. For a moment she just stared at the envelope.

"Please tell me you're about to read the nominees for Best Picture," said Ed, his face a little pale.

"I wish." Gaia leaned against the water fountain. She slid her finger beneath the flap and tugged, then pulled out a sheet of paper and began to read it aloud: "'Kudos on the successful completion of Test One.'" She looked up from the paper and frowned at Ed. "Kudos? Oh, great. So the guy's not only a maniac, he's a dork."

"A dangerous dork, Gaia. Keep reading."

Wrrrzzzzzzzz.

I am Sam Moon.

They said my name. I heard
them. Good, because maybe I forgot
it. Sam Moon, Sam Moon, Sam Moon.

Sam Moon.

Wrrrzzzzzzzz. Clank.
Wrrrzzzzzzzz.

They grabbed me. That much I
know. But who? Why?

Wrrrzzzzzzzz. Clank.

If that damned noise would
just . . . stop. It comes in
through a window I can't see.
That . . . noise. That . . .
grinding, scraping, scratching,
humming, rumbling.

WrrrzzzzzzClankWrrrzzzzzz.
NearFarAlwaysLouderSofter . . .

Wrrrzzzzzzzz. God! Numbing my
brain.

Not just the noise the questions my own questions I have
never wondered so hard it's
making me queasy all this not
knowing my blood is screaming
it's pounding in my temples I
can taste my own bile I keep

S
A
M

shaking and I want to peel my
skin off—

And I want to kiss Gaia.

Did I? Once? I did, I think.
She was soft. Her eyes took me.
Took me right in. Nothing bluer,
ever. Nothing so generous, or
alone and . . .

Wrrrzzzzzzzz clank wrrzz.

Shit, what the hell happened
to my face? Oh Yeah, Guy With A
Fist With A Ring. And the voice.
Not the Fist's voice, somebody
else's.

Pokey? Smokey? Low Key? Loki.

His voice, then the fist.
Damnthathurt.

Then how come they haven't
killed me yet? Or have they?
Maybe I'm supposed to be heading-
forthelight already.

Jesus, I'm losing it. I'm not
dead. Okay? *I'mnotdead*. Just . . .
focus. Right, that's right. Focus.

I amSam MoonI am Sam . . . Sam
I am.

Remember? Yes. I remember. I
am sitting on my mother's lap

yesterday last week now later.
Athousandyearsago. Letters are
new, words are strange. I am
small—

　　And safeAnd she is reading to
me. Something about . . . what?

　　Eggs? Yes. And Ham. Green Eggs
and Ham. Yes! And Sam I am.

　　I said,

　　Sam *I* am

　　and we laughed and laughed and
laughed.

　　God I want to laugh again.
Now. Right now.

　　*Wrrrzzzzzzzz clank
wrrrzzzzzzzz.* Laugh!

　　Do I remember how? Try. You
can't laugh if you're dead. Be
alive. Laugh.

　　Try. I must be laughing, because look how they're looking at
me.

　　Uhhg. Something burns my
throat then my tongue then my
lips. Laughing hurts.

　　And I'm vomiting. I'm puking.
That happens. Diabetic. Me.

　　It's warm on my chin slick

smearing down onto my shirt. It
reeks. Bad.

Someone comes, cleans me up.
Not gentle. Not like Mom did.

Mom?

Wrrrzzzzzzzzzclankwrrrzzzzzzzz.

The noise, damn it! It's mess-
ing up the story. Inahousewitha
mouseinaboxwithafox.

Wrrrzzzzzzzzz. Clank. Wrrzz.

Focus. Remember . . . how did
it start? Where was I before I was
here? What was I thinking before I
couldn't think? Focus . . .

Heat. And shoulders. And a
silky throat.

Heather. Me. Together. So together. Mmmmmm . . . almost good.
But I'm wishing beyond it. I'm
wishing for Gaia.

Wrrrzzzzzzzzz clank wrrzz.

And then . . . Gaia.

Gaia. Jesus. Gaia. No, don't go
. . . I'm sorry. And then . . .
running. Darkness and street-
lights and . . . where? Where did
she go? And then the arm across
my chest, the hands around my

throat.

And *wrrrzzzzzzzz* I'm here again, over the noise again. Still.

Oh, God. What the hell is happening? I don't know. I can't know. Knowing is somewhere else. And it all fades into the noise.

Wrrrzzzzzzzz clank.

Gaia?

Wrrrzzzzzzzz . . .

. . . zzzzzzzz . . .

His weird talent had been the cause of his wife's death. Would it now take his daughter's life as well?

daddy's home

TOM MOORE STARED AT HIS DESK, which was piled high with top secret government files, profiles of the world's most threatening terrorist groups, and all other manner of classified information. At this moment, though, the most important document on it was the unfinished letter to his daughter.

Father Knows Best

> *Dearest Gaia,*
>   *I was closer to you Saturday night than I've been in years. Close enough to be reminded that you have my eyes, your mother's nose, and our combined determination.*
>   *Close enough to see you nearly shot.*
>   *Close enough to save your life.*

The pen trembled in his hand. Thank God he'd been there. His bullet had only hit the punk's shoulder, but it had been enough. For the moment, at least. Gaia had gotten away. Maybe the bullet had sent a message: Back off. Stand down. Give up. Tom could only hope. And anyway, there were other dangers stalking Gaia—ones far more grave, far less predictable.

One, he knew, was a sick son of a bitch with

whom, forty-some-odd years ago, Tom had shared a womb.

The thought made him physically ill. His brother. His twin brother. A deadly psychopath with a vendetta against Tom. Loki. Tom knew the name from the research his outfit provided. But he would have known it, anyway.

When they were children, his brother had fixated on the idea of Loki, the Norse god. A Satan-like hero, consumed by darkness and evil. It was no wonder that as an adult, he would adopt this moniker, under which to pursue his hateful purpose.

Tom said the word out loud. "Loki." It literally stung his vocal cords.

But what about his own name, his undercover name? Enigma, they called him. Definition: anything that arouses curiosity or perplexes because it is unexplained, inexplicable, or secret.

He gave a humorless laugh. Yes. That I am, he thought. I am a secret to my own child.

The name was dead-on. Tom Moore was an enigma, even to himself. He had been from childhood, when his remarkable talent had begun to make itself known. Why was he able to think the way he did? Why was he capable of solving the unsolvable? Why could his brain take in seemingly random patterns of words and numbers and make sense of them?

He could decode, decipher, predict, and presume with terrifying accuracy.

In high school he'd discovered, much to his amusement, that he could open any combination lock in the building. `Handy for dropping little love notes into the lockers of cute girls` (his buddy Steve's idea, and favorite pastime). But even now, so many years later, he still wanted to know why he could work codes and riddles so easily. Not *how*. He didn't care how, but how *come*? Why should this responsibility have fallen to him?

And it was such an awesome responsibility. He had no formal, written job description. In fact, as far as he knew, there was not a shred of printed information on him anywhere. But in his own mind he'd boiled his job description down to one sentence: `Save the world.`

Perhaps it was better that this ability had wound itself into the double helix of his DNA instead of his twin brother's. At least, Tom told himself, he used his skill for good. If Loki had been born with such a knack . . . Tom shuddered to think about it. Genetic predisposition was a freaky thing.

Gaia, for example. `Her body chemistry was a source of even greater astonishment.` It was as if the gods had said, "Let's give her brains, and beauty, and charm, and grace, and physical strength, but hold the fear. No use mucking up the gene pool with that useful emotion."

Again, why?

Tom let out a long rush of breath, expelling the question with the air in his lungs. He'd wondered too hard, too long on that one. Ironic: The only other conundrum besides himself that he couldn't solve was his own daughter.

So instead, he hid from her. And hid her, too.

Apparently not so well.

Because now Loki had her in his sights. And that filthy little street punk, whose ignorance was surpassed only by his willingness to hate, was stalking her.

Tom looked down at the unfinished letter, ran his finger over the greeting.

Dearest Gaia,

His talent had been the cause of his wife's death. Would it now take his daughter's life as well?

Not while there was breath left in his body, he vowed to himself.

He picked up his pen, hesitated, then added another line to the letter.

Daddy's home.

Then, as he did with every other note, letter, and card he'd written to Gaia over the last five years, he stuffed it into a file drawer and locked it away.

Not sending it was hard.

But sending it would make things so much harder.

KUDOS ON THE SUCCESSFUL COMPLE-
tion of Test One. You are now to
commit an act of theft—a very specific act. George Niven has a computer disk that is of interest to us.
You will find this disk and drop it
off in Washington Square Park.
There will be a man there to receive

Slipping a Disk

it. He will be disguised as a homeless man and he will
have a cart. Bring the disk to him, Gaia, and do it fast.
Time, after all, stops for no man. Not even for Sam . . .

"They want me to steal from George," Gaia said,
tearing her eyes from the note.

"Huh?" Ed blurted, following along as Gaia hurried
down the hall, second period completely forgotten.

"What do they want one of George's disks for?"
Gaia wondered aloud. She'd practically forgotten Ed
was there. George used to be a Green Beret with her
dad, and they'd been in the CIA together. Were the
kidnappers somehow connected to the government?

Oh, shit. Maybe George still had connections.
Maybe he had nude photos on someone in the
Pentagon. Or maybe the disk simply contained his
recipe for barbecue sauce, and this was just another
sham test, to get her to prove she was in this 100
percent.

But what if it wasn't barbecue sauce? It was

possible. After all, she'd sensed that George had always known where her father was. He never said anything; it was just this gut feeling she had. And now that her dad was back in town . . .

Could something terrorist-related be going down in Washington Square Park? Something involving CJ and the late Marco, and all those other small-time white-supremacist swine?

And what did any of this have to do with Sam? Why hadn't they just taken her?

If only they had just taken her.

"Gaia, have you heard a word I said?" Ed's voice suddenly broke through her stream of consciousness.

"No," she answered, unfazed.

"Well, I was just wondering if we're forgetting about school for the day, since you seem to be heading for the exit," Ed said.

Gaia stopped as the automatic door swung open with a loud buzz. "I think you should stay here," she said, glancing briefly at Ed's wide brown eyes.

"No way," Ed said determinedly. "This is no time to become Independent Girl." He pushed his way through the door and out onto the street. Fortunately, the school administration was a tad lax about keeping an eye on the handicap exits.

"Ed, I'm not *becoming* anything," Gaia said, stomping after him. A brisk October wind caught her hair and whipped it back from her face. "I just don't want you involved."

"I'm already involved," Ed said, staring straight ahead.

"Ed—"

"Gaia."

The tone of his voice made her pause. She might as well let him come home with her. She'd derail his efforts then. Somehow. She couldn't have him out on the street with her, where he was an easy target.

"Fine," she said, unwilling to let him get the last word. "But stay out of my way." She sidestepped past him and walked a few feet ahead, making sure to keep up a fast pace.

Gaia and Ed were halfway to George and Ella's house before either one of them spoke. Actually, she would have liked his advice, but how could she ask for it?

A) That would make her look needy, and she'd rather be dead than needy.

And

B) He didn't have all the facts.

As far as Ed could assume, George's computer files were most likely limited to bank statements and hints on preparing tangy marinades. He didn't know about George's past, which might in fact turn out to be continuing on into his present.

The question: Was Gaia willing to turn over one computer disk, which might, perhaps (and that was one gigantic perhaps there), contain a bunch of classified government crap that could help some terrorist destroy the world?

Or could she just let Sam die?

"So . . . does this disk or file or whatever have a name?" Ed asked finally. "Maybe it'll give you some clue about what it is."

Loyal *and* smart, that was Ed. Gaia scanned the remainder of the note and found the name.

And stopped in her tracks.

The file was called Scaredy Cat.

ELLA HAD LEFT A NOTE. OBVIOUSLY

No Warrant

Gaia had overlooked it in the commotion of the morning.

She found it on the hall table when she barreled in.

Surprised George with a day trip to the country. We won't be home until late. Ella.

"Finally," said Ed. "Something goes your way."

"Lucky me," Gaia responded, crumpling the note and tossing it over her shoulder as she tore through the house toward George's office. The stupid note reeked of Ella's perfume—some one-of-a-kind, New Age concoction she paid an arm and a leg for. Some freaky witchlike person in Soho produced it exclusively for her. It smelled like dead roses on fire and it made Gaia gag.

Gaia headed straight for the disk organizer on George's desk and quickly flipped through the contents. Nothing promising.

Like there was really going to be a disk marked Scaredy Cat in big red letters. Like anything could be that easy. Gaia pulled out a drawer and dumped the contents on the desk. Papers flew everywhere, and pencils, paper clips, and tacks scattered across the smooth wooden surface. A pair of worry beads hit the floor and rolled noisily into the corner.

"George is gonna love that," Ed said, wheeling into the room.

"Somehow neatness isn't my number one priority at the moment," Gaia said, rooting around in the mess. Again, nothing. Gaia groaned in frustration and went for the file cabinet.

Ed hit a key on the computer keyboard, reviving the machine from sleep mode. "Listen," he said, not taking his eyes off the screen, "I've become pretty proficient on this little modern convenience lately. I mean, until Arthur Murray comes up with swing lessons for paraplegics, there aren't a whole hell of a lot of ways for me to kill time."

Gaia didn't want to laugh, but for his sake she forced a smile.

"So I'm gonna hack around for a while and see if I can figure out who sent that e-mail," Ed said as the computer whirred to life.

"That's great," Gaia said absently. Great was an overstatement, but Ed locked up in George's office was a lot safer than Ed out on the street with some psycho kidnapper running around.

Gaia quickly leafed through files with yuppie titles like "IRS 1994" and "Appliance Warranties." She slammed the drawer so hard a framed certificate fell off the wall and clattered to the floor.

"Gaia, you're scaring me," Ed said.

"This is taking too long," she said, bringing her hand to her forehead and scanning the room for possible hiding places.

How many tests had the kidnappers set up? What if she didn't have time to complete them all? That disk could be anywhere. His briefcase. His underwear drawer. A safe-deposit box at some random bank. It could be with George in the country, for all she knew.

She glanced at the captain's clock on the wall. There was no time.

Gaia slammed her fist into the file cabinet. It didn't hurt nearly enough. But it did knock down a picture of Ella.

The picture clattered facedown on the desk. Gaia studied it for a moment. Pay dirt.

The front part of the frame wasn't sitting flush against the backing. It was bulging slightly, and there was a gap between the two parts. Gaia turned it sideways, gave one good shake, and the next thing she knew, she was holding several floppies, one of which was labeled Scaredy Cat. God, what a lucky break.

"I'm outta here," she said, grabbing her bag.

"Wait!"

But she couldn't wait. If she waited, she might have time to think about the fact that someone out there wanted information on her. Her. Not some secret government stash of anthrax or the plans to the Pentagon.

Her.

Gaia Moore.

And Sam might die because of it.

She wasn't waiting around to think about that.

You've got a
nice ass,
for an

angel.

not
a
perfect
world

CJ LEANED AGAINST THE OUTER
wall of the arch that led into
the park. He liked that arch. It
was this big, beautiful thing—
a knockoff of some bigger
one from . . . where? France,
maybe. He'd probably know
if he hadn't quit going to
school.

One Daydream

Who cared what it was called, anyway? He just
liked it. He liked to look at beautiful things.

Like her.

Weird. He hated her. But man, he had some pretty
crazy fantasies about her. She pulled him. All that
strength and power wrapped up in all that soft sexi-
ness. It gnawed at something in him.

Sometimes he thought about killing her.

Sometimes he just thought about her.

There was one daydream in particular he returned
to over and over. In it, he'd be chasing her through the
park, and she'd be totally freaked-out scared, and he'd
grab her from behind—rough, but not enough to do
any real damage. Maybe just a small bruise. A last-
ing ache.

And he'd spin her around and her hair would get
all tangled up in his fingers.

Then she'd look up at him with those intense eyes,
those sky-colored eyes, and she'd start begging.

First just begging him not to kill her, but then it would change.

She'd be begging him to kiss her.

And damn, he'd kiss her right. And then . . . then she'd love him. And he'd have the power. All of it.

But CJ knew better. He knew to put hate in front of love every time. That was the way it was with him and his boys. Hate put you in control, but love controlled you. So he let his mind slither back to hating her.

And then, as if he'd conjured her, she was there.

Sun in her hair. And that body. Those lips . . . on his lips.

Shit! Enough of this bullshit. He had to breathe deep. Once. Twice. Steady. He had to remind himself that the one thing he wanted to do more than kiss her was kill her. He *needed* to kill her if he wanted to stay alive himself.

He adjusted the sling on his arm. The other asshole he wanted to kill was whoever the hell had shot at him Saturday night.

The bullet had punctured his biceps, and damn, it had hurt. Still hurt. One of his boys had cleaned it out and given CJ the sling. Can't go to the hospital with a gunshot wound. They report it to the cops.

But CJ was sure it had hurt even more when Tarick had twisted it that morning. That wasn't a pain CJ was going to forget anytime soon. And it was all because of the bitch.

CJ focused on Gaia.

She paused, tilting her chin in his direction, like maybe she could hear him thinking about her. His heart thunked in his chest. His hand clenched into a fist. But she didn't see him. She kept walking.

Why wasn't she in school? This chick was damned unpredictable.

He watched her walk for a moment, liking the way her hips moved, imagining kicking her hard in the stomach. In some remote recess of his mind, he knew this made him a damn sick dude. In the one remaining brain cell that could still tell good from bad, he understood his thinking was damaged.

But he'd turned on the world, and right now she was his closest target.

OKAY, NOW *THIS* WAS A PROBLEM.
There were, on this crisp October morning, eight—count 'em, eight—homeless people by the fountain in Washington Square Park. And five of them were the proud owners of shopping carts.

Guardian Angel

Why hadn't the kidnapper foreseen this possibility?

Maybe he had. Maybe he just needed a little comic relief, and watching Gaia try to find the correct one was it. Will the real undercover operative for Sam's crazed kidnapper please stand up?

Well, at least she was able to eliminate the three cartless ones right off the bat. That left only five derelicts from which to choose.

The note had said a homeless *man*, hadn't it? Yes, it had. So the two bag ladies were out of the running.

Three remaining contestants. Gaia would need a closer look.

She clutched the disk in her pocket. She should have copied it. But Ed was at the computer, and if the files really were about her, there was no way she could let him see the contents. It would have taken too long to get him out of there, get everything copied, and clear off the hard drive.

Too much time away from the task at hand. Saving Sam.

She approached the first homeless man—a guy who appeared disconcertingly young to her. Thirty-eight, thirty-nine years old at the most. In a perfect world, he'd be walking his kid to kindergarten right now, grabbing a cab to his corner office on Wall Street, making the upright decision not to sleep with his secretary.

71

But this was not a perfect world, this was New York. And the guy was rooting through a trash can in search of his breakfast.

"Excuse me . . ."

He kept digging.

Gaia stepped forward. She could smell him now, ripe with his own humanity.

"Excuse me."

The guy whirled. "Get the hell away from me, bitch!"

Well, that was uncalled-for. So much for charity. She frowned at him. "I'm supposed to—"

"This is *my* trash can," he thundered, shaking a half-eaten apple at her. "Mine! So go 'way. Go on! Get out! Mine!" He bit the apple, then placed it inside a filthy old tennis shoe in his shopping cart (presumably to snack on later).

Yummy. Next?

Gaia made her way toward a slumped figure sitting on the ground. A crudely printed cardboard sign propped up in his lap read Desert Storm Veteran.

Well, that didn't take long, Gaia mused grimly. The Gulf War took place—what? Seven, eight years ago? She would have imagined it took at least a whole decade for one's life to fall apart so completely.

Gaia approached him, then bent forward and whispered, "Are you . . . looking for me?"

The guy looked up at her. "Yes," he said.

Thank God. Gaia reached into the pocket of her jacket for the disk. She drew it out, then hesitated. How could she be sure this was the guy?

"Yes," the man said again. "I am looking for you!" He reached out and grabbed Gaia's hand, wrenching the disk from her grasp with his grimy fingers.

Please tell me this is the right guy, she pleaded to herself silently. He grabbed the disk for a reason, right?

"I've been looking for you for a long time," the guy said. "You're the angel of the Lord, ain'tcha?"

And the reason was . . . he was totally insane.

Oh, shit.

"You've come to take me on to the Promised Land. I knew it the minute I saw that hair. That's the hair of an angel, all right. Only the Almighty Himself makes that color hair."

"Yeah. The Almighty and L'Oréal," Gaia snapped. She leaned down toward him. "Give me back the disk."

"No!" he shouted, clutching the floppy. "You've come to save me!"

"No. I've come to save Sam."

"So call me Sam." He was full of logic. "Just bring me on to heaven. Lead me there, angel. Take me."

"Believe me, mister, if I brought you to heaven, we'd most likely get jumped on the way." Gaia made a grab for the disk, but the guy was quick. He stuffed it into his grubby shirt.

"Give it to me," she demanded evenly.

"No! Not until you bring me to meet my Maker."

Gaia was starting to see red. Oh, he was going to meet his Maker, all right. He just wasn't going to like the method by which Gaia would send him there.

She pressed her fingers to her temples in frustration, demanding some patience from herself. She didn't want to have to pound the guy. He was already so pathetic as it was. She glanced around the park, hoping for inspiration, and found it.

"Okay," she said at last. "I'll bring you to meet your Maker. But if I do, you have to give me back my disk. Deal?"

The man nodded.

Gaia helped him up and started walking. He followed.

"Hey. You've got a nice ass for an angel."

Gaia almost laughed in disbelief. How could she have come to this? If her situation hadn't been so totally dire, she would have allowed herself a long, cathartic laugh. "The Lord's a real stickler for fitness," she muttered.

Gaia led him straight to one of the homeless people she'd eliminated in the first round. He was taller than her Desert Storm vet, with long, flowing gray hair and mismatched sneakers. "There he is," she said, pointing.

"That guy? In the ripped-up overcoat? That's God?"

Gaia nodded, hating to lie even under these circumstances. Hadn't somebody once said there's a little bit of God in every one of us?

"He don't even have a cart!" Gaia's companion was incredulous.

"Go figure."

The man scowled at her. "Listen, angel, you better not be shittin' me."

"Angels don't shit people." That much had to be true.

"He's drinkin' whiskey."

"Yeah, well . . ." Gaia shrugged. "He's been under a lot of pressure lately."

The homeless man hesitated, then reached into his shirt and withdrew the disk. Gaia snatched it before he could change his mind. She was about to run, but he spoke, and the emotion in his voice pinned her to her place. "Thank you, angel."

Gaia swallowed hard. "No sweat."

She took off for the fountain, putting her conscience on ice.

Her real contact was seated on a bench near it. She was beyond irritated at herself for not noticing the obvious signs before. So much for maintaining her wits.

The guy was straight from central casting, with his dirt-streaked face half hidden beneath a tattered hat, the shabby clothes, the wire shopping cart filled with trash bags and empty cans. What differentiated him from the others was that, unlike "God" with his mismatched sneakers, this guy was wearing a brand-spanking-new pair of expensive lug-soled boots.

Gaia approached him, feeling hollow. This man was one of the kidnappers. This man was in some way responsible for what was happening to Sam. He or someone he knew had inflicted pain on the person she loved.

She could have killed him, but that might get Sam killed.

There was no choice. For now she would do as they said. She wouldn't ask questions.

She reached into her pocket and withdrew the floppy disk, keeping her eyes firmly fixed on the visible lower half of the man's face. There was nothing recognizable. She memorized every detail in case she needed it later.

Cleft in the chin. Small scar on the jaw. Patchy stubble. Dark complexion.

Gaia moved closer, ready for even the slightest movement on his part. But he remained motionless, seemingly unaware of her.

She stepped up to the cart, dropped the disk into it, then turned to walk away.

"Tkduhplstkbg," the guy mumbled.

She stopped. "What?"

"Plastic bag. `Take it.`"

Gaia squinted against the bright sunshine. On the handle of the shopping cart hung a small plastic bag from a Duane Reade drugstore. She reached for it cautiously. It was heavy.

She recognized the weight, and a surge of disgust filled her.

"No," she said.

The man lifted his eyes to her and glared. "Take it."

Gaia felt her free hand clench into a tight fist. One nice solid jab to the bridge of his nose and `this guy would wake up in the next zip code.`

But she couldn't. She had to think of Sam.

So she took the bag with the gun in it.

STREET SONG
for Her

Sidewalk sweet, she stands alone
In night and streetlamp
While the world sweats summer and
sirens sing
And hate pours down from the city sky
like a wicked rain,
it wets us all
until we're soaked with anger,
and fear enough
to make friends of enemies
and choices that burn like the heat
like the blades, like the bullets
like the broken promise
that I make
Even as I watch her where she stands
two steps from evil
one step from me
But in this world
You walk with danger
or you walk
alone.

He could see
the slim
silhouette
of a
switchblade
in the
punk's back
pocket.

what the hell is this?

GAIA SAT ON THE EDGE OF THE
fountain and placed the bag between her knees. She stuck one
hand in, letting her fingers
brush the butt of the gun for a
moment before fitting her palm
around it. It felt dead and
weighty.

Partners in Crime

And familiar.

Gaia hated guns. But she knew how to use them.

Her father had taught her marksmanship. While other daddies were taking their nine-year-old daughters to toy stores and ice cream parlors, Tom Moore was bringing Gaia to the firing range, or far into the woods with a rifle and a rusty tin can for a target.

And she'd been a natural. From the start, she'd rarely missed, and by the time her father had finished training her, she didn't miss at all. Even now, years away from the experience, she could still hear the report of her last shot in the forest behind their home. The deafening explosion of the shotgun, the distant screaming *ping* of the bullet hitting the can.

It blended in her memory with another explosion and another scream.

Instinctively she let go of the gun. She pressed her fingers against her eyes to make the memory go away.

80

Think of Sam. Think of him.

She fished around inside the bag, in case there was something else. There was.

A note.

"Of course." Gaia withdrew the note and read it.

Within the next twenty minutes, you will commit a crime. You may choose your victim, but you are to limit your territory to this park.

"My territory?" Gaia snarled.

You are not to go easy on this victim. The enclosed is to assist you in this task. You will also be required to en-list the assistance of a young man named . . .

Gaia felt the presence beside her at the exact second she read the name.

Renny.

She looked up and blinked. Renny was standing there, staring at her. This kidnapper had some major timing going on.

"Did I scare you?" he asked, taking a small step back.

"Not quite," she said.

He swallowed, gulped.

"Please tell me you're done with those skinhead assholes," Gaia said, looking Renny hard in the eyes, her mind leaping from one suspicion to the next.

"I am." Renny looked down at his sneakers. "But it's not that easy," he murmured. "You try living on the streets without anybody to watch your back."

"You don't live on the streets," Gaia said.

He met her gaze, his eyes almost black. "I don't *sleep* on the streets, Gaia. But I live here."

She considered his reasoning. It was true. Renny had nowhere else to go. From the sorry state of his clothes and the random bruises he was always sporting, home seemed less than appealing. So he lived for this park, those chess tables. And in how many places would a thirteen-year-old Hispanic poet be accepted? She sighed, remembering some of the verses he'd recited to her. That edgy, soulful poetry of his made her feel as though he'd scraped the words up off the sidewalk and strung them together into something that sang.

He straightened his shirt with his still small, wiry hands. Sometimes his obvious frailty pained Gaia—especially when he was trying to act tough.

She put her thumb beneath his chin and nudged it upward, so that he was looking her in the eyes. "Who sent you here?"

He shrugged.

"Don't bullshit me, Renny. This is important. Whoever sent me this . . ." She held up the bag, noting the sincerely puzzled expression in his eyes. "You really don't know?"

He shook his head hard—a childlike gesture. It made her heart feel empty.

"Tell me what happened."

He sat down on the rim of the fountain and leaned forward to rest his elbows on his knees. "I got a phone call at home."

"What were you doing at home on a Monday morning?" Gaia asked, trying to sound stern. She could barely pull it off.

"I go home for lunch sometimes," he said, shrugging. She narrowed her eyes at him. "Hey, you're not in school, either."

The boy had a point.

"Go on," Gaia said.

Renny took a deep breath. "Guy says, 'Go to the fountain in the park.' So I go."

"Did he threaten you?"

Renny gave her a lopsided grin. "Not really. 'Cept his voice sounded like he ate nails for breakfast, so I figure it's better if I do what he says."

Gaia was about to ask if the nail-eating voice had mentioned Sam, then thought better of it. The less Renny knew, the less danger he'd be in—relatively speaking, anyway. If the kidnapper knew his name, not to mention his phone number, he was already in this up to his eyeballs, based merely on the fact that he was associated with her.

"We have to pass a test," she said softly.

"A test?" He whistled low. "That doesn't sound good. That's what the guys told me just before they handed me that pistol to point in your face."

Gaia considered inquiring as to what sort of punishment Renny had faced in the wake of failing that test, but decided against it. She didn't think she could handle that at the moment.

"We have to, uh, commit a crime."

His big eyes got bigger. He said nothing.

"Something random. Something sort of rough." She held up the bag. "There's a gun in here."

"Damn."

"Yeah, damn," she said, staring across the park at a couple of fighting pigeons. "We've got to do it here. Now."

Renny mulled this over for a minute or so. "Why?"

"I don't want to tell you. Just trust me. If we don't . . ." She finished with a shrug.

"I'm in," he said.

Gaia nodded. She wasn't sure if that was good news or bad news. She had to think, to figure out the best way to go about this. Maybe there was a way to make the crime look real without actually harming anyone. She did know there was no way in hell she was going to fire that gun. She'd wield it, swing it around at whomever she ultimately chose to hassle, but she would not pull the trigger. The kidnapper would just have to settle for that.

Her eyes roamed the park, landing finally on the chess tables.

And there he was.

She recognized him immediately. The sleazebag. The well-dressed, self-important slimeball she'd played once—and only once, because he kept grabbing her thigh under the chess table. His name was Frank, she believed. He was about forty-seven, forty-eight years old but looked at least sixty with all his wrinkles. Tanning-salon regular, diamond pinky ring, woven loafers, even in October. Jerk.

Gaia despised him. He'd hustled Zolov once, taking advantage of one of the sweet old guy's less lucid moments. Gaia figured Frank had walked away with Zolov's entire Social Security check that day, then used it to pay Lianne.

Lianne. Another pathetic story. Lianne was fourteen and a prostitute. Gaia was repulsed by her, but somewhere in her heart she felt sorry for her, too. The girl must have had one horrifying life to resort to turning tricks. And Frank was her best customer. Illegal, and disgusting.

The more Gaia thought about it, the more she decided she wouldn't entirely loathe roughing up Frank.

All she could hope was that wherever the kidnapper was watching from was far away enough to make Frank look like an innocent citizen, undeserving of Gaia's attack.

Without a word, she stood and made her way toward the chess tables.

Without a word, Renny got up and followed her.

TOM WIPED HIS GLASSES ON THE

inside of his shirt, then replaced them on the bridge of his nose. He was dressed blandly, in khakis and a denim shirt. Over his reddish blond curls he wore a suede baseball cap in dusty blue. The brim was tugged low on his brow.

Downright Nervous

He was invisible, leaning there against the tree. Watching.

Watching as his daughter strode purposefully away from the fountain. There was a scrawny kid with dark hair and golden skin tagging along with her.

But what was in the bag?

He lifted the brim of his cap a fraction of an inch and squinted at the plastic bag she was clutching. His heart took a nosedive when he realized what was in it. The outline of the object bulged unmistakably against the red-and-blue lettering of the pharmacy's logo.

Unmistakable to him, at least. Tom sent up a silent prayer thanking the gods for the indifference of New Yorkers. They would probably not even notice the girl, let alone the bag, let alone its contents.

She leaned down and whispered something to the kid. Pointed to the bushes. The kid nodded and they kept walking.

He kept his eyes trained on her as she crossed to the chess tables. A small, sad smile kicked up the edges of his mouth. Chess. His favorite game. And Gaia's. The first time she'd beaten him, she'd been only eight.

Tom stepped away from the tree for a better view, looking utterly preoccupied with nothing in particular, but seeing, feeling, every step she took.

She was approaching a middle-aged guy in an ugly designer suit who was seated on the losing side of a chessboard.

The kid looked a little jumpy. This bothered Tom. Street kids didn't get jumpy without a good reason. And this kid looked downright nervous. Maybe even scared.

Gaia didn't look scared. Gaia never looked scared.

What she looked, lifting the bag and pressing it to the shoulder of the ugly suit, was determined. Tom moved away from the tree.

Why was she doing this? Had his leaving poisoned her so badly that she'd taken up petty crime? Or was there more to it?

Of course there was. He knew that was the real burden of the life he'd given her: For Gaia, nothing would ever be exactly as it appeared. Nothing would ever be simple. There would always be layers, dimensions, motives, and questions. And horrible choices.

But why was she choosing this? What had brought her here? Had her confusion and loneliness made her an easy mark for a gang? Had his absence led her to join one? Had she, in search of something resembling a "family," been sucked into their evil world?

No. Not Gaia. The girl was smart and, he knew, good. Good at her core, good in her very essence.

This was something bigger. More dangerous. Something enormous must have been at stake. And clearly her sense of urgency was overshadowing her good judgment.

This was not robbery for robbery's sake.

But it was still robbery.

Tom had to stop her, but how? Could he create some kind of distraction—knock over a homeless guy's cart, perhaps? Draw her attention away from what she was about to do, long enough to bring her back to her senses?

He took two long strides in her direction, then stopped cold.

The punk. The punk he'd shot at the other night. His arm was in a sling, and he was running toward Gaia.

Tom shuddered. He could see the slim silhouette of a switchblade in the punk's back pocket.

He meant business.

Tom should have rid the world of this menace Saturday night, when he'd had the chance. But Tom had let his emotions affect his accuracy. He'd missed his opportunity.

And now his hands were tied. This was a crowded park, in broad daylight. So for the moment, much to Tom's revulsion, CJ would have to be allowed to live.

Tom wondered what Gaia had done to piss CJ off. Maybe the kid had come on to Gaia once, and she'd blown him off. With a creep like CJ, a broken heart could easily become a fatal attraction.

There were only two things Tom knew for sure. One was that for the second time in less than forty-eight hours, he was going to have to put himself between Gaia and death. The other was that he was willing to do it.

FRANK LOOKED UP FROM HIS NEAR-

Your Money or Your Life

defeat on the chessboard and raised one bushy eyebrow at Gaia. "What the hell is this?"

Gaia, her hand on the gun inside the bag, pushed the barrel harder into his shoulder. "*This* is a gun," she told him in a matter-of-fact voice. "Let's go somewhere a little more private."

"Oh, for Christ's sake."

Renny took off for the bushes that lined the east side of the park. "Follow the kid," Gaia said. Frank just stared at her, wide-eyed.

"Let's go," said Gaia, cocking the hammer.

"Jeez! Hey. Jeez!" Frank wriggled up from his seat and slowly followed Renny. His opponent, for obvious reasons, got up and fled. Two people at a table nearby scooted farther away. Gaia didn't have much time.

She shoved Frank in the back so he would hurry up, and he ducked behind the bushes. Gaia could only hope that the all-knowing kidnapper could see them back here and wouldn't miss her command performance.

Renny went to the edge of the bushes to keep watch, and Gaia grabbed Frank by the back of his collar, jerking him around to face her. He swore, swatting at her like a cartoon boxer, managing to clip her on the chin. She released him, used the hand that wasn't holding the gun to slap his face, then grabbed a handful of his greasy hair and pulled him to her.

"Didn't your mother ever teach you not to hit girls?" she asked, her nose practically touching his. He smelled like bourbon and chewing tobacco. Gaia had to struggle to keep from hurling.

Renny turned from his post. "Give us your wallet," he demanded in a forceful voice that sounded like it came from someone much bigger and older.

"You're supposed to be keeping watch," Gaia spat out. Renny turned around again.

"Give us your wallet," Gaia echoed.

"Yeah. Yeah, sure." Frank shoved a trembling hand into his breast pocket, withdrew a fat billfold, and slowly offered it to Gaia. For a moment it just sort of hung there between them, off the tips of his fingers.

It was almost too easy. Gaia had a feeling the kidnapper had been hoping for a bit more drama. The asshole had thought this out well. Do this too quickly and easily, and the kidnapper probably wouldn't be satisfied.

Take too long and she'd end up stuck in jail.

And Sam would die.

Gaia swallowed hard and narrowed her eyes at Frank. "Look petrified," she ordered. "Cry."

Sweat poured from his temples down his cheeks. "What, are you kiddin' me?"

"Does it look like I'm kidding?"

He gave a nervous laugh. "No, sweetheart. It don't."

His use of the word *sweetheart* nearly caused her to

slap him again. "Cry," she repeated dryly, casually lifting her knee into his groin.

"Uhhnnfff!" Frank doubled over. "You little . . ."

"I don't see any tears," Gaia hissed, taking hold of his fleshy neck and applying a firm grip to the pressure point.

"Ahhh . . ." Frank's face contorted in pain, then he let out a satisfactory sob.

Gaia didn't let go. "No more sharking Zolov or anybody else," she commanded fiercely from above.

"Yeah," moaned Frank. "Yeah. Okay."

"Gaia?" Renny said tentatively. "I think we have to go."

She let go of Frank's neck and took a small step backward. He straightened up cautiously and handed over his wallet.

"This never happened," she hissed.

To her surprise, Frank gave her a cold smile. "Aye, yo. You think I'm gonna tell anybody I got held up by two little shits like youse? A freakin' Rican who ain't got hair on his chest, and his partner, the prom queen?"

At that Gaia shoved the bagged pistol right under his chin. "You *ever* insult me like that again, and I'll kill you!"

Then she grabbed Renny and ran.

Prom queen, my ass.

CJ WAS HEADING TOWARD HER LIKE

Meanwhile, Back at the Arch . . .

a tiger running down a wounded gazelle.

Gaia had no idea, focused as she was on committing her felony. The guy in the ugly suit was doubled over.

But Tom's eyes were trained on the tiger. The tiger had his hand on the knife.

Tom sprang into action. He hurdled a park bench, dodged someone on skates, and connected with the tiger in a check that would have done Lawrence Taylor more than proud.

CJ hit the pavement.

Tom kept running.

And Gaia was gone.

THE COP SKIDDED UP TO THE CURB

Two Blocks Later . . .

and got out of the car as though he were auditioning for a walk-on in *NYPD Blue*.

"Hey! You two."

93

Damn.

Gaia could feel the change in Renny as he walked alongside her. He tensed, and his body temperature climbed at a rate that was actually detectable.

Fear, she thought. So those are the symptoms, huh? Her own body was cool, her heartbeat slow and steady. Even when faced with losing Sam, the guy who made the future seem worth living, still she didn't feel fear. She felt anger, determination, frustration. But no fear. If she couldn't feel fear for Sam, couldn't feel the heartrending, temperature-raising emotion that every other human being felt, could she really love him?

She was drifting. She had to focus. She had to make use of the capabilities she had, not mourn the one that was missing.

"Don't panic," she whispered to Renny. "They can smell it." Or so she'd heard.

"Young lady . . ."

Gaia turned and graced the cop with an innocent smile. "Were you talking to me, Officer?"

"Yes."

He was really young. It could have been his first day on the job. He had one of those square chins that was pretty much a prerequisite for joining the police force.

"Is something wrong?" Gaia asked. She made no

attempt to hide the plastic bag. Both the gun and Frank's wallet were still in it.

"I've just come from the park."

She looked suitably blank, patient. Renny, however, was bouncing, shifting his weight, preparing to split. She wished he'd just stand still.

"There was a mugging," the cop continued.

Gaia gasped. Nice touch. "Oh my God."

"Nothing too serious. Guy's wallet was stolen. Couple of eyewitnesses said it was two kids. Boy and a girl." He cleared his throat, an unspoken apology.

He hated this. Gaia could tell. A serious young law enforcement officer like him should have better things to do than hassle a couple of kids. Gaia could actually see him thinking this. She wasn't sure whether to be thankful for or repulsed by his obvious attraction to her. It might just get them out of this.

"Well, we didn't see anything," she said with a dainty shrug. "We weren't even in the park."

The cop nodded. "Why aren't you two in school?" he asked, as if it had just occurred to him.

"We're home-schooled." Gaia fired this out so quickly that even she believed it. "My mom teaches us." She put an arm around Renny's shoulder, pressing down ever so slightly, to get him to quit fidgeting. "This is my stepbrother."

Another nod from Glamour Cop. He hesitated, as if he might ask for their names, but didn't. He turned to get back in the car, then turned back.

"By the way, what's in the bag?"

"The bag? What's in the bag?" Gaia knew she sounded like an idiot, but the question had caught her off guard. She'd thought they were home free.

"What's in the bag?"

Nothing. Just a gun and a stolen wallet.

Then she heard Renny say, "Tampons."

It was all Gaia could do to keep from laughing out loud.

"Tampons," Renny repeated, snatching the bag from Gaia. He held it out to the cop, but his eyes were on Gaia. "I hope I got the right kind," he said in the most disarmingly innocent tone Gaia had ever heard from him—maybe from anyone. "Superabsorbent, you said, right? The deodorant kind?"

He turned his doe eyes back to the cop. "She gets embarrassed, see, so I go into the pharmacy and get 'em for her." He gave the bag a little shake. "Wanna check?"

The cop, looking embarrassed himself, shook his head. "No," he said with a slight croak. "Not necessary."

He ducked back into his car and drove off.

Gaia was gaping at Renny in disbelief. "Where'd you learn to lie like that?"

"I dunno." He threw her a crooked grin. "Home school, maybe?"

Gaia wanted to hug him, but of course she didn't. Instead she pressed her index finger forcefully into his chest. "Lying. Bad. Stealing. Worse. I only did this because somebody's life is in danger, and I had no other choice."

Renny opened his mouth, probably to ask whose life, but Gaia barreled right along.

"From now on, I want you to stay the hell away from that stupid gang. You don't need them to watch your back." She paused, hoping she could pull off the next sentence without sounding like a total Hallmark card. "You've got me, all right? I'll . . . watch your back."

She didn't wait around to see the expression on his face.

Media people who have a
problem with rap music, contro-
versial movies, or premarital sex
like to throw around the term
"family values."

I don't mind saying I don't
even know what the hell they're
talking about.

I mean, okay, I'm not an
idiot. I *know* what they're talking about—two parents with college degrees, kids in clean
sneakers, mass or service or temple (whichever is applicable)
every weekend, meat loaf on
Monday night, freshly cut grass,
and a minivan. Yeah, I know what
they mean.

I just don't know it from
firsthand, personal experience.
Anymore.

Consider my family, for example. My current one, that is.
Absentee (big time) father, well-
meaning concerned guardian,
bitchy wife of guardian, chess
geeks whose last names I don't
even know. That, at present, is

as close as I come to having a
family.

Can you imagine this crowd
sitting down to meat loaf and
mashed potatoes some evening?

And what about Renny? He's
been so brain-poisoned he actually thought he could purchase
himself a family (of violent,
hate-obsessed misfits) with a
bullet to my face. What makes me
ill is wondering how majorly
screwed up the kid's real family
must be in order for violent misfits to constitute an upgrade.

But the only family I can seem
to think about right now is
Sam's.

They've got to be somewhere in
the realm of decent, don't they?
Or else how could they have produced such a perfect human being
as Sam?

All right, so he's not
perfect—there's that 108-pound
wart on his ass (you know her as
Heather), and the guy's a master
of the mixed signal. But if he's

not Mr. Perfect, he's certainly
Mr. Pretty Damn Close.

The thing that's turning me
inside out now is the fact that,
for all I know, his parents are
sending him a package of homemade
peanut butter cookies baked by
his little sister (for some reason, I imagine he has one), with
a note saying that Uncle Mort
says hi and they'll see him on
parents' weekend. Maybe they are
at this very second dialing his
number, calling him up just to
say hi, and since he's not answering, they'll simply assume
he's at the library, studying for
some huge exam.

Maybe they're eating meat loaf
and mashed potatoes, and com-
plaining that he only calls home
when he needs money.

But the point is, their son's
life is in danger and they have
absolutely no idea.

That's killing me.

I mean, okay, *my* life is in
danger and *my* father has

absolutely no idea. But somehow
that doesn't bother me as much as
Sam's family not knowing.

I guess maybe because I'm figuring if they knew, they'd actually care.

Whereas if my father knew,
he'd have to stop and think to
remember who I was before he
could go back to whatever it is
that he's been doing all these
years and continue to not give a
shit.

It wasn't that she didn't want to pray for Sam. She just wasn't sure how.

she's no angel

IT DIDN'T MAKE SENSE.

Ella had dragged him all the way up to Greenwich, cooing and purring about some private time together, enjoying the romance of the countryside on an autumn morning.

Cozy in Connecticut

So what did she do the moment they arrived?

She dropped herself into a chair at the most Manhattan-like cafe she could find and ordered a double martini. At ten forty-five in the morning.

George ordered coffee for himself, then reached across the table and took her hand.

"This was a great idea," he said, hoping to divert her attention away from her drink. "You and me, the country . . ."

Ella nodded, glancing around the cafe.

"So what's on the agenda? Picnic on the Sound? A little sailing, perhaps?"

Ella sighed. "Oh, I don't know. Shopping, maybe."

"Shopping?" George raised an eyebrow. "Honey, you can shop anytime in New York. I thought the idea was to come up here and do something that involved grass and trees and quiet country lanes." He'd known when he married her that she wasn't exactly an outdoorswoman, but surely even the most pampered Manhattanite would be enchanted by the old-time New England charm of this town.

Ella wrinkled her nose. "Country lanes, George? Really."

"Sure. Me and you, the breeze, the sunshine. Some cozy little grotto somewhere . . ."

She looked as if she was considering it. "Well . . ." She sighed, lifting her dazzling eyes to his.

A wave of pure attraction washed over him. The truth of it was that he didn't really much care what they did, as long as they were together. He would try to talk her into doing something slightly more romantic than signing credit card receipts, but he wouldn't push. Whatever she wanted was, in all sincerity, fine with him.

So he was smitten with his own wife. So sue him.

The beverages came, and George let go of Ella's hand to allow the waiter to deliver her martini. When he reached for it again, she made a quick grab for the drink.

George sat back in his chair, telling himself she was just thirsty.

"What time is it?" she asked.

He checked his watch. "Close to eleven. Why?"

Ella lifted one shoulder in a shrug. "We'll take the two-thirty train back to Grand Central."

"Back?" George tore open a sugar packet and poured it into his coffee. "We just got here. Listen, there's supposed to be a beautiful little horse farm just a few towns away. I read about it in the travel section of the *Times*." He gave his wife what he hoped was an irresistible grin. "How about we shop this morning, then we can spend the afternoon cantering through some of those sprawling open fields we passed on the way into town?"

"Those weren't open fields. Those were people's yards."

He laughed. She didn't.

"C'mon. What do you say to a little horseback riding?"

She sighed again, causing her ample chest to swell against the satin of her blouse. "I'm not exactly dressed for riding," she said, then gently, seductively caught her lower lip between her teeth. "But if you really want to . . ."

She had him. And they both knew it.

"Shopping it is." George lifted the cup to his lips, tramping down the prickle of disappointment. A moment or two passed before he spoke again. "Have you noticed that Gaia's been acting a little distracted lately?"

"Distracted?" repeated Ella, as if she herself hadn't been paying attention. She looked over her husband's shoulder and out the window.

"I'm worried about her."

"Don't be." Ella traced the rim of her martini glass with one slender finger. "She's a teenager. They're a species unto themselves. What looks peculiar to us is perfectly normal for them."

"Normal, huh? Saturday night she came home sweating, panting, all out of breath—"

"Oh?" Ella pursed her lips in disdain. "Were you waiting up, George?"

"No. Well, not exactly. I just happened to be awake."

This time she did laugh. "And did you go to her? Ask her if all was well? Tuck her in?"

George shook his head. "Maybe I should have."

"She's seventeen!" Ella exclaimed in a patronizing tone. "And as far as the sweating and panting goes, well, that's exactly the kind of reaction a teenage girl would experience after spending hours teasing some poor boy in the backseat of his car!"

"C'mon, Ella," said George, his face flushing at her inference. "I don't think Gaia —"

"Oh, please! She's no angel, George, as much as you'd like to believe she is." Was it his imagination, or was there bitterness behind her voice?

"She's been through a lot," George said, eyeing his wife warily.

Ella rolled her eyes. "So you've said—often."

"I still think I should have talked to her the other night," George said, turning his profile to her and staring out the window. "She's lost so much." George had no idea what it was like to be a teenage girl. He could barely recall what it was like to be a teenage boy. But he knew what it was like to have someone he loved snatched away. He remembered that vividly.

"We're all she has," George said, finally turning back to Ella. "Maybe she's lonely—"

"Fine, George," said Ella, sighing. "Gaia's lonely. Not horny—just lonely. The point is, she probably would have told you to mind your own business, anyway." She paused, then said pointedly, "She's not our child."

At this George felt a familiar jolt—a longing. *Our child.* His, theirs, hers. His eyes searched Ella's questioningly.

"Oh, no." She held up her hand like a traffic cop and laughed again. "Don't even go there, George Niven. We've discussed it." Her other hand went to her firm, flat tummy. "This figure is not to be tampered with." She cleared her throat, then added, "Yet."

It was the most unconvincing "yet" he'd ever heard in his life. The waiter returned with more coffee for him and a fresh martini for Ella. Three olives this time, instead of two. Clearly he hadn't heard her remark about flat-tummy maintenance. Or maybe he just liked her.

They sipped their drinks without further conversation until the silence was interrupted by the bleating of her cell phone.

She flipped it open. "Yes?"

George watched her near-expressionless face as she listened. After almost two full minutes, she said, "Fine." Then she hung up.

"Who was that?"

"No one important," she said, plucking a plump olive from the toothpick in her glass.

George smiled teasingly. "No one important who?"

She looked at him. "If you must know, it was Toshi. My feng shui appointment has been canceled for tonight."

"Oh." George lowered his gaze to the table.

Toshi, huh? He wanted to believe her, but at the same time he had a very strong hunch that the call had had nothing to do with feng shui.

If Ella had any hunches regarding his hunch, she didn't show it.

She went right on drinking her martini.

And, he imagined, waiting impatiently for five fifteen.

GAIA STUFFED FRANK'S TACKY EEL-

Another West Side Story

skin wallet into the pocket of her faded sweatshirt jacket and shoved the gun into the bottom of the messenger bag. She took a deep breath and let it out slowly.

So she'd just conducted her first mugging.

It was not a good feeling. Gaia kicked at a crumpled-up McDonald's bag as she walked along the cracked sidewalk. She didn't like playing the part of a lowlife, even if the joke was on Frank.

But it was all about saving Sam. Gaia booted the bag into the sewer. The end justifying the means, and all that. Very Machiavellian.

So where was the next test? Once again she was left with downtime while Sam was sitting alone somewhere, suffering. Gaia felt her heart squeeze painfully as she remembered Sam's swollen face. She pressed her eyes closed, as if she could block out the image. Could she find fear—even a tiny shred of it—if she kept that image in her mind's eye?

This was torture. Maybe that was the point.

Trying to distract herself, she pulled out Frank's wallet again and flipped it open. There was a stack of bills inside, and Gaia pulled them out, counting quickly so that no street thugs would spot her and get any ideas. Three hundred and fifty bucks. Not bad. What the hell was she going to do with it?

When she looked up, Gaia noticed she had stopped right in front of St. Joseph's Church. That couldn't be a coincidence. She stuffed the money and wallet back into her pocket and ducked inside the church.

The place was perfectly quiet. There was no one in sight, and the sunlight streaming through the stained-glass windows revealed dancing particles of dust. Gaia found herself thinking how weird it was that all churches always smelled the same. Not that she'd been to very many—just enough to know they all had that same damp, smoky smell.

As Gaia wandered down the carpeted center aisle, she wondered how many times "Amen" and "Please, God" had been whispered in there. She got the feeling that if she listened carefully enough, she might hear the echoes.

It occurred to Gaia that if the kidnappers were still watching her closely, a deserted church would be the perfect place for them to attack. Gaia wished they would. It would be nice to get this over with. Kick some ass, find out where Sam was, get him, and then go the hell home. She was tired of this already.

There was an alcove toward the front of the church with a brass stand in it. On the stand were rows upon rows of stubby white candles in little glass holders, some red, some blue. Gaia smirked. Religious *and* patriotic.

Gaia knew what the candles were for. One night when she'd first moved in with George and Ella, she'd stayed up late, unable to sleep, and watched a rerun of *West Side Story* on TV. Natalie Wood, as Maria, had a little setup like this one with the candles and everything, right in her apartment. She was lighting candles and saying prayers.

Gaia went to the alcove and found what she was looking for—a worn wooden box with Donations painted painstakingly across the front. Gaia was pretty sure she was supposed to make a contribution before lighting a prayer candle. Someone had to pay for all that wax. Fine with her. She stuffed Frank's money into the box. She figured that $350 bought her the right to start a bonfire. But she wasn't exactly good with prayers. She wasn't even entirely sure of what religion she was supposed to practice. Her family was one big melting pot.

Next to the candles there were a bunch of skinny sticks, like extralong toothpicks, sticking out of a little pot of sand. The ends on some of them were charred.

Okay, I get it, she thought. You use a lit candle to light the stick, then use the stick to light your own candle.

She picked up one of the long, fragile sticks. Should she or shouldn't she?

Part of her felt like a serious hypocrite. But a bigger part of her felt she needed help from wherever she could get it.

She breathed in the church smell and thought about Sam. He didn't deserve this. No one deserved this. It was all her fault.

Then she poked the stick into the flame of one of the burning candles. What prayer went with that one?

she wondered. Had it been bigger than hers? Had it been answered?

She held the stick over an unlit candle and for a moment just watched the flame dance. Then, in spite of her $350 donation, she slammed the burning end of the stick into the sand and got out of there.

It wasn't that she didn't want to pray for Sam. She just wasn't sure how.

GAIA RAN ALL THE WAY HOME,

A New Video Release

hoping at every turn that she'd be stopped by another crazed fake homeless man with a note. No such luck.

She was ready to scream with frustration when she rounded the corner onto Perry Street and caught a glimpse of George and Ella's front stoop. There was a package. Time for a sprint. It seemed like forever before the box was in her hands, but the card had her name on it. And since she didn't belong to the Jam of the Month club or anything, she was pretty sure it was from her friendly neighborhood kidnapper.

She let herself inside (still no Ella, thank God) and took the stairs to her room in threes. After slamming her bedroom door and locking it behind her, Gaia pulled the Duane Reade bag out of her messenger bag and shoved it, gun and all, under her bed.

Then she tossed her messenger bag on her mattress, sat down at her desk, and opened the box. Wonderful. There was another video inside. And, of course, another note. This was getting old.

"Wonder what this movie's rated," Gaia muttered.

Gaia gathered up her stuff again and jogged back downstairs to the living room. She shoved the tape into the VCR and hit play.

Gaia's eyes narrowed as an image of her own face—so close up she could count her own pores—flickered onto the screen. The camera panned back to reveal her and Renny sitting by the fountain. She felt the blood start to rush through her veins, bringing an angry flush to her face.

Whoever had filmed this had been so close. How could she have missed him? How stupid was she?

Lowering herself onto the plush couch, Gaia watched as she and Renny crossed the park. It was like some kind of morbid home movie.

Isn't Gaia adorable, sticking that pistol into Frankie's shoulder, stealing his wallet, kneeing him in the groin?

She hit the off button, pulled the cassette out of

the slot, and proceeded to `tear its celluloid guts out`. After that, she did the same to the tape of Sam and Heather, which was still in her messenger bag. Then she unfolded the note that had come with the new tape, and read it.

Then she read it again.

Suddenly Gaia really wished she'd lit that candle.

You are doing surprisingly well. Your next test may not be so easy. Your friend in the wheelchair is to be your next victim. No violence is necessary. What we want is for you to HUMILIATE him. In public.

This humiliation, Gaia, is to be thorough. Uncompromised. You will emotionally destroy this young man.

And if you are wondering why . . . don't. You need no reason other than that I require you to do it.

IF YOU FAIL, SAM MOON WILL DIE.

TOP TEN WAYS TO EMBARRASS A
KID IN A WHEELCHAIR

10. Buy him a pogo stick.

9. Ask him how often he has to have his tires rotated.

8. Tell him you'd like to borrow his chair to guarantee your-self a good seat for *Cats*.

7. Attach a bumper sticker that reads Warning: I Break for Orthopedic Surgeons.

6. Totally fawn over him, and tell him how sorry you feel for him.

5. Totally ignore him and pretend he doesn't exist, like every-body else does.

4. One good shove down the handi-cap ramp.

3. Invite him to visit the top of the Statue of Liberty.

2. Ask him, "You must really feel
   like a loser during the
   national anthem, huh?"

1. Say something—anything—of a
   sexual nature, implying that
   it's not just his legs that
   are permanently limp.

  I can't believe I am even capable of coming up with these
things. It makes me sick. I make
me sick.
  How am I going to do this?
  Why are they making me do
this?

And then the world went surreal on him. Because Gaia was not Gaia.

like lox?

ED ROLLED HIS CHAIR OUT OF HIS

eighth-period class and into the crowded hallway. He'd made it back to school in time for the chem exam, which, unfortunately, had been even more difficult than he'd expected. With all of the in-

Seduction 101

sanity running through his head, he'd be lucky to pull a C plus. Of course, in light of what was happening to Gaia and Heather, not to mention Sam, a C plus didn't sound too terrible.

The good news was that the morning's searching had yielded major information.

It was the noise. A noise he knew. Or used to know.

He'd sat there in George's study for over an hour, viewing the video e-mail of Sam over and over. Just as he was about to pack it in Ed had noticed a noise in the background. It had been there all along. He couldn't imagine how he'd missed it, unless his eyesight was shutting down from all the staring and his ears were taking over. But as soon as he detected it, he recognized it.

Wrrrzzzzzzzz. Clank. Wrrzz.

It was a noise he himself had made for years. A noise he'd never make again.

And he knew there was only one place in New York

City where that noise could occur precisely the way it sounded in the background of the e-mail.

Wrrrzzzzzzzzz. Clank. Wrrrzzzzzzzz . . .

"Ed, man! Totally nice ride. You got serious air on that one, dude. Is this the most bodacious ramp in the city or what? Let's see it again. Go for it!"

Wrrzz. Clank.

Yeah, Ed knew the noise.

He pushed aside the memory and gritted his teeth at the way the crowd in the hallway parted for him.

At least it meant getting to a private place to use his phone faster, although the chances of Gaia being home were slim to none. If the girl was going to insist on being the `reluctant superhero,` the least she could do was invest in a cell phone.

Ed rounded a corner, and there she was. Right in the middle of the jostling, locker-slamming crowd. No dialing necessary.

His smile was automatic. (Not to mention the re-action from a more southern portion of his anatomy.) He waved, `relishing` the way he could see her eyes burning like blue flames, even from this distance.

"Good news," he began, but the rest of his greeting caught in his windpipe. She was striding—no, more like stomping—in his direction. Panic engulfed him. What had happened? Had Sam been hurt? Worse thought: Had she?

She stopped about a foot in front of him.

And then the world went surreal on him. Because Gaia was not Gaia. Everything about her said hatred—the rigidity of her shoulders, the tightness of her face.

"Hey," she barked. Yes, barked. It was a horrible sound, one he couldn't reconcile with the sexy, slightly raspy voice he loved hearing over the phone every night.

He stared at her, peripherally aware that people were slowing down, glancing their way. They were curious, but not committed just yet. School was over, after all. There were soccer balls to dribble, lattes to drink, boyfriends to kiss.

"Hey . . . freak."

Okay, now she had their attention. Ed opened his mouth to say something but hadn't the slightest idea what that something should be. His eyes slid over her carefully. Was she bruised? No. Drugged? Didn't seem to be. Brainwashed? Not likely.

What was going on?

She said it again. "Hey, freak."

Ed wished he could make himself meet her gaze. "Something I can do for you?"

A strangled sound came out of her mouth. It took him a second to understand it was supposed to be laughter.

"I doubt it," she said. "In fact . . ."

He noted that her fists were clenching and unclenching.

"In fact, I doubt there's anything you can do for any girl in this school."

This earned her an "ooh" from the onlookers, and she let her eyes fall purposely to his midsection. Ed felt scalded by the heat of them. His heart hit the badly scuffed floor. She couldn't possibly have just said that.

"So am I right, Ed?" she prodded. "I mean, we all know you're paralyzed from the waist down, but I'm curious. Does *anything* still work?"

Horror filled him as she came closer. She placed one hand on each of his chair's armrests and smiled wickedly. "Aren't you going to tell me?" she asked in a seductive tone he might have liked under different circumstances. "Or am I going to have to find out for myself?"

This piece of cruelty was rewarded with another "ooh."

Ed's brain vaguely registered that not one single son of a bitch in the crowd was making an attempt to defend him. But he didn't actually care about them. He cared about her. Too much.

And she was destroying him. Why?

His voice decided to work without his permission, and he heard himself say, a bit pathetically, "You're enjoying this, aren't you?"

"Yes," she assured him, still smiling. "I like torturing you. About as much as I like lox."

Lox.

"Like lox?"

"Hate them."

His heart surged. This wasn't real. She was faking. He pulled his eyes to hers at last. And she answered him. It wasn't a word, or an action, or even an expression. It was something deeply unnameable in her eyes.

This was her next test. For some inexplicable purpose, the kidnapper wanted her to hurt him. So be it. He'd play along.

Unfortunately, one of the male spectators chose that moment to get righteous. He stepped forward and said, "Leave him alone."

Ed wouldn't have believed it, but in that second he could actually *see* her resolve falter. One word from a pseudo-Samaritan and she was ready to crumble—her belief in this heinous charade was that fragile.

He felt her begin to back away, and he knew he couldn't let her. Too much was riding on it. Sam's life. More important, possibly her safety.

So Ed lifted his chin. "You wanna know if it still works?"

She blinked, clearly taken aback by this reaction. He kept his eyes glued to hers. *Don't quit, Gaia. I understand. Don't back down.*

One corner of her mouth twitched.

"Yeah," she said, her reluctance audible only to him. "I wanna know if you're still man enough to do it."

"Well, that depends." Ed reached forward, catching

her around the waist and pulling her onto his lap. "Are you woman enough to make me want it?"

The crowd's "oohs" rose to a crescendo now, and the applause that erupted froze her.

"C'mon, Gaia," he urged, knowing she had to bring this full circle to satisfy the kidnappers. "Make me."

"Fine, I will."

"Fine. So do it."

"Fine."

She leaned toward him—somehow the movement was at once gentle and violent—until her mouth was dangerously close to his.

"Principal!"

Suddenly the crowd scattered like rats, leaving Ed unkissed and alone in the hall with Gaia, who was sitting sidesaddle across his thighs. Now that they were alone, she made a move to exit his lap, but didn't get far.

"I think maybe you should get off me now," Ed suggested calmly.

"I'm trying!" Gaia snapped in reply. The zipper on the outer pocket of her cargo pants was caught on his sweater, and she was struggling to disengage herself. "I promise you this is not what I want to be doing right now."

He chuckled. "Yeah, you just keep telling yourself that, Gaia."

Ed could hear the principal's footsteps approaching the corner of the deserted hallway. Gaia let out a little yelp of frustration.

"Scared?" he baited.

"Annoyed," she said. She let go of the zipper and met his eyes for a second. "And very sorry," she added under her breath. "Not scared."

She tried jerking her leg sideways, and wound up straddling him.

"We might want to wait until *after* the principal's come and gone," he said.

The sound of the principal's whistling floated toward them. "I really think you should get off me, Gaia."

"Hey, nobody told you to put me on your lap," Gaia said calmly. She stopped struggling. Was she just going to let them get caught like this?

"Well, nobody told you to seduce me in the middle of the hall!" Ed said, trying to push her off him. She really was stuck.

"As a matter of fact," she hissed, lowering her face to his until their noses were touching, "you're wrong. Somebody did."

Then came the principal's booming voice. "Mr. Fargo! What is the meaning of this?"

Suddenly his head contained more than its allotted share of blood. Ed toyed with the idea of making a joke—something about extra credit for biology class—but decided against it.

"Miss Moore, kindly remove yourself from Mr. Fargo's . . . er . . . lap."

"If you get me a scissors, that just might be possible," Gaia said.

Sarcasm. Ed closed his eyes. Good strategy, Gaia.

Principal Reegan gave them his patented I've-seen-it-all-already-so-don't-even-bother stare. "I'll inform Ms. Strahan that she can expect you both in the detention hall," he said. He turned on his heel and walked off.

"Good one, Gaia," Ed said with a sigh.

Gaia stared after Reegan. "Do you think that means he's not going to get me a scissors?"

Heather
Gannis was
nothing if
not brave. **armor**
She proved
that every
day, didn't
she?

BY THE TIME GAIA AND ED ARRIVED

at the detention hall, Ed had a hole in his sweater, and Gaia had a chunk of blue cotton sticking out of a zipper on her thigh.

Detention

Apparently it was a slow day for the school rebels. The place was practically deserted. Of course, Robbie Canetti was there because Robbie Canetti was always there.

He looked up from his notebook when Ed and Gaia entered. "Hi," he said.

Ed said hi. Gaia didn't bother. Ms. Strahan glanced at them, then went back to correcting papers.

Ed wheeled himself to the back corner of the room, and Gaia flung herself into a chair, letting it scrape against the floor loudly. Her leg immediately started to bounce up and down. There was no way she was staying trapped in this box for the next hour.

She leaned forward, pressing her elbows into her knees to stop her legs from spasming. "I have two things to say," she said, looking Ed in the eye. "One, I didn't want to do what I did out there. I really am sorry."

"I know," Ed answered seriously. "What's the second thing?"

"The second thing is that I'm outta here." She stood up and started past him, but Ed grabbed her wrist.

"I know where Sam is," he said.

Gaia froze. Relief, confusion, and disbelief rushed through her, clouding her vision. She fell back into her chair. "What?"

Ed shot his eyes toward Ms. Strahan, then Robbie. When he was sure neither was listening, he whispered, "I know where they're holding him."

It was all Gaia could do to keep from screaming. She wasn't sure if she should hug him or kill him. "Why didn't you tell me this before?"

Ed actually blushed. "You didn't exactly give me a chance back there, G."

"Where is he?" Gaia demanded, feeling a strong urge to hold him upside down and shake the words right out of him.

Clearing his throat, Ed pushed his hands against his armrests and shifted in his chair. The gesture took forever. "He's in Tribeca. I actually pinpointed the street." Ed's expression was all self-satisfaction. Gaia was leaning away from hug and toward kill, but she kept her cool.

"How did you figure it out?" she asked in a whisper.

Ed leaned forward. "I just kept replaying the e-mail," he said excitedly. "By, like, the nine billionth time, I started to register this sound in the background. Over and over, this sound. And I recognized it. It's skateboarders."

"Skateboarders?" Gaia hissed, her shoulders so

131

tense they were practically touching her ears. "Ed, skateboarders can be anywhere."

"No." Ed shook his head. "This noise was distinct. It was boards on a ramp—an extreme ramp, with a major slope. And I know for a fact there's only one ramp like that in this whole city. I practically used to live there."

His eyes were glassy, and she could tell he really missed this home away from home.

Gaia would have loved to let him slip into a fit of nostalgia, but this wasn't the place, and it definitely wasn't the time.

"Ed."

He rubbed his hand over his face. "Anyway, I heard that sound in the background, and I realized that Sam's got to be somewhere in the vicinity of that ramp. He's gotta be in one of those buildings."

Gaia stood up. "So let's go."

"Go? Gaia, we can't go."

"Ms. Moore?" Ms. Strahan warned. Gaia didn't care.

"Why not?" she asked Ed. "Because we've got detention?" She looked around the room, holding her palms out like a balance, pretending to weigh the options. "Let's see. Sam's life, detention. Detention, Sam's life." She frowned at him. "I'm going."

She started for the door, but Ed reached out and grabbed her wrist.

"Ms. Moore," came another warning.

Ed actually yanked on her arm, tugging her backward and forcing her into her seat. She looked at him for a moment, stunned.

"No, Gaia. Not because we have detention," Ed hissed, his eyes flashing. "Think about it. You know the kidnapper's watching every move you make. You're at his mercy. If he figures out you're planning a search-and-rescue operation, he might just kill Sam on the spot."

"Yeah, but . . ."

"I know you want to swoop in there and rescue Sam," Ed said. "But you have to make sure you're thinking straight."

Gaia sighed in exasperation.

"Even if you could get to Sam without having the lunatic kidnapper catch on, how are you going to get him out?" Ed asked. "The guy's a mess, Gaia. He's weak, remember?"

Gaia felt as if her head were being pumped full of molten lava. She pressed the heels of her hands to her temples and squeezed her eyes shut.

"So why'd you even bother to tell me where he was?"

"Because I knew you'd want to know," Ed whispered, shaking his head. "Look, Gaia, I'm aware you're not going to let me tell you what to do. I'm just telling you what I think."

She gave the desktop a good slap. Everyone in the room jumped but her.

"Okay, I've had about enough of this, Ms. Moore," Ms. Strahan said in what Gaia assumed was supposed to be a threatening tone.

"You got something against hearing what I think?" Ed whispered with a grin.

"I've got something against being trapped in a classroom when I should be out doing something constructive," Gaia answered, standing again. "And don't ask me what, because I don't know, but I have to get the hell out of here!"

"Gaia—"

"That's it, Ms. Moore."

But Gaia barely registered the warnings. She was already halfway down the hall.

HEATHER DID NOT LEAVE SCHOOL immediately following first period.

That would have been

Rent-a-Cop

the cowardly thing to do, and Heather Gannis was nothing if not brave. She proved that every day, didn't she? Swimming with the sharks (as she secretly referred to her friends) with only her Almay pressed powder for armor.

So she'd stayed at school and toughed it out. She'd handled all those pitiful looks they threw at her, the feigned sympathy, the understanding hand pats. It was so patronizing. Didn't they know she knew? Didn't they realize she could see through them like a Victoria's Secret peignoir? They loved that she'd been humiliated. They got off on it.

As soon as the final bell sounded, Heather escaped them all.

And now she was on her way to Sam's dorm.

She walked—all right, so it was more like a subdued run—toward Washington Square Park, taking the opportunity to think. There hadn't been a clear thought in her head all day. The rigors of maintaining a stiff upper lip, seeming to be grateful, and acting suitably flustered had taken all her energy. She had also been forced to accept hug after hug after hug from all those guys who said they only wanted to comfort her, but really just saw her grief as perhaps their only chance to press their deprived bodies against her legendary one.

Pigs. Idiot pigs. But, she reminded herself for the twelve zillionth time, she'd invited popularity, worked for it, and now had to live with the consequences. What was that old saying? Live by the sword, die by the sword. Yep. Same went for popularity.

By the time she reached Fifth Avenue, Heather was convinced she had it all figured out. Sam had secretly filmed them, and then somehow had carelessly allowed the tape to fall into the wrong hands. The hands of Gaia Moore.

Or maybe it hadn't been carelessness on Sam's part. Maybe it had been part of a horrific conspiracy. Maybe—for some reason she could not even begin to imagine—Sam had taped their encounter, then *given* the tape to Gaia to screen in econ.

That would explain why Gaia had shown up that night. That would explain why Sam had run after her. They were working together to ruin Heather's life.

Why? She had no idea. But she was definitely going to find out.

Heather reached Sam's dorm, stomped into the lobby, and was met by the security guard.

Right. She'd forgotten about that little roadblock.

"Can I help you?" he asked.

Heather smiled automatically. The guy was beefy, maybe in his late twenties. She could tell this rent-a-cop position was probably a dream job for him—second only to his lifelong fantasy of changing his name to the Raunchy Raider and becoming the darling of the professional wrestling circuit.

136

"Hi," she said. "I'm just going up to visit my boyfriend."

He drew himself up tall. He was obviously very important. "I'll need to see your university ID."

Lucky for Heather she could blush on command. "You think I'm in college?"

The guy smiled. "Aren't you?"

Heather shook her head coyly. "I'm only in high school. But he's expecting me. . . ."

"Sorry, sweetheart."

Don't *sweetheart* me, you pumped-up piece of shit. "Please?" She smiled and gave him her best little head tilt. "Look. He gave me a key."

She produced Sam's dorm key from the back pocket of her jeans. Okay, so he hadn't actually given it to her. She'd stolen his spare copy in a fit of immaturity back when they'd first started getting serious. It had made her feel special to have it—her boyfriend's college dorm room key. And her friends had thought she was beyond lucky. Now her petty crime was about to come in handy.

"Look, honey," meat-for-brains said, "I don't care if the guy gave you his key. I don't care if he gave you his tuition money, all right? The bottom line is, you're not getting in here without a valid New York University ID."

Heather ground her teeth. "Can't you call him? He'll come down and get me."

137

The guard's eyes slid over her body like maple syrup on a stack of pancakes. "I'm sure he will." He picked up the phone. "What's his number?"

She gave it to him. He dialed.

"Busy."

"What?"

"The line's busy."

This threw her. Sam's line was never busy. A black hole formed in her stomach. Maybe he had it off the hook.

Maybe he was so desperate to avoid her that he'd instructed this steroid-shooting side of beef who used too much hair gel not to let anyone fitting her description anywhere near the elevator.

Disgusted, Heather turned on her heel and stalked out onto the cold street.

"SO NOW WHAT?"

Gaia shrugged. "I don't know." Ed had followed her out of detention, and now she was following Ed down the handicap ramp. A late afternoon chill crept into the neck of her sweatshirt, causing goose bumps to break out on her skin. "Maybe they're gonna have me

The Works

scale the Empire State Building in my underwear."

"I'd like to see that," Ed joked.

"Seriously. There's got to be another test, doesn't there?" Her eyes made a wide sweep of the area. "But what? When?"

Bring it on, she willed silently. Come on! It was like waiting to throw a punch, or waiting to have one thrown at you. Come and get me. Come and get me.

When they reached the sidewalk, Ed angled his chair to allow a food vendor to pass by with his stout, steaming cart.

"Y'know what's weird?" Ed asked. "The last tests came at you like rapid fire, so where the hell are they?"

"Maybe the guy's taking a coffee break," Gaia deadpanned. "Maybe he's a union kidnapper."

Ed's face became tentatively hopeful. "Or maybe you're done."

"Done?"

"Yeah. Maybe they're satisfied," Ed said with a shrug. "Maybe the next message is gonna be, 'You may reclaim your diabetic boyfriend at your earliest convenience.'"

"Don't call him my boyfriend," Gaia said.

"Yes, ma'am."

Absently Gaia watched the hot dog vendor drag his moving eatery to a halt. When he banged open a metal compartment, the uniquely New York aroma of frankfurters and sauerkraut reached her. Her stomach growled fiercely, and she realized she hadn't eaten a thing since the three bites of bagel she'd had at breakfast.

"Hungry?" she asked Ed.

"Sure."

Gaia approached the vendor. "Two. With the works."

"The works," the guy mumbled, grabbing two empty rolls and placing the hot dogs into them.

Gaia watched as he clumsily spooned relish and onions onto them. More of the condiments wound up in his hand than on the dogs. Well, maybe if the jerk took off those dark glasses and pulled his hat up from over his eyes, he'd be able to see what he was doing and—

"Sam says hi."

Gaia's eyes snapped up to the vendor's face.

He thrust the hot dogs into her hand. Her first instinct was to shove them both up his nose. The guy pulled off his sunglasses and gave her the hands-down wickedest stare she'd ever seen. Anyone else would have passed out from the ferocity of it, but Gaia met his gaze. And, since she *had* been born with whichever chemical component created hunger, took a sloppy bite of the hot dog.

The sham vendor was obviously thrown by her calm.

"Sam says hi," he repeated, less icily. He reached into his apron, removed a piece of paper, and held it out to her.

She glanced over her shoulder at Ed. "He's out of hot pretzels," she said sarcastically. "Will you settle for a ransom note?"

Ed was wide-eyed. "God. Are they everywhere?"

Gaia took the note, and seconds later the phony hot dog guy was gone.

She handed Ed his hot dog, which he just sort of stared at, as if he'd never seen one before. Gaia decided to read to herself and give Ed a couple of seconds to recover.

Clearly you did not understand what I meant by HUMILIATION, as you and your friend in the wheelchair are still on speaking terms. Momentary embarrassment in the school corridor was not what I had in mind, Gaia. I wanted him out of your life, but I see this has not happened. For this reason, you will perform another test, the most difficult thus far. Before I return Sam to you this evening, you will be required to . . .

Gaia looked up from the note and blinked at Ed. "What? What does it say?"

"Uh . . . it says I'm doing really well. Listen." She skipped to the final paragraph, cleared her throat, and read aloud. "'Sam will be turned over to you this evening at 10 P.M. in Washington Square Park. Choose any pathway. I will find you. FYI—Mr. Moon's health is failing, so I suggest you be prompt.'"

"Is that all it says?"

She swallowed hard and nodded. No reason to tell him how personal the kidnapper was getting with his notes. No reason to tell him—

"Man. He must be pretty sick." Ed was looking pale.

"It says I have to get his insulin from his dorm room," Gaia murmured. His room. Like she wanted to revisit that memory anytime in the next century.

Ed nodded. "Hope we can get into his room."

"You'd be surprised how easy it can be," said Gaia, frowning.

"That's if it's unlocked," Ed reminded her.

"True." Her eyes dropped unwillingly to the note, that one sentence . . .

Ed lowered an eyebrow at her. "You okay?"

Gaia nodded.

"Well, you might not be after I make this next suggestion." He took a deep breath. "I think we're going to need Heather."

"Need Heather? For *what*?" Gaia asked. "Fashion advice on what to wear to a hostage rescue?"

Ed tossed his untouched hot dog into a nearby trash container. "For the key to Sam's room. I'm guessing she's the only person we know who might have one."

Gaia felt her muscles tighten with anger. He was

probably right. And the last thing she needed was to get nabbed for breaking and entering. She wouldn't be helping anyone from jail. Having Sam's room key was crucial.

She ate the rest of her hot dog in two angry bites, then glared at him. "Heather it is," she said with her mouth full.

Ed watched her swallow with a look of near disgust. He'd never looked at her like that. But then, she figured she was doing a pretty good impression of a boa constrictor.

"Are you sure you're all right?"

"I'm fine," she lied, glancing at the note again—at another part she hadn't read out loud. At the part that said, "*Kill CJ.*"

Loki hovered
there
another
moment,
allowing his
icy laughter
to rain down
on Sam.

a
little
buzz

"HI."

CJ turned. The woman was talking to him. The beautiful woman in the tight blouse.

He did his little shoulder thing—loosened himself up. Slouched. "Wus'up?"

She smiled. "I've seen you around, you know."

It's a Date

"Yeah? Well, I ain't seen you." At least not in a while. She used to walk through the park every day, but not lately. It was hard to forget a body like that. She smelled great. Expensive. And her legs went on till Tuesday.

"What's your name?"

"CJ."

"Nice to meet you, CJ."

She reached for his hand and shook it. Talk about silky skin.

"Listen, CJ, I don't usually do this sort of thing, but I was hoping you might like to go out with me. Tonight." The way she fixed her eyes on him made things inside his body stir. Things he didn't even know were there.

Brain cramp! This gorgeous, uptown piece of ass was asking him out? Sure as hell sounded like it. For a moment there was no Gaia.

"Uh . . . uh . . ." Damn, he had to get it together.

"Well?"

Shit, this one was friendly. She was pressing her palms against his chest now.

"You don't have plans, do you?" she asked in a husky voice.

Well, as a matter of fact, he did. He was going to kill Gaia tonight. But then again, maybe he could do both.

The woman was giving him this very seductive little pout. "Please say you'll meet me tonight. There's a band playing in the park. And I love to dance. . . ." She pushed her hips against his and swayed. "Do you like to dance?"

CJ nodded. He liked her perfume. It was giving him a little buzz. Smelled like burning flowers or something.

"Good. So it's a date, then?" She tossed her hair back and looked up at him through her thick lashes. "We'll meet tonight, in the park."

"Yeah. Yeah." He backed up from her slightly, trying to play off the fact that every inch of his body wanted to pounce on her right now. No use letting the lady know she had the power. "That'd be cool. In the park."

"I'll meet you at the fountain," she said, making even the word *fountain* sound dirty. "Say . . . nine-thirty?"

"Yeah. sounds good."

"Till then . . ."

"Yeah."

She turned to walk away, and he remembered that walk. He and Marco used to study it. When she'd gone half a block, he called out to her. "Yo, girl. What's your name?"

She didn't bother to answer.

TO: L
FROM: E
RE: CJ

Arrived in NYC early and met with pawn. He'll meet me in the park at nine-thirty.

If all goes as well as this, he should be dead before the band plays its first set.

LOKI CRUMPLED THE FAXED MEMO AND

dropped it into the wastebasket.

"Dead before the first set?" He smiled sardonically. "That's what I like to hear." His laughter was an ugly, guttural rumble in his throat. He turned to Sam.

Poor, poor Sam.

Dying, really, right before his eyes. A shame.

What the Kidnapper Said

Loki walked toward his hostage, who was huddled in a shivering heap on the floor, and studied him in silence for a long moment.

Well, he could understand what his niece saw in

the boy. He was certainly nice-looking. At least, he had been, before that unfortunate incident in which his face collided with that fist. Tsk, tsk. And, of course, his medical condition was really taking its toll.

"Sam?" Again, louder. "Sam!"

The boy lifted his head slightly and let out a ragged breath.

"Sam Moon," said Loki thoughtfully, rolling the name over his taste buds as though it were a new wine he was tasting. "Tell me about yourself, Sam."

The only reply was the shuddering of Sam's body.

"Cat got your tongue, boy?" Loki sneered. "Ah, yes. Just as well. I generally prefer to do the talking in situations such as these. I do so enjoy being in control."

He was circling Sam now, like the predator he was. "You're aware, I imagine, that my niece is quite taken with you?" His eyes turned hard as he stared at the prone form before him.

Loki stopped walking, folded his arms across his chest, and glared down at Sam. "That, as you must understand, is not an easy thing for an uncle to accept. I wonder, would you be worthy of her? Because an uncle has certain expectations for his only niece, Sam. He wants the best for her, wants only her happiness. I know it may not seem that way, given current circumstances, but it is true. Gaia, you might say, has become my whole world."

Loki lifted his foot and used the toe of one of his three-hundred-dollar wing tips to give Sam's languid body a hard nudge. "So tell me, Sam Moon," he demanded. "Are you the boy who will make Gaia's dreams come true?"

Loki hovered there another moment, allowing his icy laughter to rain down on Sam.

Then in a voice so slick and close to silence that Loki barely heard it himself, he asked Sam Moon `one last question`.

After that he walked away, the heels of his expensive shoes drumming the highly polished floor of the loft.

He didn't turn around.

He should have.

What the Hostage Heard

HE FELT THE LAUGHTER BEFORE HE heard it. An ugly rumble from across the room. Guttural, like an animal choking.

The first footsteps—approaching. A presence, near. Then, words:

`Sam Moon.`

`I enjoy . . . control.`

Gaia . . . taken with you . . . my whole world.

A kick to his rib cage. A shouted question:

. . . dreams come true?

And then, in the slightest whisper:

Do you love her, Sam?

Sam's bruised eye throbbed as he lifted his head. He had not attempted to use his voice in nineteen hours, but with what he sincerely believed might be the very last breath in his body, over the sound of fading footsteps, Sam answered.

"Yes."

Gaia and Heather.

When you look at them and take them at face value, one might wonder how one person (namely, me . . . and possibly Sam) could love them both in one lifetime.

Gaia is tall, blond, powerful, and favors brown clothing.

Heather is shortish, brunette, a slave to the masses, and never wears brown unless a respected fashion writer tells her it's the "new black."

But Gaia and Heather are more alike than the general public might think.

The first similarity? They'd both kill me if they heard me say that.

The list goes on.

Neither one of them is as brave as she thinks she is. They both have a lot of secrets. (Heather's I pretty much know, Gaia's I'm not sure I want to know.) They both have trust issues. I've never known two people with such a gift for sarcasm. They are both extremely beautiful.

And they both have a thing for college guys.

So it's not hard to see why one guy could love them both in the same lifetime.

The real question is, why do I bother?

"Heather? It's Jeff Landon. . . . So, uh, are you busy Saturday night?"

phone tag

RRRING. CLICK. BEEP.

"You've reached the Gannis residence. Please leave a message at the beep. Thank you."

Sex in School

"Heather! It's Megan. Oh my God! I am still so totally freaked out by what happened at school today! I cannot believe Sam, like, actually taped you guys doing it. And gave it to *Gaia*? That's like—ugh—*so* unbelievably tasteless. It's like, okay, why don't we all just go on *Jerry Springer*? I mean, like, what if you were wearing weird underwear or something, y'know? Okay, so, like, call me as soon as you get in. Bye."

Click. Beep.

What kind of idiot was Megan? She knew Heather didn't have her own phone line. She knew Heather's answering machine was in the family room, where anyone could overhear a message coming in. Heather's parents were actually really good about not snooping, and they would never purposely listen to an incoming call. But what if they happened to be passing through the family room while Megan was ranting about she and Sam "doing it"? Idiot.

Rrring. Click. Beep.

"Hi, it's Ashley. I skipped school today to get my hair highlighted, but I just heard the best dirt! This

156

morning somebody actually showed a video of people having, like, *sex*—in school! Well, no, I mean, they weren't having sex in school, they showed the video in school. The sex was, like, someplace else. I don't know who was on the tape, though, 'cuz I heard it from Jen, who heard it from Mallory, who heard it from . . . I dunno, like, somebody. But now I'm, like, so bummed that I dropped AP econ! Oh! Hey! You're still in that class, aren't you? So *you* must have seen it. Cool. All right, so call me with the info!"

Click. Beep.

It had been going on all day. She'd already erased at least twenty messages on this very topic. But she refused to take the phone off the hook, in case Sam tried to call.

To explain himself.

To apologize.

To tell her he'd had nothing to do with that damn video.

She'd come home from the disaster at the dorm and spent the last hour lying on the family room sofa, screening calls.

Rrring. Click. Beep.

"Heather! It's Jeff Landon. Heard about your film debut. Whoa. Didn't know you were into that kind of thing. So, uh, are you busy Saturday night?"

Beep.

Heather chucked a throw pillow at the answering

157

machine. It missed by about three feet and bounced off the top of the television. She sighed, then rolled over onto her stomach. Sam's dorm room key bit into her hip. It was still in the front pocket of her pants. She pulled it out and stared at it for a second before flinging it, too, across the room, where it knocked over a framed photo of her and Sam at a Yankees game.

Rrring. Click. Beep.

"Heather, it's Megan again! Are you there? Pick up! I just heard that band Fearless is playing in the park tonight. The drummer's a total hottie! Wanna go? Maybe it'll, you know, cheer you up or whatever. Call me."

That was it! Heather had officially had it. She was taking the phone off the hook, and for all she cared, Sam could go to hell. Let him call. Let him get a busy signal. Let him come over with a dozen long-stemmed roses and apologize in person, like a normal boyfriend!

She was just reaching for the handset when the phone rang again. She jerked her fingers away as though she'd been shocked, then listened.

Click. Beep.

"Hi, Heather. It's Ed. Fargo. Listen, I realize this call must come as a shock, but I have something really serious I need to talk to you about. It's important. It's . . . uh . . . about Sam. He's in trouble. Well, actually, not trouble. More like danger. There's something we have to get out of his room. We're talking life and death here. Sam's life and death. So we were thinking, since you probably have a key to his room, you would bring it to us. Heather, you've got to help us. . . ."

Heather picked up the handset. The machine shut off, routing Ed's voice directly through the phone as she pressed it to her ear.

"Heather? Are you there?"

She had two words for him: "Who's us?"

The Key

"WHAT DO YOU MEAN, SHE DOESN'T want me involved?"

"I mean," said Ed, wheeling fast to keep up with Gaia's furious pace, "she's all for helping Sam, but she doesn't want you to be a part of it."

"*Part* of it? Part of *it*?" Gaia punched her right fist repeatedly against her thigh as she walked. "Doesn't the airhead realize that I *am* it? Didn't you explain that to her?" Gaia slammed directly into a man in a business suit, sending him sprawling. "Sorry," she mumbled over her shoulder. The guy swore after her but was too busy restuffing his briefcase to give chase.

159

"No, I didn't. I'm guessing it would have done more harm than good." Ed stopped at the corner, waiting for the light. He glanced warily over his shoulder. Gaia half hoped the suit would come yell at her. She needed a good excuse to hit something.

When Ed had explained that Gaia was involved, the news had, naturally, sent Her Royal Heatherness into convulsions. After some careful negotiations, Ed had managed to get her to agree to discuss it in person—without Gaia.

"So she's not expecting me?" Gaia asked, holding her hair back from her face to keep it from whipping into her eyes.

"No," Ed answered, staring at the rushing traffic.

"Great."

Gaia stopped fuming long enough to check out the neighborhood. It was a little to the east of the area that was really upscale. It wasn't bad. But there was nothing much to recommend it, either. The streets were lined with smallish apartment buildings that were falling into disrepair—chipping paint, cracked moldings, windows scratched with graffiti. Plus it seemed like the garbage hadn't been hauled off in weeks.

"Where are we going?" Gaia asked.

"Heather's."

Gaia lifted an eyebrow in the direction of the

nearest worse-for-wear apartment building. "You mean she doesn't live in some yuppie co-op somewhere in the eighties?"

"Not anymore," Ed said flatly.

They continued in silence for two blocks, then turned a corner and found Heather waiting for them on the sidewalk in front of a nondescript, graying apartment building.

Ed waved.

Heather fired Gaia a hateful look from thirty paces off.

"I told you not to bring her," Heather said, crossing her arms over the front of her suede jacket.

"This is important," Ed told her. "Gaia's involved, whether you like it or not."

Heather looked like a rabid alley cat. She ignored Ed, focusing all her attention on glaring at Gaia. "Are you sleeping with Sam?"

Gaia rolled her eyes. "Oh, give me a break—"

"Are you?" Heather's mouth contorted with fury.

"Heather!" Ed blurted. He wheeled his chair between the two girls. "This isn't about you," he said firmly, leveling her with a stare. "This is about Sam."

Heather glanced at him, a flicker of interest in her eyes. "Right, so what's going on? How do you even know him?"

Gaia let out an exasperated sigh. The girl had a talent for pointless questions.

"It doesn't matter how I know him," Ed said. "What matters is he's been kidnapped."

"Kidnapped?"

The color drained from Heather's face, and Gaia felt her stomach flop.

That was what fear looked like. Gaia found herself fighting back a wave of what could only be called jealousy. She cared for Sam more than anyone would ever know. Yet again she felt deep discomfort at the knowledge that when his life was threatened, she couldn't feel this most basic emotion. But a conscience-free zone like Heather Gannis could. Heather could have natural feelings when the guy they both loved was in danger.

Gaia felt like a voyeur as she watched the tears forming in Heather's eyes. She made herself look away.

"By who? Why?" Heather asked.

"We're not sure," Ed said. "Somebody's holding him hostage."

"Oh my God!"

"We think we can rescue him, but we're running out of time."

"Rescue him? When?"

Probably needs to check her Week-at-a-Glance, Gaia thought cynically. "*Sure, I can pencil in Sam's rescue for tonight—unless there's a sale at Abercrombie.*"

"Tonight," said Ed.

Morbidly curious, Gaia watched Heather closely, feeling an inexplicable loneliness. Heather's eyes were so huge, so filled with terror, they threatened to overtake her whole face. She was actually quaking. Gaia couldn't pull her eyes away. She knew what fear looked like. But what did it *feel* like? *What?* And would she ever know the extent of what she was missing?

"Oh my God," Heather said, her voice quivering. "Oh my God, oh my God!"

"Calm down," said Gaia. "Freaking out isn't going to help anything."

"Shut up!" Heather glared at her. "Just shut up and go away."

"She's not going anywhere," said Ed.

"I don't even want to look at her!" Heather sputtered.

"Then don't," snapped Gaia. "Just give us the key so we can—"

"You're not going without me!" Heather exploded. "Sam is still *my* boyfriend. And besides, it's not the key that's the problem. It's the pit bull of a security guard."

Gaia remembered the guard. She'd slipped by him without much trouble on her own, but all three of them? A towhead, a homecoming queen, and a Boy Scout on wheels. They weren't exactly an inconspicuous bunch.

Heather turned to Ed, and her voice ironed itself into a reasonable tone. "I have to do *something*. I want to help him."

"You'll be helping him by giving us the key," said Ed. "That way, we can get his insulin and bring it to him tonight when they release him in the park—"

Gaia brought her hand down hard on Ed's shoulder, effectively shutting him up, but not soon enough. She watched Heather's face as the information was sent to her mental mainframe.

Damn.

"I'm coming with you. I have to be the one to bring it to him." Suddenly she was overcome with either real emotion or really good acting technique. Her eyes filled with tears again, and her breathing was fast and shallow. "He'll need me," she cried. "He'll need me to take care of him. I'm going with you."

"Oh, no!" Gaia exploded. "No way."

"Heather," Ed said calmly, "it's too dangerous."

She glared in Gaia's direction. "Why is it too dangerous for me and not her?"

Gaia wouldn't have minded showing her. Instead she said, "It's dangerous for everyone. Especially Sam. But I'm going because the kidnapper contacted me in the first place."

Something shifted in Heather's eyes as she digested

this information. She seemed to suddenly grow smaller. "Why you?"

"I don't know," Gaia said honestly.

Heather crossed her arms over her chest. "Who do you think you—"

"Yo! Enough." They both snapped their heads around to face Ed. "This isn't helping Sam."

Gaia swore under her breath. Sam's life was in jeopardy, and here she was arguing with Bad-Attitude Barbie. She had to let Ed work on Heather alone for a minute. She turned and headed back toward a small convenience store she'd noticed near the corner.

If all else failed, she could knock Heather's lights out and just take the key.

But something told her that wasn't going to be necessary. Ed would be able to convince her. Maybe it was the residual tenderness she heard in his voice every time he talked to her or about her. Maybe it was the way Heather changed—almost indiscernibly, but still, *changed*—when Ed looked at her, as though something were happening inside her that she didn't want or expect. It was as if Heather were locked out of her own soul and somehow Ed still had the key.

For the life of her, Gaia could not figure out why that annoyed her so much.

But it did.

GAIA WAS COMING OUT OF THE
store, finishing up her Mars
bar, when Ed appeared.

"I've got good news and
bad news," he said.

"Is the bad news that
you couldn't think of anything more original to say

The Ripple Effect

than that?" Gaia asked through a mouthful of nuts
and chocolate. She crumpled the wrapper and shoved
it into her sweatshirt pocket with the two other
chocolate bars she'd bought. Gaia didn't know much
about diabetes, but she thought Sam might need
them.

"So where is she?" Gaia asked, glancing past Ed.

"She'll meet us here in a few minutes," Ed said, stu-
diously avoiding eye contact. "She went inside to get
the key."

Gaia's body rippled with relief. "She's
going to give it up?"

"More or less," Ed answered, picking at the hole in
his sweater.

"I'm not sure that's possible, Ed," Gaia said impatiently.

"She's coming with us to the dorm," Ed said, pushing his shoulders back, trying to look defiant.
"There's no way around it."

Gaia tilted her head back, staring up at the rapidly

166

darkening sky. "Do you think she's gonna be able to keep her head when she sees Sam in the park, all beaten and bloody, being shoved around by some guy in commando gear who's holding a sawed-off shotgun to his head, and who knows what else?"

Ed looked a little white. "She'll be long gone before we get to the park."

Gaia had to bite her lip to keep herself from commenting on his use of the word *we*. He didn't know it yet, but *he* was going to be long gone, too. There was no way she was going to drag Ed into that little scenario. But perhaps it was best not to mention that just yet.

"What makes you so sure she'll be gone?" Gaia asked, leaning back against the brick wall of the convenience store.

Ed smiled and his eyes filled with mischief. Gaia knew what was coming before he said it.

"Because I have a plan."

He didn't
think he
could handle
the humilia-
tion if his

brainless

first-ever

covert-

action plan

crashed and

burned.

ED WHEELED HIS WAY INTO THE

dorm and took a look around. The lobby smelled of beer-dampened carpet and the bottle's worth of CK One with which the guard had obviously drenched himself.

Mission: Not-So-Impossible

Hmm. Ed would have pegged this one for a Brut by Fabergé type. Go figure.

"Hi."

Behind his desk, the guard averted his eyes and gave him a nod.

Typical. Can't look the cripple in the eye.

Ed aimed for the elevator.

Waiting . . . waiting . . .

Okay, so gimme the ID speech already. He checked his watch. Seven twenty-eight. C'mon, buddy. Ask for the card.

Nothing.

Ed hit the elevator button hard. The Neanderthal glanced in his direction and dredged up an awkward grin.

Damn! Don't tell me the quasi-cop is too soft-hearted to hassle a guy in a wheelchair.

Above the elevator, the number 3 lit up. It would

reach ground level any second, and Ed would be able to roll right on. No distraction, no clear avenue for Gaia and Heather.

Over his head, the number 2 blinked orange.

"Excuse me," he said. "I'm heading up to see a friend, but I'm not sure I'll be able to find his room. Those letters and numbers are kinda confusing. Can ya help me out?"

Not until you see my ID, right? Go ahead, say it!

"The letter stands for the wing," the guard explained. "A is to the right, B to the left. There are four rooms to a suite and they're all clearly marked."

"Thanks," Ed muttered. He was starting to sweat. He didn't think he could handle the humiliation if his first-ever covert-action plan crashed and burned.

For a second the guy just looked at Ed and seemed to be trying to decide what to do.

C'mon, brainless. Card me, already. Then the elevator announced itself with a loud *ding,* and the door opened.

"I've never been in any of these dorms before," Ed said. He raised his voice a few decibels louder than necessary. "I don't go here."

There! Now he's got no choice.

The Neanderthal cleared his throat. "Listen, pal," he said in a regretful tone. "I really can't let you up if you don't have an ID."

Finally! Ed narrowed his eyes as the elevator door slid closed. "What do you mean?"

"University policy. Sorry." The guard shoved his beefy hands into his pockets. Damn, he was uncomfortable. "Nonstudents can't—"

"Nonstudents?" Ed challenged, spinning his chair toward the guard. "You sure you don't mean people in wheelchairs?"

The guy looked at him, waylaid. "Huh?"

"C'mon, man. You know the real reason you're not letting me get on this elevator is because I can't walk into it on my own two feet," Ed said, his face growing red. He should get an Oscar for this one.

"No. That ain't it." Now the Neanderthal was sweating, too. "It's just—"

"Yeah, right! I've seen this crap before," Ed shouted, gripping the armrests on his chair. "It's always the chair. It's discrimination."

Now the guy was getting pissed. "It has nothin' to do with the chair. It's the rule. No ID, no admittance."

Ed gave him a disgusted look, then turned his chair again and reached for the elevator button.

"Hey!" barked the guard, hurrying out from behind the desk. "I told you—"

"What are ya gonna do?" Ed chuckled wickedly. "Hit me?"

With that, they began to argue in earnest.

"ALL RIGHT, WE'RE GOING IN," GAIA

7:31 said from her position outside Sam's dorm.

Heather rolled her eyes, but when Gaia pushed through the lobby door, Heather followed. Ed had managed to lure the guard out from behind his station, so Gaia and Heather tiptoed behind the guard's back and slipped into the stairwell.

All politeness, Gaia held the door open, allowing Heather to go through first. No idiot, Heather shot Gaia a suspicious look, but Gaia could practically see her train of thought. Heather didn't want Gaia behind her, but the thought of getting to Sam's room first was tempting.

Heather sneered at Gaia and brushed past her.

"You're welcome," Gaia snapped in a whisper.

Heather started to jog, and Gaia followed close behind. It was torture having Heather's scrawny ass in her face, but it was going to be worth the sacrifice in about five seconds. Gaia let Heather get up three half flights of stairs before she made her move.

Gaia reached up and grabbed Heather's ankle, sending the girl sprawling on the concrete landing between the first and second floors.

"Get off me!" Heather yelled.

Holding Heather down with one hand, Gaia seized the key from Heather's grasp with a mercury-fast action that would have done even the most seasoned New York purse snatcher proud.

Gaia pulled Heather to her feet. "Sorry, but it was necessary," Gaia muttered.

"I-I'm going to-to *kill* you," Heather shrieked, struggling to no avail.

"Me first," Gaia said, trying not to enjoy the terror in Heather's eyes. She wasn't going to kill her, of course, though it was tempting. She did, however, need to shove Heather down a few steps, both so she could get to Sam's room without further interference, and so the overweight guard could catch Heather.

Gaia gave Heather one hard push, and Heather yelped. She stumbled down the half flight and landed at the bottom with a thud. It looked like it hurt at least a little.

At that moment Gaia heard Ed yelling at the guard. Right on cue.

"Some chick just snuck into the stairs! Yeah! Yes! I swear! Brown hair! Pink shirt!"

Heather was struggling to her feet as Gaia heard the sound of the lobby door to the stairs banging open.

It was time to get out of there.

"Later, Heather!"

Gaia took off up the stairs. She heard Heather start after her, but the guard had already caught up.

"Where do you think you're going?" he asked, panting.

"Get *off* me!" Heather screamed. "Gaia! *Gaia!*"

Gaia smiled as she sprinted down the fourth-floor hallway.

GAIA STOOD OUTSIDE THE DOOR OF

Dorm Room Revisited

room B4 and held her breath. The last time she'd been here Sam had been making love to Heather.

How could she bring herself to go in there?

"Don't be such a sentimental idiot," Gaia told herself, shaking off the self-inflicted melodrama. "This is a college dorm room. I should have a nickel for every sexual encounter that's taken place in here."

She slid the key into the lock.

The doorknob fell off in her hand.

For a moment she just stared at it.

Son of a bitch!

The damn thing had been broken all along! Not even lockable. So they hadn't needed the key after all.

And, by association, they hadn't needed Heather. What a waste of time!

Then again, it had provided the opportunity for Gaia to give Heather a good hard shove. Truth be told, that had actually been kind of cathartic.

She opened the door. And there it was. `Sam's bed.`

Gaia stepped into the room, keeping her mind on her task. Insulin. Must find insulin. Don't even look at that framed photograph of Heather over there on the dresser. Could she possibly be wearing any more lip gloss?

`Insulin,` damn it! What was the matter with her?

Gaia seemed to remember the stuff had to be refrigerated. Her eyes swept the room and found a minifridge in the corner. She opened the door. Two bottles of mineral water, a small mountain of those plastic packets of duck sauce that come with Chinese takeout, and a small zippered nylon case.

She opened the case. Pamphlet of instructions. Vials. Syringe.

A wave of emotion washed over her. It was like holding the definition of *vulnerable* in her hands. Sam—perfect, brilliant, gorgeous Sam—had this to contend with. This frailty. This tiny physiological flaw, this infinitesimal defect in body chemistry. This burden. This disadvantage.

Tell me about it.

She stuffed the case into the oversized pocket of her cargo pants, then got up to leave. But there was that damn bed again.

Gaia hesitated perhaps a fraction of a millisecond. Then she threw herself onto the bed. Don't think about the fact that the last time you saw it, Heather was between the sheets. Think about Sam.

Sam's bed.

Sam's sheets. Sam's pillow. Gaia buried her face in it, breathing deeply. Maybe there was something of him still clinging to the pillowcase—an eyelash, maybe, or an echo of a dream.

"Oh, God, Sam . . . I'm so sorry."

She clutched the pillow to her body.

I don't want to kill anybody, her brain said for the hundredth time since she'd read the last directive. *I don't want to kill. I don't want to kill.*

Images flooded her mind, drowning her brain: Sam at the chessboard. Sam coming to see her in the hospital. Sam on the park bench.

And then it was CJ. CJ chasing her down Broome Street. CJ in the police lineup. CJ holding a gun to her head. And firing. And . . .

Gaia sat bolt upright.

She knew what to do.

Rook to knight four.

Queen's knight. Castle. Pawn.

Wrrrzzzzzzzz. Clank.

I see Gaia's fingers on a chess piece. She pushes the smooth, angular knight with her index finger. And Zolov clicks his false teeth in appreciation of her genius.

The sound bullies me.

Wrrrzzzzzzzzz, clank, wrrzz. I only want to sleep. Sleep. But my levels are off, and my own blood poisons me.

Time is running—check.

Checkmate.

Blackness surrounds me, cold, flat, then it erupts into a pattern of squares. Clean, sharp-cornered red bruises interrupt my blackout. The board spins in its own dimension until I am above it, leaning, knowing, playing. I hear the sound of the plastic piece scraping the cardboard squares.

Wrrrzzzzzzzz.

The hunger is huge. The blackness quivers. I place my hand around Gaia's on her knight.

And sleep.

S A M

Oh, God. Is this what forgiveness feels like?

bring it on

GAIA FOUND ED WAITING AT THE

southwest corner of Fifth Avenue and Tenth Street—the designated meeting spot. It was dark out, and he sat in a square of light pouring out of the lobby of the building behind him.

Liar

"Get it?" he asked.

"Got it." She nodded, patting the nylon case inside her pocket. "C'mon, let's go. There's somewhere I have to be."

Gaia started walking toward the park, and Ed quickly caught up with her.

"How'd it work out with Heather and the guard?" Gaia asked, hoping to keep him from asking where exactly she had to be.

A shadow of guilt crossed his face. "It got pretty hairy. She was ballistic when they tossed her out."

"Tossed her out, huh?" asked Gaia, savoring the image. "You mean that literally, right?"

"Pretty much," Ed said. "From what I overheard, it seems our little Heather tried to get in to Sam's room earlier today. The guard recognized her and thought she was some crazed stalker, so he totally ignored her when she was shouting about you getting away. They took her to the main security office. She fought him like you wouldn't even believe, kicking, swearing, snorting. . . ."

"So she didn't get around to implicating you?" Gaia asked, glancing up at the arch at the north end of Washington Square Park. It was illuminated at night, and Gaia couldn't help thinking it was beautiful. It was kind of like a beacon.

"I'm sure she tried," Ed said, following her gaze. "But no way were they gonna believe her." He shook his head. "Man, I feel sorry for the guy who had to interrogate her."

"What time is it?" she asked. If he noticed she wasn't really paying attention to the conversation, he didn't say anything.

He checked his watch. "Only eight ten. We've got plenty of time before we have to go to the park."

"Excuse me?" Gaia said. "*We've* got plenty of time?"

"What is it with you women and pronouns today, huh?" Ed asked.

Gaia shoved her hands into her pockets. Her fingers automatically closed around the candy bars. "I'm serious, Ed. I'm going to do this alone."

Ed scoffed. "No, you're not."

"Yes, I am."

"No, you're not."

"Yes, I . . ." Gaia threw up her hands. "Ed, this isn't open to debate. You said it yourself, to Heather—it'll be dangerous."

He had no idea how dangerous, of course, because

181

he was unaware of the last note's final directive. But she wasn't about to tell him she'd be murdering a gang member in cold blood this evening, which wasn't exactly the sort of thing that required an escort.

He stopped wheeling. "And you think just because I'm in this chair . . ."

"Oh, please! Save the politically correct guilt trip for somebody who gives a shit, okay?" Gaia spat out. "Yes, you're in a wheelchair. Yes, in this case it's a liability. It makes you slow, and obvious, and a real easy target."

Ed looked at her a moment, then turned away.

Damn. She hadn't meant that the way it sounded. Well, no, actually she'd meant it exactly the way it sounded. It was the truth, for God's sake. Of course, she'd neglected to mention her most important reason for not wanting him there.

"Listen," she said, not quite gently, but as close to it as she could stand to get. "I'm not saying this stuff to hurt your feelings—if I wanted to do that, I'd tell you what I really think of your taste in clothes." He didn't face her, but she could feel him smiling. "I've got to do this myself, Ed. Because . . ."

At last he turned. "Because?"

"Because if anything happened to you . . ." Gaia pulled her jacket close to her as the wind picked up, and sighed. "If anything happened to you, the world would be a much sadder place," she finished so quietly she wasn't certain the breeze had left any of her words for Ed to hear.

A few hundred years went by before Ed finally spoke. "Thanks, Gaia."

"Yeah, whatever." Gaia picked at a hangnail. "Let's not make this a mush fest, okay? You know you're, like, my only friend on the planet. So what good would it do me to let you take a bullet to the skull?"

She handed him Heather's key, careful not to let her hand touch his.

"Get this back to her," she said.

"Don't you want to keep it?"

Gaia shook her head. "He gave it to her, not to me."

"Yeah," Ed replied softly, lowering his eyes. "I know exactly what you mean."

She figured he was thinking back on his bygone relationship with Heather, because his tone was tender in the extreme. She sighed again.

"I gotta go," she said, looking off toward the center of the park.

He raised his eyes, surprised. "Now?"

"Yeah, well . . . I have to stop back at my place. I've gotta get something." Something she really didn't want to get. Something that should just have been left in its uninspired hiding place forever.

"What?"

Gaia hesitated, waiting for an appropriate lie to shove its way to the front of her brain. Then her mind zoomed back to the Duane Reade bag, the cop, Renny.

"Tampons."

"Oh." Ed's face flushed faster than Gaia had ever thought possible. "Well, uh . . . be careful."

She grinned. "With the tampons?"

"Gaia!"

"I'll be okay." Her brows knitted together, and she stared at Ed seriously. "I'll be okay as long as you stay far, far away from the park tonight."

Ed sighed and shook his head. "Fine."

She was three steps away when she turned around again. "Promise me, Ed. Promise me you will *not* come to the park."

He nodded. "I promise."

If she hadn't been thinking so hard about killing CJ, she might have recognized that Ed was as good a liar as she was.

ELLA WOULD NEVER GET TIRED OF
doing Loki's dirty work.

Especially when it involved her running her hands over the bare chests of well-built young men like CJ. Okay, so they were rolling in

Seduction 201 (AP)

the dirt behind a bush off some pathway in the park—not exactly a classy setting. But she knew how to make the best of any situation.

This one was as sexy as he was mean. She'd always liked that combination.

Marco was good. CJ was much, much better.

And he was amazed by her. Well, of course. He was probably used to teenage sluts with grungy hair and too much black eyeliner. He'd never seen actual silk this close before, let alone touched it.

Now, here's where I sigh for him, nice and deep—make him think I've never had anything this good before.

CJ smiled hungrily.

He's so proud of himself. Look at him showing off! It was almost cute.

That's right. One more button.

He breathed her name. Or what he thought was her name. So amazed. So grateful. He had no idea there was a blond assassin on her way there to murder him.

Well . . . if you've gotta go, this is definitely the way to spend your final hour.

He asked why she was laughing.

"I always laugh when I'm ready," she said seductively. "Are you ready?"

Over his shoulder, she checked her watch. Ten till ten. Then there was a sound from a nearby tree. It was a miracle she even heard it over CJ's moaning and heavy breathing. It was a signal: She's here.

Okay, you darling, dangerous boy . . . let's make this quick.

"Yes, CJ! Yes . . . *Yes!*" Perfect timing! And then . . .

"CJ, I hear someone. . . ."

He rose to his knees with a nice lazy smile, tugged up his jeans, and peered through the leaves.

"Shit!"

"What is it?" He was looking for his shirt. No luck.

"Shit. It's her. I gotta go. Sorry."

The "sorry" threw her a bit. I suppose I have to act like I care. "Don't go, CJ! Wait!"

He didn't even realize she'd taken his gun.

He leaned down and gave her a hard kiss on her mouth and told her he'd see her again; he *promised*—in this rough, almost heartbreaking voice—that he'd see her again. Then he took off. She sat up, buttoning her blouse, surveying the damage to her skirt.

Gaia, he's all yours.

GAIA ENTERED WASHINGTON SQUARE
Park.

It was nine forty.

The concert was supposed
to start at ten. The band was
already doing sound checks.
The squeal of feedback from

Parks and Wreck

186

the microphones echoed above the gathering crowd. Gaia watched the arriving fans with a combination of interest and longing.

What must it be like, she wondered, to have nothing else to do on a Monday night besides go to a concert in the park? No gangbangers to ice, no hostages to free . . .

What's it like just to be normal?

Well, she decided, looking around at the crowd, *normal* was a relative term—this was the West Village, after all. Tattoos and navel rings required.

So where the hell was CJ?

It was almost funny that she was looking for him for a change. The problem was, she hadn't expected to actually have to look. He'd been like clockwork in the past, always just sort of there—lurking, looming, stalking. Tonight, though, when it was absolutely imperative that their paths cross, he was a no-show.

How nauseatingly ironic was that?

Reasoning that even a brainless wonder like CJ might find the band concert too public a place to hunt his prey, Gaia plunged into the semidarkness of the pathway that led to Washington Square West.

She'd noticed that morning that a few leaves had begun to change. Change. Die. It was all in how you looked at it, but where just weeks ago there had been nothing but thriving greenery, there were now little glimpses of color. Throughout the expanse of billowing green, the brown-red leaves clung like scabs. They drew the eye automatically, as though to remind you that death refused to go unnoticed.

The shadows engulfed her, and the trees muffled the sound of the band and the band watchers. It was odd—even after all the horrific stuff that had happened to her in this park, she still liked it, liked the way it smelled, liked the way it rustled. She marveled at the weird, restless peacefulness of the place.

Even tonight. Even with a .38 in her waistband and CJ on the prowl.

And Sam . . .

Was he here somewhere? What if the kidnapper wasn't really going to release him? What if . . .

No. She couldn't dwell on that possibility. Sam was here. He had to be.

Did the kidnapper have him in a half nelson behind some tree, a rag stuffed in his mouth to keep him quiet? Then again, if Sam was in as bad shape as the last note had indicated, none of that would be necessary, would it?

So maybe he was writhing in the dirt in unbearable agony, clinging to his gorgeous existence by a mere thread, closer—like the drying leaves—to death than to life.

Gaia's skin prickled; her heart was practically doing the lambada in her chest. She wouldn't have

Sam back until she dealt with CJ. So where was he?

"C'mon, you dirtbag. Show your ugly face."

Even as she whispered it, she heard him. He was maybe fifteen feet behind her but approaching fast. And then he was on her, his hand slamming down on her shoulder, jerking her around to face him.

She reached out with both hands, grabbed him around the neck, and yanked his face down to connect with her head.

Nose—busted. No question. Good. It would go nicely with the sling on his arm. He staggered backward, groaning. "You bitch!"

"Whatever." Gaia nailed him with a series of front kicks to his gut, then spun around, swinging her left leg in a high arc that landed like a wrecking ball against the side of his jaw.

He fell sideways, hitting the pavement with a rib-bashing thud. Gaia pressed her foot between his shoulder blades, pinning him to the ground while she reached into the waist of her pants for the gun.

"You know," she said through clenched teeth, pressing the gun into the flesh behind his right ear, "as much as you really do deserve to die a very painful death . . ."

He flinched as the sole of her sneaker dug deeper into his back.

"As much as you deserve it . . ."

She sighed and lifted her foot. It took him a second to recognize he was free. As soon as he did, he leaped to his feet, and Gaia found herself making the very incongruous observation that this idiot was running around the park at night in October without a shirt on.

He stood very still, staring at her. She held the gun about an inch from his chest.

She had to make it look real without actually killing him. Had to make it look as though she'd tried and failed.

She cocked the hammer. "Hit me," she said, slicing her voice down to a whisper.

"Huh?" He was looking at her as though she were nuts. Maybe she was.

"Hit me," she snarled again, waving the gun.

CJ, obviously, was not very good at following directions.

She leaned closer to him. And wanted to gag. *Smoked rose petals.* Another divergent thought: The freaky witch in Soho is scamming Ella good. Unless . . .

Gaia ducked. CJ's heavy fist caught her in the cheekbone, throwing her slightly off balance. Good enough. She aimed the gun into a tree and fired.

Apparently CJ was only just realizing he'd left his own firearm elsewhere. He froze.

Gaia stumbled a little for dramatic effect, then pointed the gun at him. "Look out, asshole. This one's gonna be closer."

She aimed and fired. The bullet passed so close to CJ's face he could have kissed it.

"That's two," she whispered, watching as CJ fell to his knees and covered his head with his arms. He was begging her not to shoot.

Again she pulled the trigger.

CJ winced.

And Gaia whispered, "Bang!"

She had to. Because the bullet that should have been loaded in the third chamber of the gun's barrel was safely hidden in a Duane Reade bag under Gaia's bed.

It was as if eternity made itself visible, swelling around her, slowing the spin of the earth. Gaia swore she saw leaves changing in the chasm of time that elapsed between the steely click of the trigger and CJ's moment of recognition.

No bullet.

She gave him a wicked smile. "Déjà vu, huh?"

That's when he ran.

Gaia let out a huge rush of breath, then swung her gaze across the shadows that shrouded the path. She knew the kidnapper was out there somewhere, watching. "Hope you fellas got all that," she muttered. "Hope you bought it."

Her answer was two heavy hands coming down on her shoulders. Hard.

Evidently they hadn't bought it at all.

She could
fight like a
machine,
full force,
pumped on
fury and
desire.

eyes
like
hers

OKAY, SO MAYBE LYING RIGHT TO

her face wasn't exactly the best way to make her fall in love with him. But what choice did he have?

911

"Promise me you will *not* come to the park tonight."

Yeah. Right.

Sure, she was gutsy. Sure, she was powerful, and capable, and—all right, he'd even give her deadly. But she was his. At least in his heart she was his, and even a—what was it she'd called him? A liability? Yeah. Even a liability like him knew that you absolutely, positively did not let the love of your life do something like this alone.

So he followed her.

The band crowd was a good cover. He had to keep his distance on the path, though.

She still hadn't spotted him. He was at least twenty yards behind and to her left, in the shadow of a rest room building. He didn't have a weapon; he didn't even have the use of his legs. He did, however, have a cell phone, which he would use to dial 911 the minute it looked like Gaia was in trouble.

What was he thinking? It always looked like Gaia was in trouble. What he meant was, the minute it looked like Gaia was out of her league. That's when he'd call for help.

Ed watched as a figure emerged from the bushes, and when he recognized it, he felt fear more intense than he could ever have imagined. It was that gang punk CJ. The one who'd tried to kill her.

"Shit!" Keeping his eyes glued to Gaia, he flipped the phone open. *(Power ... 9 ... 1 ...)* "Whoa! Nice head butt!" *(End)* Man, could she kick! Bam, bam, bam!

She had the looks of a supermodel and the speed of Jean Claude Van Damme. Ooh! Right in the jaw. Nice. CJ went down.

Another cramp of fear gripped Ed when he saw Gaia reach into the waistband of her pants. What the hell was she doing with a gun? And what the hell was she standing there *talking* to CJ for?

Ed's heart jerked in his chest, and then he was watching CJ hit her! The bastard!

(9 ... 1 ...)

Holy shit! She fired, missed, but ha! The sound had sent CJ to his knees. Okay, she was back in control. *(End)*

The next shot was close! And then she was pulling the trigger again. And ...

No bullet?

(9 ... 1 ... 1 ... Send)

"Ed?"

He looked up. "Heather?"

GAIA'S ARMS WERE PINNED BEHIND

her back when the man appeared
from out of the bushes. He was
dressed—appropriately enough, Gaia
supposed—in black. Black slacks, very
expensive black sweater, and black
shoes, also pricey. She immediately
discarded any assumptions that the

Men in Black

kidnapper was somehow connected with CJ's scrubby
little street gang. These guys were big-time crime.
Money. Maybe even brains.

"You failed!" growled Mr. Monochromatic.

Gaia shrugged as best she could with the compromised use of her arms. "I tried."

"Not good enough!"

"It's not my fault you boneheads loaded the gun
wrong!" Gaia reasoned.

"Shut up!"

She rolled her eyes. "Fine, I will."

Gaia struck like lightning. She shoved her elbow
upward, a nice crack to the underside of her captor's chin, freeing her arms. Before the man in black
even had time to advance, she'd delivered one
powerful jab to the back of guy number one's
neck, knocking him out. He hit the ground like a
rag doll.

Then, in one graceful sweep, Gaia turned and
wrapped the man in black up in a headlock, pressing

the gun—the fourth chamber of which did contain a bullet—to his temple. "I'd prefer to let this do my talking for me, anyway."

The guy grunted.

"I want Sam!" she called to the darkness. "Now. Or this guy's dry cleaner is gonna be looking for a way to get brains out of cashmere!"

Somehow, impossibly, this little corner of the park seemed to be deserted. Had they cleared the area or something?

The guy laughed.

Gaia made herself ignore it. "A trade!" she shouted. "Sam for this guy. Right now. Or I blow his freakin' head off."

The guy laughed again. Gaia arched an eyebrow. He wasn't supposed to be laughing. He should have been begging his buddies to make the trade, save his life.

"What's so funny?" she demanded.

"Shoot me," the guy said. "He won't care."

"What's that supposed to mean?" Gaia asked. "Who won't care?"

"I mean," gurgled the man in black (because Gaia's forearm was still crushing his esophagus), "my employer won't give a damn." The mirth had vanished from his voice now. "He'll probably kill me himself for this."

Damn it! Gaia loosened her grip but didn't release him. She had to think. She had to . . .

Sam!

He was there. Being pushed out from behind a stand of broad oaks by another black-clad villain.

Gaia's heart lurched. Oh, God, Sam! He looked half dead. Gaia had never seen skin so pale before in her life. His face was covered with a sheen of sweat that matted his dirty, greasy brown hair to his forehead. One of his eyes was swollen shut, and the other twitched like a dying bee's wing. There was a spot of blood beneath his right nostril. The jerk in the suit was dragging him like a sack of flour.

Gaia was so overwhelmed with grief that she almost let go of her own charge. She caught herself in time, though, gave him a nice whack with the butt of the gun, then let him crumple to the ground, unconscious.

"Sam!" she screamed.

Did he flinch? Had he heard? Hard to tell. She made a move to go to him, but his captor had suddenly produced an automatic weapon.

And he was aiming it directly at her heart.

"JESUS!" IF ED WEREN'T ALREADY sitting down, he might have passed out. "Heather!"

She was standing there, holding **Hysteria**

198

the cell phone she'd just snatched out of his hand. He could hear the operator's voice coming through the mouthpiece.

"Hello? Nine-one-one emergency? Hello?"

Apparently Heather was oblivious. She punched the end button.

"How dare you feed me to the wolves like that!" Heather fumed, hands on hips.

He quite seriously wished he could strangle her. "Heather, listen. I'm not kidding around. You have got to get out of here!"

"You can't tell me what to do, Ed," she spat out, her eyes wild. "It's not like we're going out anymore."

Like he'd ever told her what to do when they were together. He decided to chalk that inane remark up to hysteria, which she was clearly on the verge of.

"Heather . . ."

"Where the hell is that little bitch?" she demanded. "And where is Sam? He'd better be all right, or I swear I'm holding you and Gaia responsible. Now, where are they?"

Ed clenched his teeth and jabbed his finger in the direction of a spot on the pathway, roughly twenty yards ahead. "There they are."

Heather looked.

Fortunately, he was able to reach up and flatten his hand over her mouth in time, or her shriek would have certainly given them away.

HE SLAMMED THE SILENCER ONTO

his .44, then stepped out onto the path in front of CJ, who skidded to a flailing halt. The kid had his gun now. He must have found it and grabbed it so that he could go back and finish Gaia off.

That wasn't going to happen.

Blood still gushed from his nose, and his bare chest was scraped raw. When he saw the gun, his dark eyes got huge. He lifted his hand and aimed at the gunman's chest. That was all that was needed.

Perhaps the last thought ever to register in CJ's brain was something along the lines of He's got eyes like her.

The bullet hit him just above the bridge of his ruined nose, right in the place where all thoughts began.

And ended.

He remained on his feet a good five seconds, a tiny rivulet of crimson trickling from the corner of his mouth, his eyes bulging with what looked more like surprise than anything else.

Then his knees buckled.

And he began to fall.

And with the soundless echo of the boy's last, unspoken plea raging in his mind, Tom Moore disappeared into the darkness before CJ even hit the ground.

GAIA HEARD IT, LIKE SOMETHING OUT

Boogie Knights

of a dream.

A song. What was it? She knew it. Her father used to like it. An oldie. The lead singer's intro over the sound system came floating through the cool night to reach Gaia.

"A classic from the seventies . . . 'Rescue Me,' by Aretha Franklin . . . so let's boogie!"

Boogie? Oh, please.

And then the bouncy tune, and in the singer's gravelly West Village voice, the lyrics: "Rescue me, I want your tender charms, 'cause I'm lonely, and I'm blue. I need you, and your love, too. . . ."

Great. So now the hostage rescue had a sound track.

A surge of memory nearly blinded Gaia as the familiar song wrapped itself around her. Her mother and father, one night in the cozy family room of their house. The radio blaring. It was a classic even then. "Rescue Me." She was six. Laughing. So were they. Dancing. All of them. They were dancing.

Rescue me. Rescue me.

The scream ripped itself from her throat, drowning out the distant melody. Gaia threw herself at the man with the gun, slapping his arm out of the way, sending the gun spiraling into the night sky. He

201

lunged for her, and Sam, unsupported, slipped to the ground.

Her fist plowed into the guy's abdomen, lifting him off his feet. Her foot slammed into his rib cage. She heard him grunt. "Ugh!"

Ugh. We have an ugh. Do I hear an ummphff? She grabbed a handful of his hair and shoved his face down hard against her knee.

"Ummphff!"

We have an ummphff, ladies and gentlemen!

The guy dropped forward, landing on his hands.

Gaia closed by giving him a good old-fashioned kick in the ass. His chin hit the pavement with a sound like breaking glass.

And then her own breaking began—the breaking down, the shutting off, the surrender of all strength. She was familiar with the experience; it happened every time. She could fight like a machine, full force, pumped on fury and desire. Her might was boundless, but only as long as that fuel was in supply. This fight had sucked up every ounce of energy she possessed.

And now she was spent. Her knees softened. Her limbs tingled. Breathing took on an entirely new caliber of effort.

And the lead singer of the band sang, "Rescue me."

It wasn't just in her head, as it seemed. It was blasting through most of the park. She staggered toward Sam, fumbling in her pocket for his insulin, and went down on her knees beside him.

"Hang on," she whispered. At least she thought she whispered it. Maybe she just thought it. He opened his good eye—just a slit, but still, it opened. "Hang on."

She prepared the syringe according to the directions she'd forced herself to memorize on her way from her house to the park. In her weakened state, the needle seemed to weigh a thousand pounds, and then it was entering Sam's flesh. Swift, smooth. Strangely intimate. She was injecting life back into him.

She withdrew the needle. The night spun in slow circles. The singer sang, "Rescue me." Gaia told herself to get up. Stand. Run. For help. But she couldn't seem to lift herself from the pavement.

As it turned out, she didn't have to. The guy in the black sweater was on his feet again. He grabbed Gaia and hauled her up. Her legs buckled. He was crushing her against him, her back to his chest.

Oh. A knife. At her throat. How inconvenient.

And Sam. On the ground, stirring now.

The shot came from behind her. An excellent shot, piercing her captor's shoulder but leaving her untouched. He went down, screaming.

She staggered forward a few steps and landed in the grass.

A man—a golden-haired man—thundered onto

the scene. A police officer? No. The Incredible Hulk?

A knight. Yes. A valiant knight.

To rescue me.

Gaia wanted to smile but couldn't seem to send the message to her face.

The knight was standing over her now. His face was so concerned, so familiar. *Dancing in the living room, and laughing with Mom. Rescue me.*

The knight was her father.

He crouched beside her, lifted her head, stroked her hair.

Oh, God. Is this what forgiveness feels like?

"Gaia?" he whispered. "Gaia, I don't want you to misunderstand. I'm not who you think I am."

She squeezed her eyes shut. *Please don't say that.*

"I'm not Tom. But I'm your family. I'm . . . your father's brother. His twin."

She finally made her mouth work. "His . . . brother?"

The knight nodded. "I've wanted to find you, and take care of you. But I wasn't sure how you'd react. So I waited. Tonight I had no choice but to show myself. I'm sorry if this is painful, Gaia. I'm so sorry. But I'm here now. I'm with you. You're my brother's child. And I love you."

Gaia drank in his words. An elixir. A potion.

She had a family. She could feel the strength returning to her body, with the hope. With the love.

"There's a lot to explain," he whispered, "but I can't now. I have to go. As long as you're safe . . ."

Gaia opened her eyes and looked at him. "No . . ."

He nodded, stroking her hair. "It's all right. You'll understand soon. I promise, I won't be far. I'll come back for you. I swear it."

Gaia struggled to sit up. It was as though her nerves had turned into live electrical wires.

Then her uncle placed one gentle kiss on her forehead, and he was gone.

Don't cry, she told herself, greedily pulling air into her lungs in quick, sharp breaths. Don't.

Her uncle had saved her. Her family.

"Gaia!"

She turned. "Ed?" But before she could ream him for following her, she spotted a figure flinging itself toward Sam.

Her eyes widened. "Don't . . . even . . . tell me."

"She saw the whole thing," Ed said.

Gaia watched Heather pick up the nylon case from where it lay on the ground beside Sam. She watched her place her perfectly manicured hand on his forehead, her perfectly glossed lips on his cheek.

And she watched Sam open his eyes.

She was a good twenty feet away, but even from that distance, Gaia heard his whisper. It seemed to explode in the deepness of the night. "Heather?"

"Yes," sobbed Heather. "I'm here, Sam. I'm here."

Gaia saw him try to smile and she saw his grateful eyes move from Heather's face to the nylon bag and then back to her face. His voice was trembling with exhaustion and emotion when he asked, "Did you . . . save me?"

Gaia closed her eyes. This wasn't happening.

To her credit, Heather didn't say yes. But she didn't say no, either.

Sam is okay.

He thinks Heather saved him, but he's okay.

CJ's dead.

I didn't kill him, but I saw them zipping up the body bag and hoisting him into the ambulance, so he's dead.

I have an uncle.

I'd never heard of him before today and he's been absent for my entire life—even longer than my dad—but I have an uncle.

Before today I hadn't thought it was possible for life to get any more surreal.

Today proved me very, very wrong.

SHOCK

To Isabelle Stevenson

Some mornings I wake up and everything seems okay. It's something my brain does. I suppose everyone's brain does it. You're in dreamland, and the wish fulfillment fairies take over and douse you in their bogus happy dust. Peek into your hidden desires and make you believe that you've satisfied them. Paint pictures that your eyes, flicking back and forth behind your closed lids, devour with an embarrassingly ravenous greed. And by the time you open your eyes, you're full of ill-gotten endorphins, convinced that all is well with the world.

Sometimes I can float there for thirty seconds, a minute, two minutes. I can will myself to believe I'm just a regular teenager whose biggest problem is figuring out how to sneak out after curfew. I can look at the sky outside my window and think, *Good morning, sunshine! Are we ready for another fabulous day?*

But reality always gets me in the end.

Before I can even wipe the boogers out of my eyes, I start to remember.

That's when the fairies take off. The minute they see my eyelids flicker, they start laughing like a bunch of punky eight-year-olds and take off out the window. And all the good feelings they gave me get slowly squished by the lead-and-tar mixture of the very real mess that is my life. I sink under the weight of reality. And pretty soon the bright colors of my dream fade to the dismal black-and-white of facts.

Fact one: Ed, my boyfriend up until last night, but more important, the person who's been my closest friend through all of this. . . well, he hates me. Wants to keep distance between us, where there used to be nothing but the best of friendships.

Fact two: Sam, my first love—as in the person you never fully get over—turns up just long enough to ruin things with Ed and then turns out to be a two-faced killer. Just like George Niven and everyone else I tried to trust.

And worst of all, fact three: My dad is missing. A particularly gut-wrenching fact that should make all boyfriend troubles irrelevant. He's out there somewhere, and nobody seems to know the first thing about how to find him. I might be his only hope. Which just makes me that much more of a target for whoever is trying to kill me.

Oh, yes. Trying to kill me. Shots fired, life in jeopardy. Someone actually wants to take this dismal life from me, and I'm damned if I'm going to let them. My father needs me too much.

For one brief moment I had everything I wanted: a family—two parents and a sister. A boyfriend. And I let myself believe it was mine, that those stupid dreams had really come true. And it all fell apart.

Note to self: Never fall for that one again.

Period.

End of story.

Beginning of day.

Rise and shine!

This was so WEIRD. Like a new reality show: *When Best Friends Go Bad.* **human obstacle** They didn't speak to each other like this.

GAIA MOORE EXITED THE BUILDING SHE

Electronic Dork Tool

lived in, on East Seventy-second Street, in a foul mood. She didn't even know where she was heading; she just knew she had to get out of that apartment and go somewhere, anywhere. It was stupid to stay in one place for long if her would-be killers—with or without the help of Sam—were looking for her. She wanted to search for her dad, but with nothing to go on, her energy just floated around in a hyper haze. It made her feel wired and weird.

To make matters worse, some asshole was letting his cell phone ring. Probably an idiot yuppie fresh from his morning workout getting a frantic call from the office asking what was going on with the Hooper account. Or a frazzled mom with two bratty kids who left her phone in the diaper bag and couldn't find it. Or some "boutique" dermatologist avoiding her needy patients jonesing for their Botox fix.

What Gaia couldn't understand was, why did people carry cell phones if they didn't want to answer them? And if they knew they were going to blow off a call, why not turn off the ringer and save everyone from having to hear that incessant, bleating whine? The worst part was, whoever the phone belonged to seemed to be following Gaia down the street. She glared at the people passing her, trying to shame whoever it was into turning off that annoying ring, but it kept going and going. Jesus, it sounded like it was coming right from her own backpack. Who the hell. . . ?

Crap. It was Gaia's cell phone. She kept forgetting she was one of the wirelessly enhanced masses!

She dropped her backpack to the ground and quickly unzipped it, yanking the zipper up so that the grimy pack flopped against the ground. She spotted the cheerful silver phone in the dank recesses and reached in to get it, at which point it finally stopped.

Aaah. Sweet silence.

She checked the incoming-calls screen and saw that the phone number was for Dmitri's apartment. She hit the talk button twice and stood in the middle of the sidewalk, legs planted on either side of her open backpack, listening intently. She'd never get used to this tiny electronic dork tool. It clicked a few times, then beeped. She tried again, but the damn thing wouldn't connect. She waited to see if the little envelope would pop up—maybe he was leaving a message—but after about a minute and a half she realized that nothing was happening. Maybe Sam had signed her up for one of those low-rent plans.

Sam. As she closed up the phone, Gaia was disturbed to realize that her heart was thudding. Despite all evidence that he was a two-faced, double-crossing, wanna-be

6

killer, there was still a part of her that just didn't get it. That wished he was calling. How dumb was that? The guy had given her instructions to meet him at a Ukranian church the night before, and as soon as she got there, *bam*, gunshots were headed straight for her gut. He had to be involved. He'd obviously been the willing bait to bring her there. But some small, idiotic part of her still felt a connection to the guy she had fallen for long ago.

The human heart was undeniably the stupidest organ in the body.

Forget it, she thought. *There's nowhere to go and nothing to do. I might as well go to school.*

Stuffing her nonworking phone into her backpack, she disappeared down the yawning maw of the subway tunnels. She'd try calling Dmitri again when she got to school.

GAIA WALKED UP THE CONCRETE STEPS

Festive

to her high school in her usual state of bored irritation and inward concentration. Even if she were actually thinking about nothing more interesting than paper plates, it kept people from talking to her. But as she stepped through the wide metal doors, she stopped. Something was distinctly different.

There was a weird buzz in the air. Something undeniably festive was happening.

Gaia hated festive.

"What's going on?" she murmured to no one in particular.

"It's intramural week, silly," Megan shrieked. Megan was a particularly loathsome friend of Heather's. That is, she had been a friend of Heather's before Heather had gone blind from one of Loki's experiments and been whisked off to a hospital. Now she was a friend of Tatiana's—Gaia's roommate and almost stepsister had stepped into the part with barely a ripple—who looked surprisingly fresh, considering she'd been partying it up in Gaia's apartment just the night before. In fact, Megan was just as perky as she'd ever been. A cynical observer might even have said that Megan could barely tell the difference between Heather and Tatiana and didn't care which one was head of the proud crowd as long as Megan was among the top bananas. That FOH and FOT were all the same to Megan the Shallow. But that observer would have been a very, *very* cynical person.

"Intramural week." Gaia didn't state it in the form of a question, but Megan didn't let that stop her from expanding on her dementedly exciting news.

"I wouldn't expect you'd know about it," Megan said with a sigh. "I mean, Gaia, you're not exactly Miss School Spirit. But intramural week is when everybody forms different teams, and we play against each other."

"For what?" Gaia asked.

"For fun!" Megan squealed. "And trophies. But mostly for fun!" She moved in close, so close that their noses almost touched. Gaia caught a whiff of her very specific scent: a combination of fabric softener, Chanel Coco Mademoiselle, and spunkiness. "I formed a swing-dancing team," Megan said confidentially. "We have three couples. I mean, anything goes."

"Swing dancing is a sport?"

"They're trying to get it into the Olympics," Megan said sadly. "It's hard to get respect, but swing dancing takes a lot of athletic ability."

"Hm. Yeah, if curling gets to be in the Olympics, there's pretty much nothing that can't be considered a sport. Even golf," Gaia said.

"Exactly!" For a moment Megan seemed to feel very vindicated. Then she saw the complete lack of expression on Gaia's face and remembered who she was talking to. The freak of the school. "Oh, Gaia. You're being sarcastic again."

Gaia shrugged.

"I wouldn't expect you to understand," Megan complained. "But just look at how excited everyone is." With a sweep of her hand she gestured to the groups of chattering girls and on-a-mission guys crowding the hallway. "You'd do yourself a lot of good if you joined in, Gaia."

"Sure." Gaia hoisted her backpack higher on her shoulder and gave a little nod as she walked off. Wow, Megan had no clue. About anything! *Maybe I should start a dad-finding team,* she thought. *Would that make me more normal in your eyes? But who would I compete against?*

In her rush to get out of the main hallway Gaia took a quick left and felt herself collide with someone. She backed up and muttered an apology, but the someone wouldn't move his lanky frame out of her way. She looked up, about to spit out a withering insult, when she saw that her human obstacle was Jake.

Why did Gaia always call him "snake" in her mind? Despite his friendly words to her the night before, somehow this guy seemed inherently untrustworthy. He was new to the school, and his ridiculously movie-star-level good looks made him a prime target for the FOHs (or FOTs or whatever they were). The most desirable divas in school were working themselves into a group frenzy over him, and he seemed to enjoy the attention—but part of him seemed to stand back, not quite joining in, not quite playing their games.

Of course, Gaia herself was the definition of stand-offish, but she wasn't used to seeing other people hold back like she did. And he did it so subtly, she wasn't even sure she was right about her feelings. She couldn't get a read on him, and that made her suspicious. That plus the fact that he'd challenged her to a karate competition and had very nearly beaten her. That was just not normal. His eyes narrowed as he fixed her with a smile that could only be described as sly.

"Trying to escape the epidemic?" he asked her.

"What epidemic?" she asked warily.

"The school-spirit epidemic," he said. "It's spreading like wildfire. I think they put something in the cafeteria Jell-O."

"That wouldn't spread anything," Gaia informed him. "Nobody in their right mind would eat the cafeteria Jell-O."

"Good point. So you're going to join in, right?"

"Yeah, right." Gaia made a move to pass him, but Jake blocked her way and put a firm hand on her arm. His grip was surprisingly strong.

"I'm serious," he said. "I'm putting together a karate team. We'll beat the pants off of everybody if you and I are on the same team."

"Wow, I so would prefer to see pants remain *on*."

"Don't you want to win? Don't you want to beat these clowns at their own game—literally?"

"You're so goal-oriented," Gaia told him. "I thought intramural week was all for the *fun* of the games."

"Come on," Jake said. "Those were some wild moves you pulled on me. You humiliated me, for chrissake. The least you could do is make it up to me by being on my team."

"Sorry, but I don't need to show off," Gaia told him. "Besides, I've got a new hobby taking up my time."

"What, you're a secret agent?" Jake asked.

Gaia didn't let her surprise show on her face. She

11

studied Jake carefully secretly, exactly as her father had trained her to do. She took in his body language: His muscular arms, crossed over his chest, said he had something to hide, but he was leaning toward her with his head tilted—which was supposed to indicate that he was friendly and unthreatening. She noticed he was actually just a little too close—was he trying to intimidate her by invading her space? His pupils were dilated, a sure sign he liked what he saw. But his eyes wouldn't quite meet Gaia's, flicking away when she gazed back into them. Damn it. The guy was a walking pile of conflicting information. There had to be something in what her dad told her, some way to read what was behind Jake's words: He seemed to be kidding. She *hoped* he was kidding.

"Secret agent? Right," she said, sliding her own eyes to the side so he wouldn't see how rattled she was. "No, I just really feel that watching paint dry is my true calling," she went on. "It satisfies some deep inner passion."

"That's just how I feel about watching grass grow," Jake retorted, without skipping a beat. "It's so meditative. Almost as good as watching concrete set."

"Ha ha." Gaia almost included a smile in her response. Almost. But Jake seemed happy just to have gotten the "ha ha" out of her.

"Think about it," he said, and walked away.

"Yuh-huh," Gaia said noncommittally, and continued down the hall to her locker. She wondered what was really going on there. Jake wanted something from her. He seemed to be curious—a little too curious. Then again, he could just be flirting with her.

Yeah. Right.

She mulled over the Jake question as she walked down the hall, trying to untangle the strands of information she had from him. She was so distracted, she didn't really notice Ed Fargo walking straight toward her. In fact, she almost said hi to his familiar, loping form.

Then she remembered: The argument. The dismissal. The double-sided promise that they'd keep their distance from each other. Seeing Ed made Gaia feel like hydrogen peroxide had been dumped in a fresh gash in the middle of her gut: It burned and bubbled and ate away at her. Somehow the pain she felt when she saw him was exactly proportional to the closeness they used to have. It was amazing. Best friend had turned to boyfriend and then to total enemy in less time than it took for one of the FOTs to relax a perm. It made Gaia feel sad, sadder than almost anything else in the world, but she wasn't about to let anyone else in on that little secret. Least of all Ed, the guy who was the cause of it.

And here he was. Duh. Of course she was going to have to see him around school. She was going to have to be polite. If not out of respect for their old friendship, then out of the dim hope that the FOTs wouldn't get more fodder for their gossipy bitchfests.

13

Ed's face didn't betray any emotion. Well, it did, but for him, he was being pretty stoic. Trying to show Gaia a mask of calm. She knew that underneath he was hurting as badly as she was. Stopping about five feet away, his skateboard tucked under his arm, he stood there uncertainly.

"What's up," he said.

"Nothing," she answered, not looking at him.

Gaia's skin felt like it was on fire. The last time she'd seen Ed, he'd been standing on the sidewalk, half drunk, calling her a liar and a cheater and demanding she stay the hell away from him. Her guts turned into a colony of cockroaches, skittering around inside her. She wanted nothing more than to just go back to being friends. But the way he'd spoken to her last night? That wasn't just going to go away. And she had to be honest: She had lied to him. Having Sam show up out of the blue had really knocked her for a loop, and she had been lying to Ed when she'd said she didn't have feelings for Sam anymore. That made her feel horribly guilty. Like maybe Ed was right for wanting to keep his distance. Like maybe she needed to be on her own until she sorted out her unbelievably annoying jumble of emotions.

"So how's Sam," he said, as if he'd been reading her mind and the guilty feelings that were blotched all over it. He was convinced she'd been canoodling with Sam behind his back.

14

"I don't know. I haven't seen him," she told him, emphasizing the last half of her sentence.

No need to tell him that he'd just tried to kill her. And no need to tell him that before that, Sam Moon's return to the land of the living had made her feel confused. Still, as far as Gaia was concerned, she hadn't *done anything* about her confusion—that was what counted. And Ed was supposed to trust her. And he didn't. Which was why she was pissed.

"So, I'm doing a skateboard clinic as part of intramural week," he said.

"Uh-huh," she murmured. No congratulations, no questions—not even a little bit of teasing about how he was joining in with the school-spirit masses.

This was so WEIRD. Like a new reality show: *When Best Friends Go Bad.* They didn't speak to each other like this. Except they did now. Gaia felt horrible. But this conversation had to end. She needed him to get away from her, fast.

"Yeah. I thought it'd be fun," Ed said. It was a limp, nondescript sentence, and it plopped onto the floor between them and lay there. For Gaia the silence that followed was full of unspoken accusations. *You can't be part of anything, you freak,* he seemed to say. *Like a family. Like a couple. Like anything you desperately want and won't let yourself have.* It stung to hear him say it—stung for the words to be there, sandwiched

15

between the lines in glaring, accusing, ten-foot-high red letters. Without another word Gaia turned back to her locker, hoping he wouldn't see the slight tremble of her chin as she listened to his sneakers squeak down the hall away from her like the turns of a screwdriver driving a rusty screw deep into the soft flesh of her heart.

I wish I didn't have buttons. The same way I don't have fear. I wish nobody could push my buttons the way Ed does, making me feel like everything I do is wrong and useless and mean. I wish that nothing would infuriate me, or make me feel insecure, or rattle my cage.

It's my fault, though. If I hadn't shown Ed where my buttons were, he wouldn't be able to push them.

I thought I was okay, not being close to anyone. I thought I had taught myself not to wish for what I can't have. After my mother died and my father took off, I shut myself off. Personally, I think it was a pretty impressive feat for a kid that young. After a while I didn't know what I was missing.

Well, now I know, don't I? What I'm missing.

Being close to Ed felt like. . . what did it feel like? It wasn't like he was my other half or anything doofy like that. Plato had this whole thing in the *Symposium*

GAIA

about how everyone used to be smushed-together couples with four legs and four arms and their sex organs locked in a constant erotic knot. Then something happened to blow us all apart, and now we spend our whole lives looking for our other halves. I guess some couples feel that way, but not me and Ed.

Still, there was something in the way we were together that was so easy. It felt like *home*. Being with him, being his friend, filled something in me that I didn't know was empty. And then having him become my confidant and my actual boyfriend—that made the connection so much deeper. But the best part was always having him as my friend.

It was a blessing and a curse. The blessing part is what I just said. The closeness. The comfort. The home.

The curse part is that once you've felt that comfort and it's taken away from you, all of a sudden you miss it—even though you never knew you wanted it

before you had it. All these
nerve endings flapping in the
breeze, looking for the tooth
that just fell out.

But there's something bigger—
something worse. Once someone has
been that close to you, he's got
too much on you. He knows how to
hurt you, how to push those goddamn buttons. Hell, he can push
them without even realizing it.

I want to be calm, cool, button-
less. No way in, no way out. Not
even a zipper.

Not fearless, feelingless.
That's a genetic mutation I could
really get behind.

Here is the thing I have to
get through my thick, stupid
head: The Gaia I fell in love
with obviously *does not exist*.
Therefore, I do not care that
she's gone. Right? WHO CARES? NOT
ME. I don't care that she lied,
snuck around, maybe even cheated
on me with Sam. Since the depend-
able, honest person I thought she
was never existed, technically, I
can't miss her. How can you miss
a mythical creature? Do I miss
unicorns? No. Do I miss the Yeti?
No. Do I miss Anna Nicole Smith's
dietician? No. And why is that?
Because none of those creatures
can exist, do exist, will exist.
And I don't miss Gaia-my-best-
friend because she doesn't exist,
either. Now I should be cured.

Except I'm not. The feelings I
had for her—the ones that just
yesterday were a huge, comfortable
blanket around my heart—they just
won't get out of me. No matter how
much evidence I tally up to the
contrary, those feelings want to

swim around in my consciousness.

The word *love* keeps floating around inside my head, like the afterimage of a flashbulb. Except in my head the word *love* is purple, and it looks kind of like a balloon. When I met Gaia for the first time, I saw that love balloon in my head. It was small then and just hovered around in the background as I thought about calculus, and history, and my Regents exams. I got to know her better, and I started to think, *Maybe I love her. Maybe this word I've heard about all my life has a new meaning, maybe it's something I feel for this girl.*

That's when the love balloon started getting bigger. But the color of a real balloon gets paler as it fills with air. The love balloon in my head just became a richer shade of purple, and when I thought of Gaia, it got bigger. The night we spent together, it got huge. And whatever I was doing in my day, that purple balloon would bounce around and make me feel great, because I knew what it meant and I felt all this love for this weird, annoying, funny, crazy girl. I'd say to myself, like I was trying it out, "Oh, I love Gaia," and it made me feel so great.

Well, now I don't love Gaia. I was wrong about her and I was wrong about feeling that way about her. But the big purple love balloon DOES NOT GET THE MESSAGE. It still bounces around in my head, but now, instead of being comforting, it's annoying, like Barney.

I try to poke it with an imaginary needle, but it's made of some really tough kind of rubber. I try to make it burst into flames and hit the ground, like the *Hindenburg*. Oh, the humanity! But the damn thing won't deflate and it won't burst. It's still hanging out in my head, looming and bouncing like a permanent purple storm cloud.

Oh my God. What was that conversation? We're worse than strangers. It's like we hate each

other. She actually *hates* me.
This feels terrible. Cutting off
Gaia is like cutting off my own
leg—losing it completely, not
just having it paralyzed. But
she's been lying to me, and I've
got to get rid of her now, before
I get in even deeper. It'll be
better this way in the long run.

The trouble is, how do I make
a long run with only one leg?

She should
have been
able to tell
the **plausible**
difference
cover
between a
masked oper-**story**
ative and the
president of
the Shakira
fan club.

THANK GOODNESS GAIA HAD OTHER

things to occupy her mind. Her phone finally snapped out of its reverie and went through to Dmitri. Gaia thanked the God of Unpredictable Cell Phone Service and put the phone to her ear.

"Dmitri," she said. "It's Gaia."

"How are you this morning?" he said.

"I'm all right," she lied.

"I thank you again for rescuing me and bringing me back," he said. "My apartment is very comforting to be back in. It is not so much dustier than when I left it."

"Well, good," she said. Was this why he had called? To chat about his one-bedroom in Chinatown?

"I wonder if I can ask for your help," he said, answering her unasked question with his polite segue. "I think I have some information that may be of assistance in finding your father. But I need you to help me get to it. Are you opposed to a little breaking and entering?"

Now this was getting interesting. "Not if it means getting more information about my father," she told him.

"That is good. Your father trained you well."

"I guess. So what's the deal?" she asked him, impatient.

"I don't want to say on the phone," he said. "I've sent you instructions via e-mail. You can go retrieve them."

"Why won't you just tell me?" she seethed.

"Too much to tell," he said. "Too many details. You need to see them and commit them to memory. You should know that this is how things are done in the Organization."

"Yeah, but the Organization should know that e-mail is never secure," she retorted.

"This one is. It's encoded and contains a self-destructing virus. It can only be read once."

"Okay, fine."

"You can check in with me if you have any questions. Otherwise I will expect a visit from you when you've completed the task I've laid out for you."

"Okay." Gaia snapped her phone shut and started to head for the front doors of the school just as the bell rang.

"Gaia Moore," a voice boomed from behind her. She turned to see Vice Principal Lorenz—the grooviest school administrator on the entire East Coast. Lorenz never wore suits, preferring jeans and a sweater, or khakis if he really had to dress up. His thick salt-and-pepper hair had only recently lost its extra ponytail length. Most students liked his get-to-know-you attitude—he acted like the tormented poems of the literary-magazine crew were genius and even thought the cheerleaders were following their bliss. And he liked everyone to call him Bob. Even Gaia thought he seemed cooler than your average schoolhouse bureaucrat—on a normal day. But at this moment he had a distressingly

26

friendly look on his face, like it was time to have a *talk*. And Gaia didn't have time for one of those.

"It looks like you've got somewhere to go," he said.

"No. No, I was just walking. . . past the front door, to my next class," she said. She had to get to a computer and then bust out of school to complete Dmitri's assignment. She wanted to do it now. But Bob Lorenz had a different task in mind.

"I've noticed you've been missing a lot of classes," he said, putting a reassuring hand on Gaia's shoulder. "And even when you're here, you don't really seem *present.* Is something going on?"

Well, let's see. My dad has disappeared, a mysterious old man is sending me on a secret mission, and both my ex-boyfriends are haunting me, in their own special ways.

"No!" Gaia said. "Nothing's going on."

"I know you have an unsettled home life," Bob went on, clamping that hand onto her shoulder and strolling down the hall with her. . . away from the front door. "It must be really tough. If you want to talk about it, you know my door is always open."

Yeah, or I could just watch Dr. Phil, Gaia thought. "I know," she said aloud. "I was actually planning to stop by later this week."

"Well, why don't we just chat now?" he asked, steering her into his office. "I mean, you're here, I'm here. We can talk about all the classes you've missed." He pulled a file out from a stack on top of his desk. It had a yellow sticky on it. Clearly he'd been watching Gaia for a while. . . . She cursed silently. *Should have played my part better,* she grumbled to herself. *I'm setting off alarms left and right.* If the school's administration thought she was some kind of tormented teen in need of intervention, then intervention was what she was going to get—and that meant less freedom to come and go as she pleased. Less freedom to defend herself and find her father.

This was not good.

Every muscle in Gaia's body felt poised for action. Finally there was something she could do about the Mystery of the Missing Parent——and all she had to do was get to a computer to find out what it was. Instead, she was sitting in the vice principal's office, being gently scolded for missing assignments and not being more "proactive in her educational advancement." Ugh.

The intense irony of it was, with one *thunk* of her leg she could have had Vice Principal Bob on the floor and stepped on his unconscious body on the way out the door. But he was a nice guy. And she didn't want to get herself arrested. No, she had to play her part for now; nod and smile as if she understood her shortcomings and really, *really* wanted to better herself. She'd bide her time, make it through this meeting, and check her e-mail in the school library. Whatever was waiting in her in box, it would have to keep for an hour or so.

"STUPID ORGANIZATION," SHE MUTTERED

Constant
Skitz

as she waited impatiently for the infuriatingly slow 56-K modem to connect her to the Internet. "Left over from the Cold War. About as updated as Tang or the Fonz. Like this stupid modem," she added, giving the pesky peripheral a whack.

This was a serious breach of security as far as she was concerned. Sending sensitive information over the Internet? Duh. Any twelve-year-old with a Dell could hack into it, encoded or not. Forcing Gaia to read it here, at school? Double duh, ha-doi, and a dah-hicky. This was public property. Maybe the fact that it was teeming with innocent civilians would make a less cynical operative think she was safe here, but Gaia knew her enemies better than that. Her classmates were in as much danger as she was, and whoever was after her—whoever had her father—wasn't going to let a few hundred teenage martyrs stand in his way.

Gaia swallowed hard, the knowledge that she was in constant danger peeking above the surface of her consciousness again. She couldn't live in a state of constant skitz. But she couldn't stop being vigilant, not for even one second. They were after her. Whoever they were. And they'd used something as innocent as a bite of chicken potpie to get her father.

29

When anything could be a weapon, the world could start looking exceedingly twisted.

The modem finally connected, and she maneuvered through web pages till she got to her e-mail program.

To: gaia13@alloymail.com
From: ruskie@acenet.net

The Worldwide Travel Agency at 53 West 35th Street is a front for the Organization. In there are files pertaining to your father's disappear-ance. They are labeled *Moorestown* and are enclosed in a brown cardboard accordion folder wrapped with a thick brown string. The label is red. The exact location is not known, but it's most likely in the top drawer of file cabinet A (see map below). Also central to your search is a travel dossier. This is in a yellow file folder in a drawer on the right side of the desk marked *FF*. It is labeled *Places of Interest*. Break in and deliver the files to me today at 5 P.M. at my apartment. Be careful.

Gaia eyed the e-mail with total and complete con-centration. She had a photographic memory. The image of the words seared into her frontal lobe as the distrac-tions of the library fell away. There was something meditative about this action: The words became more than black and white on the screen; they took on a life of their own, the shapes of the letters forming patterns that Gaia recognized apart from the meaning of the words themselves. Wow, her brain was freaky sometimes.

A pensive haze settled over her for a moment. There was nothing but the words and the message they brought her. Until a hand clamped over her eyes and the world went dark.

SAM'S POSSESSIONS LAY IN A TANGLED

Stupid Cell Phone

heap on the floor, looking like they'd been ransacked by a couple of angry prison guards. He surveyed the mess with frustration and fury. He couldn't blame anyone but himself for it. He'd been tearing through his own stuff for half an hour, trying to find his cell phone.

He picked up the regular phone and was greeted, yet again, by the incessant whine of an Internet connection. Dmitri was still on-line, and all Sam wanted to do was call Gaia. The guy had been locked up for so long, he hadn't even heard of DSL.

31

Whatever he was doing, he was doing it at a crawl, and Sam was itching with impatience.

He had an almost physical need to speak to Gaia—it pained him as much as the red scars of the gunshot wounds and operation incision that were the legacy of the time he'd spent in Loki's prison. The last time he'd seen her, she'd been trying like hell to get him out of her apartment while her boyfriend—*her boyfriend!*—read her the riot act in front of her building.

It just killed him. All Sam wanted for Gaia was for her to be happy, and she seemed miserable. Okay, he had to be honest: all he wanted, really, was for Gaia to be happy *with him*. Of course he was jealous that Ed got the title of boyfriend and everything that went with it. *Everything that went with it.* An image of Gaia wrapped in the thin sheets of his dorm-room bed flashed through Sam's brain. He pushed it back into whatever corner it had jumped out of. He was not going to think about that. Gaia had too much going on in her life to deal with Sam's feelings for her. She'd made that much clear. If he'd never been shot, if he'd never disappeared from her life, then things might be different. But they weren't. They were like they were, and he had to keep his distance and give Gaia her space.

But he wanted to call her, anyway. He had to speak to her today. Not to get in her way or push his feelings on her. Just to make sure she was okay. The whole party-packing-fighting-leaving thing the night before had been a situation of such relentless awkwardness, he hadn't been able to relax since.

Forcing himself to take a deep breath and try to relax while he waited for the phone to become available, Sam flopped onto the floor and started doing stretching exercises. The wounds on his back were still raw and painful, but he knew his best chance of healing was to get strong and keep his skin from atrophying into more scar tissue. He could even manage a few push-ups if he really focused. And all through his long imprisonment, there was one image that had helped Sam truly focus: Gaia. He saw her sitting on the edge of his bed, her knees drawn up, the toes of her sneakers pointing toward each other. If he worked out harder, he could even hear her voice.

Very impressive, Sam's inner Gaia said in a flatly sarcastic, teasing voice. *What was that, half a push-up?*

Sam stretched harder, feeling his muscles scream with the effort, but his inner Gaia was right: It wasn't hard enough. This was what he had done the whole time he'd been in that prison. Pictured Gaia to get him through the days. Used the memory of her to force himself to survive. And now he was back in the world with her. Come to think of it, this was probably none too emotionally healthy for him. But he really didn't give a damn: Healthy or not, he needed Gaia to be with him, *really* with him, his girlfriend. They'd had a brief moment of perfect bliss before he'd been captured, and he knew that she could bring him back to that earlier, more innocent, less troubled version of himself. The Sam Moon who was premed at NYU and played a little chess. Who didn't suffer from prison-flashback nightmares. Who wasn't reduced to living in a busted-up apartment in Chinatown where the air smelled like the "fresh" fish store downstairs and the paint on the walls flaked off in lead-filled hunks.

"You picked up the phone again!" Dmitri growled from the next room.

"I need to make some calls," Sam said, stopping his workout and looking up. Sweat poured from his slick skin and his breathing was labored. He was glad to have an excuse to stop, inner Gaia or not. She vanished in a poof from her spot on his bed.

"Use your cell phone," the old man told him, not even turning around from his post at the monitor.

"I told you, I can't find it. I need the phone to at least check my cell's voice mail."

"I am sorry. I must get some things in order."

Sam stood leaning against the doorway, and observed the gnarled fingers tapping away at the keyboard. "I thought you were in that prison for a long time," he said.

"I was, yes," Dmitri said impatiently.

"This iMac is a brand-new model. Did someone buy it for you while you were inside?"

Dmitri turned to him, giving him a baffled, hurt

stare. The old guy had taken a long shower, cut what was left of his thin gray hair, shaved, and served a freedom feast for the two of them the night before, bringing in food from an old-school Romanian restaurant a few blocks away. He was no longer the frail scarecrow that he and Gaia had freed from Loki's prison. His blue eyes had taken on a sharpness, and his muscles seemed to have gained strength overnight. But he was still an old, old man, and one who had just survived a hell of an ordeal.

"Sorry," Sam rushed to say, but Dmitri put up a hand to stop him.

"No, my boy," he said. "I am sorry. I know what it is like to be brutalized the way that you were. I know what it does to you. And I know I am not an ordinary person. All I can tell you is, the years I spent in the Organization left me with many resources. I am not the only one who has used this apartment, though it is my home. Trust me when I say there are certain things you should not know." He shrugged.

Sam nodded and left the room. But the truth was, he really didn't feel any better off here than he had in his cell at the prison. At least there he'd been able to see the bars that held him inside; here, in this apartment, he simply knew that there was danger lurking outside—people trying to recapture him, maybe, or just kill him—and that his life might never get back to normal. Then there was the Gaia question. Which wasn't really a question. It was more a screaming need that wrenched his heart the way his scars wrenched his chest.

He kicked over a milk crate full of his clothes and muttered a stream of curses. He wasn't in school, he had no job (what was he going to put on his resume for his lost semester—"professional prisoner kidnapped by shadowy spylike organization"?), and he didn't even know who he was anymore. *And* he still couldn't find his stupid cell phone.

I used to think that there was good and evil and that good would always win out over evil. That's what we're taught to believe, right? That's what always happens on the cop shows on TV. The bad guy might be clever, but *clang clang! Law & Order* will win in the end.

I don't know if I believe that anymore.

I did everything the way I was supposed to. I mean, I wasn't always perfect. I didn't always drive the speed limit, and if the check was wrong, the waitress wasn't going to hear about it from me. But on the whole, I think I tried to do the right thing.

And for most of my life it worked out pretty well.

I don't know, maybe I should have gone to Tufts. Because it was in my second year of NYU that everything started spiraling out of control. I started dating Heather, then she dumped me. I

SAM

got seduced by Ella, this older
woman, and then she disappeared,
too. Classes? With all that was
going on, organic chemistry
wasn't exactly foremost in my
mind. And then my roommate got
killed.

And before I could say,
"Prozac, please," my entire existence was basically wiped from
the earth.

I was shot, sewn together, and
cooped up in a jail cell for no
reason. I got no phone call, no
due process, not even a hint of
what I'd done wrong. . . . or
right. I tried to train myself
not to stare up into the sky,
looking for a helicopter full of
good guys who'd rescue me. Not to
look for Superman, or Spiderman,
or even Charlie's Angels.

Sometimes I think about this
guy who lived on my floor in the
dorms. He claimed to be a
nihilist: someone who believes in
nothing. He said no good and
evil, there was no justice or
crime. I thought about him a lot

when I was locked up. I thought,
If I can be like that, if I can
believe there's no reason or pat-
tern in the world, then I'll stop
believing there's hope, I'll stop
hoping for release. Because it
was the hope that was killing me.

But I never managed to believe
in nothing. And you know what?
Neither did the guy on my floor.
Because when he got a phone call
telling him his father was dead,
I saw him cross himself. Even the
nihilist believed, just for a
moment, when things got bad
enough. And I did, too. I
believed I'd get out of there.

And then I did. Okay, so it
wasn't an action hero who rescued
me, it was Gaia and Dmitri. But
the thing I had hoped for? It
came true. That should tell me
that there is good in the world,
right? And that good triumphs
over evil, setting the innocent
free and bringing justice in its
wake?

But the big day of my rescue
was just like any other day. The

sun set, and it rose the next day, and I still didn't have any answers about why this had happened to me. And I'm not any more free than I was behind bars. And worst of all, the bad guys are still out there.

So what does that mean, Bosley?

All I know is, the last time I felt good, the last time the world made sense, I was with Gaia. Wrapped in my sheets and feeling her strong body next to mine, watching her let go of all that tough-bitch bullshit and just melt into my arms. I want to feel that way again.

Can being with her bring me back to that place? I don't know. But nothing else seems to be working. I guess I'd really like to find out. I guess I need to see for myself if Gaia can bring the world back into focus for me.

GAIA WHIPPED HER ARMS BEHIND

Bigger Fish

her and grabbed whoever had their hands clamped over her eyes. With one brisk movement she had her attacker slammed on a library table, faceup, with her forearm against their throat, ready to rip out their...

It was Megan.

Her hazel eyes were wide with surprise, and she was making a faint choking noise. Gaia let go of her throat and stood up, snapping off the monitor behind her with her other hand.

"Hucccch," Megan said, rubbing her throat and giving Gaia a confused and angry stare. She sat up on the table. "You're such a freak. What the hell is wrong with you?"

"Why did you attack me?" Gaia asked flatly. The truth was, she felt like a total idiot—she should have been able to tell the difference between a masked operative and the president of the Shakira fan club, for chrissake. And that made her even more aggressively angry.

"I was just trying to goof around with you," Megan snapped, her hand still fluttering protectively around her throat. "Jesus. You were so wrapped up in the computer, I thought it was funny. I was just going to say 'guess who.'"

"You can't sneak up on people like that," Gaia told her.

"Oh, please. Would you give it up already?" Megan

seemed exasperated. "When are you going to learn that you're not fooling anybody?"

"What the hell is that supposed to mean?"

"I mean, nobody buys your 'I'm so mysterious, try to figure me out' act. Like you're the tormented star of some movie of the week. Everybody just thinks you're pathetic. Your psycho party-pooper routine last night went a long way toward convincing everyone you've got serious emotional issues. And when I tell them you attacked me just to increase the faux mystique, your stock'll take even more of a nosedive."

"Well, thank you so much for the insight," Gaia said. "It's really comforting to know I'm being psycho-analyzed behind my back by someone who thinks swing dancing is a sport."

Gaia didn't know whether to be relieved or insulted. Okay, she was both. Relieved that she *was* fooling everybody. And insulted that they thought she was a stereotypical tortured teen. Well, at least she had a plausible cover story.

"Why don't you do yourself a favor and take some advice," Megan said. "Stop assuming I'm an idiot just because I'm popular. And join a team—*any* team—before you become one of those lonely old people with twenty cats whose only close personal relationship is with a phone psychic."

"Yes, I'm sure spending time with people who share my intense interest in bowling will really draw me out of my shell and provide me with the life skills I need," Gaia snapped.

"Suit yourself," Megan told her. "You know, frankly, I don't give a crap what you do. I just felt sorry for you. When you're a lonely thirty-year-old writing memoirs about how miserable your younger days were, like Janeane Garofolo or Margaret Cho, don't you dare say nobody ever tried to get through to you." She stalked off.

Gaia stared after her. *Well, well, well,* she thought. *Little Megan was on a mission to do some good works. I hope she gets a gold star for trying.*

Whatever. Gaia had bigger fish to fry. She still had the information in her head, which was good, because when she turned the monitor back on, she could see that the message had already self-destructed. With a few flicks of the mouse she emptied the computer's cache, just to be on the safe side. The fun was over. Now she had to get to Midtown—fast.

"I SWEAR, ONE OF THESE DAYS WE'RE

Ready to Spring

going to see Gaia on the cover of the *New York Post,* being led into a squad car in handcuffs," Megan complained to Tatiana five minutes later. "No offense, but I don't know how you can be friends with her. Let alone Heather. She's totally nutso."

"It is not easy," Tatiana agreed, checking her lipstick in her locker mirror. Her lilting Russian accent was still apparent, but her English improved by the day, and as it did, her shyness seemed to melt away. So much so that her position as nouvelle Heather seemed completely natural. "She can be a most unusual roommate," she added. "Sometimes I expect to see her sleeping upside down, like a bat. Has she done something to you today?"

"Well, yeah. I just went up to her in the library and tried to be friendly—for your sake, I guess," Megan answered. "But she was so wrapped up in her geekoid computer world that she flipped out the minute I touched her. I mean, it was so totally over the top, I could have had her arrested for assault. She must be involved in one of those on-line role-playing games. She probably forgot about reality for a second and thought she was really Astrella, Queen of the Dark Demons." She gave an evil titter. "Do you think she dresses up like an elfin waif on the weekend and meets up with Renaissance Faire weirdos for some naughty jousting?"

Megan let out a loud guffaw at the thought of Gaia in a green doublet and hose, but Tatiana just turned to her with a blank expression on her face.

"What was she doing on the computer? Did you see what was on the screen?"

"No. It was probably naked pictures of the cast of *Buffy the Vampire Slayer*."

"Was it e-mails? Did you see what any of them said?" Tatiana asked in a curiously intense voice.

"I don't know, maybe. It did look like she was reading e-mails, and she was totally focused, like they were full of secrets or something."

"Are you sure you didn't see what any of them said?"

Megan looked at Tatiana. "Jeez, no, Tat. I mean, come on, who cares, right?" She gave a little laugh, then looked expectantly at Tatiana, who fixed her eyes on her new friend for a moment longer, then gave in and laughed, too.

"I just thought it would be such good gossip if you saw something." She shrugged. "I never can figure out what Gaia is up to. I thought you might have seen what the big secret was."

"The big secret is there is no big secret," Megan said decisively. "Are you hung over? I'm hung over huge, and I think I'm going to run to Starbucks between classes. You want to come?"

Tatiana turned away and seemed to be staring into the black recess of her locker. Megan didn't notice that Tatiana's spine was curiously tense, that she was wound as tight as a coil ready to spring.

"No, thank you." Tatiana's voice drifted over her shoulder. "I just remembered, there is a phone call I must make."

Tatiana closed her locker and stepped toward one of the wide windows that would afford her cell phone the best reception. She flicked it open, murmuring into it in serious Russian tones that seemed out of place in the teeming high school hallway. If Megan had noticed, she might have found it odd. But she didn't notice. No one did. And after a little while Tatiana snapped her phone closed. Then she pulled a second cell phone out of her bag, checking closely to see if any messages had popped up on its small screen. Then she put both phones away and strolled down the hall as if she didn't have a care in the world.

The jangling
bells of the
antitruant
alarm
exploded in **rules**
her ears.

ED STRODE PAST THE LIBRARY, AND

for the second time that day he caught the familiar sight of Gaia's long, straight blond hair. His reflex reaction was to rap on the window and say hi, but he stopped himself just in the nick of time.

Off-limits

When was he going to get it through his thick head—or his thick heart? Gaia: off-limits. He knew it intellectually, but the rest of him—every bit of him from the neck down, including the heart and various other regions—hadn't yet gotten the news.

Without realizing it, Ed leaned his head against the window of the library and sighed.

"Oh, my goodness, who is sad today? Perhaps you are hung over like Megan. Would you like to get some coffee?"

The musical Russian accent, the friendly voice—he hated to admit how good it felt to see Tatiana coming up to him.

"Hey!" he said. "How are you doing? You were pretty wrecked last night."

"Oof!" Tatiana waved a hand in the air. "I have almost no memory of the party. My apartment is such a mess, I have to have someone help me clean. I hope you had a fun time?"

Ed shrugged. Actually, the party had been a nightmare: obnoxious girls, too much Sam Adams, guys

48

who thought "woo!" was a conversation aid, and of course his horrible confrontation with Gaia after he'd found her in a love knot with Sam. He hoped Tatiana really didn't remember much. Jeez, she'd been so drunk, she'd come on to him, and he'd been so drunk, he'd almost let her. But as he studied her face, there didn't seem to be any awkwardness in her gaze.

"I had a fine time," he said. "I don't remember much, either."

There. They were both off the awkwardness hook, using the age-old beer-amnesia excuse. Gosh, it was handy. Now all the awkwardness he felt was the regular old I-don't-know-you-well-enough kind. Which was kind of okay, actually. Interesting. Possibly even a little exciting.

"Are you going to do an intramural?" Tatiana asked him.

"Yeah, a skateboarding clinic," he told her.

"Oh, that is so perfect for you!" Tatiana cried, slapping him on the arm. "And after you couldn't do it for so long, now you'll be teaching it to the younger students—Ed, that is really cool."

Now, see? How hard is it to just be happy and supportive? Is Gaia just lacking this skill altogether? This is how friends are supposed to act together.

"I'm actually pretty psyched," Ed admitted. He shifted his feet, feeling self-conscious, not sure if he needed to explain. "I never thought I'd be teaching anything, but when they asked me, I was just like, what

49

the hell. I'm sure they'll regret ever considering such a thing, especially when I take a bunch of freshmen into the abandoned pool in Williamsburg and we all get arrested."

"Ed, don't be silly. They wouldn't have asked you if they didn't think you could do it. You'll be a great teacher."

The way that Tatiana looked at Ed with her big blue eyes made him feel ten feet tall. Never mind that the eyes he'd prefer to see gazing at him were ice blue and belonged to Gaia. Never mind that Tatiana didn't hold quite the same fascination for him—that she was sweet and funny but didn't have quite the same spark as Gaia. Gaia had taken herself out of Ed's circle of friends. And Tatiana clearly wanted to be in that circle. Could you blame a guy for feeling good about that? It was just the antidote Ed needed.

"Yeah, well. So what about you? Starting a ski team or something?"

"I'm going to do something, but I'm not sure what," she said. "Perhaps running track or something boring like that."

"That's not boring," Ed told her. "And it comes in handy when you're running late to catch a bus."

"Now, you see, that is good common sense," Tatiana told him. "I knew I would learn good life skills in your American high school."

The banter between them was easygoing and fun,

good-natured and friendly. After a while the heart-break Ed was feeling receded from the front of his consciousness. Without realizing it, some of the lead in his chest leaked out, just a little. Tatiana had some kind of effect on him. Enough to make him stop seeing Gaia everywhere he looked and start having fun again. For a moment. For a little while.

And it felt—if not all better, halfway normal. For Ed, that was the hugest relief of all.

GAIA'S NEXT CLASS WAS AP ENGLISH.

Low-Rent Drug Deal

The class was about halfway through a long discussion of *Hamlet*; today they were going to watch scenes from the movie versions starring Ethan Hawke, Kenneth Branagh, and Mel Gibson and compare them to one another. Literature via Hollywood.

Gaia had read *Hamlet* in sixth grade. She really didn't care what Hollywood had done with it. And quite frankly, the story of a guy whose father was d-e-a-d dead and whose son was haunted by the need to avenge him was completely not what Gaia needed—or wanted—to think about.

51

It shouldn't bother me, she told herself. *Because my dad is not dead. He's just missing.*

Right. And she was the one who had to find him. Pronto.

Before the between-class bell could ring a second time, Gaia was clear of any part of the school where she might be spotted by someone other than a stray mouse. Contrary to what Vice Principal Bob thought, she had done a lot of studying in high school. But the knowledge she'd squirreled away had nothing to do with *The Red Badge of Courage* or pi-*r*-squared—stuff she'd mastered years before and didn't feel the need to show off about. The most useful information she had acquired in recent months had more to do with blueprints—as in, the layout of her school, from top to bottom, complete with emergency escape routes for times just such as this.

She admired the purpose of the antitruant rules that were supposed to keep her here. But they were getting in the way.

Most of the doors to the basement were wired with alarms, but Gaia had noticed that the school janitors were easily annoyed—particularly by oversensitive bells that went off accidentally when they were just trying to clean up a chem lab spill. At least half of the doors were disabled, a fact she'd noticed when a gang of ersatz bad-kid freshmen had gone through a phase of daring each other to set off the alarms on purpose.

It had kept not working. Gaia had noted the location of the dead doors for future reference.

That knowledge came in handy now. She made her way to a corner of the school near the sidewalk and hit the red lever of the door smack in the middle of the word *warning*. Seconds later Gaia Moore vanished from the smooth tiled hallways of her high school and into the dusty dank basement below.

She heard the metal stairs clank under her feet as she made her way down into the gloom. It was so gross down here, even the most hot-blooded adolescents wouldn't want to use it as a make-out spot. The heater and water boiler were ancient and had sprung quite a few leaks over the years, creating the kind of moldy environment that silverfish and millipedes found irresistible.

Gaia was sure nobody would be down here. Too sure.

"Who's that?" she heard a voice say. She froze, cursing herself for not having tiptoed down the metal stairs. The silence around her was broken only by the throbbing hum of the boiler. As her eyes adjusted to the gloom, she looked out into the open space of the basement and saw three nervous-looking students peering around, a triptych of paranoid self-preservation. One of them—a kid Gaia recognized as a self-styled wanna-be wise guy—was holding out a couple of mini-baggies of what looked to be weed. The other kids were holding money. This was nothing more than a low-rent drug deal, and it was none of her business.

But before she could melt back into the shadows, something conked her on the head from behind. Her relief turned to fury as she hit the ground, knocked off balance by the sneak attack.

"What the—"

Gaia saw an overgrown hulk standing over her with a lead pipe still held over his shoulder like a softball bat.

"What the hell are you doing down here?" he demanded.

Gaia saw the two buyers race up the stairs and disappear through the door back into the school, a momentary sliver of light announcing their departure. The back of her head burned, and she could hear a loud ringing in her ears. But the dizziness retreated almost immediately. The blow to her melon might have trounced a normal kid, but Gaia was anything but normal.

"Crap, they took their money with them," the dealer groaned. As he turned toward her, Gaia got a good look at him. His mussy hair was in dire need of a bottle of Pantene, and he wore a denim jacket emblazoned with Megadeth patches over a hooded sweatshirt. Worst of all, his upper lip held a smudge of peach fuzz that she was sure he intended to pass off as a mustache. "Who messed up my deal? Brick, man, what do I keep you around for?"

Brick just glared down at Gaia. His bulk was the

most noticeable thing about him: Some pituitary mis-fire had given him the body of a wrestler, and his shaved head only served to enhance the impression that he had absolutely no neck whatsoever. "She came out of nowhere, Skelzo," he complained. "I didn't see her till she was practically on top of you."

Skelzo walked over and glared at Gaia, who was patiently waiting for these two nonentities to get tired of talking so she could get out of there.

"Girlfriend, you wandered into the wrong part of school," he told her.

"Oh, no, I'm petrified," she said. "Can I leave now if I promise never to come back?"

"You'll run straight to the principal's office," he scoffed.

"I won't, I swear." Gaia was finding it increasingly difficult to play the part of terrified teen, however half-assed her attempt already was. "I'll get in as much trouble as you if anyone finds out I was down here," she pointed out. "Just let me go and I promise I'll forget anything ever happened."

"Oh, you'll forget, all right." Skelzo's scraggly mouth twisted into a grin. "You'll forget because I'll make you forget."

She rolled her eyes. "What does that even mean?" she asked.

"What?"

"I mean, *you'll make me forget?* What, did you read

that in a comic book and think it would sound good? It doesn't even make sense as a threat."

"Look, bitch, you better—"

"No, you bogus tool, *you'd* better." Gaia kicked directly up and into Skelzo's crotch, lifting him into the air with the force of her blow. He gave a kitten-like mew of pain as he arced backward, and when he hit the ground, he curled into a ball without another sound.

Brick was faster on his feet than Gaia had expected, and he brought the lead pipe down toward her. She rolled to get out of his way, but the pipe still glanced off her shoulder, creating a searing white-hot flash of pain instantly.

"Ow," she complained, rolling into a crouch and eyeballing her opposition. "Brick, why don't you just run? I promise you'll be better off."

Brick only stared at her, crouching slightly as he poised to swing at her again the second she moved. He was a good fighter, she noted. Or he could be if he trained. This self-taught tough guy was about to find out that brawn wasn't the only thing he needed to beat some ass.

"I really don't have time for this," she complained. Then she shot forward, grabbing him around the waist and pushing him backward onto the floor. Landing on top of his massive frame, she straddled his chest and grabbed both sides of his head, bringing it down to smack against the cold concrete. She heard an "uggh," but when she leapt to her feet, the stupid doofus still wanted to come after her. Stealing a glance at Skelzo, she saw he was puking up his guts and clutching his stomach; at least she didn't have to worry about him. She stopped Brick with a foot to the chest, then moved her foot six inches higher to smack him back down with another shot to the forehead.

Blood splattered where his scalp scraped the concrete. "Shit," Gaia muttered. These were just a couple of kids in her way, not a true threat, and she didn't want to do real damage to them. "You total idiot, why didn't you just back off before I hurt you?" she asked.

Leaving the Moron Twins flat on the floor, Gaia turned toward the trapdoor to the sidewalk that would lead her to freedom. Then she heard a groan. She turned back to look and saw more blood leaking out from Brick's head wound.

Forget him, she told herself. *You have a job to do.*

But some sneaky little sliver of conscience yanked her mind back into the basement. These weren't Loki's henchmen. They were a couple of stupid pot-dealing teenagers. And if she left them bleeding in the basement, they might not be found for hours—even days.

She gave a hefty sigh and ran across the basement, leaping up the metal steps of another set of stairs toward a door that would trip the alarm. She leapt up and snapped her foot out, hitting the door with percussive force and shoving the door open with whatever was the direct opposite of delicacy. It slammed open with a clang, and the jangling bells of the alarm exploded in her ears.

It would only be a matter of moments before someone came in the open door. She raced back across to the trapdoor set into the ceiling under the sidewalk, throwing herself against it with the strength of a bucking horse. It held fast. She cursed, then threw herself against it again. Obviously it was padlocked from the outside. Gaia looked around wildly, feeling her adrenaline rise as the alarm bells continued to jangle. She wasn't worried about being punished. She was worried about how this would slow her down. And getting slowed down was not an option.

Her eyes rested on a red fireman's ax. Never mind that a high school was a horrible place to leave a lethal weapon; she was glad to see it. Angling it between the door and its frame, she placed the sharp edge against the crack and whacked it. Once, twice. . . and on the third hit she felt the metal hinge snap and give above her hands. She pushed the door open and leapt up, swinging her legs and pushing her arms down so she could reach the sidewalk. She rolled away from the gaping door and came face-to-face with Karl, the hot dog vendor who tortured the students with his heaven-scented Sabrett cart.

"Now, I know you're not supposed to be out here," he said, giving an amused shakeof his head.

"I'm not planning on sticking around," she told him.

"Hey, you want to cut school, go right ahead," he said. Without another word Gaia stood, kicked the door closed, and raced uptown.

"But you oughta go back," Karl yelled after her. "Unless you wanna be selling wieners for a living when you're my age!"

By the time anyone noticed she was gone, Gaia was halfway to Midtown on the 1 train.

Tatiana —

What is up? I just had a mocha latte and I am buzzing from a sugar high and caffeine, but guess what? I am still hung over! I am chugging vitamin water to escape this hell. If you have any Motrin, please chuck it my way.

DWI = drunk woman intoxicated.

So by the way, I saw you talking to Ed! <u>What is going on there, girlfriend?</u> It looks like you two are already BFGF. You've got more chemistry than seventh period HA HA! You'd better watch out for the psycho beast known as G. M! Make sure she's done with that toy b/f you play with it! Otherwise you might find yourself picking teeth out of your ass <u>or worse</u>!!! DSIDWY (don't say I didn't warn you).

Seriously, I think u 2 (ahmigod! My favorite band!) would be the cutest couple. You should jump on that. When Heather was with him, she said he had a way with his tongue — I mean when they were kissing!!! I hope Heather is OK. I keep meaning to call her, but I'm being such a flake about it. I want to tell her about the benefit, but first I want to find out how much $$$ we made. Thanks to you and your connections, girlfriend! You are the best!

Uh-oh I can see Mrs. Hochman giving me the evil eye. If she busts me I'll get detention for sure! TTYL!

  — Megan

GAIA HAD NEVER BEEN TO CALCUTTA,

Chubby Airplane

but she had heard about the wall-to-wall throngs on the sidewalks, the makeshift bazaars where people sold fruit, the crowds that slowed foot traffic to a crawl. Midtown Manhattan on a weekday—especially here, in the part of town called the Garment District—had to be a lot like it, she thought. There were just so many people going to their jobs, from their jobs, delivering things from one job to another. Entire racks of clothes bumped down the sidewalk, bright colors standing out against the gray and grayer buildings, sleeves billowing out as if they were being strutted down a catwalk instead of being wheeled by poverty-income dudes who barely noticed the fabulousness they transported. If she'd wanted to, she could have bought batteries (*Energizer!*) or a watch (*Bolex!*) or pirated DVDs of the top ten movies playing in the theaters that week. Or she could have ducked into Macy's and joined the tourists going up and down the building's ancient wooden escalators to buy Charter Club ties and sweaters. Or she could've gotten on a train bound for suburban New Jersey heading out of Penn Station. But she had no interest in any of this. She was headed for the travel agency.

The avenues in this part of the city seemed impossibly long, probably because they were sandwiched between tall, looming buildings that barely left a wedge of street between them. In some places the sunshine barely hit the pavement; the sunniest day could feel like an overcast mess if you never walked west. The address she was looking for was here, right in the middle of the block, in a storefront that seemed almost abandoned among the bustling wholesale clothing stores and office buildings whose revolving doors never stopped turning.

The travel agency's storefront was grimy, and the only decoration was a once cheerful cardboard sign in the shape of a `chubby airplane` announcing new low fares to Yugoslavia. It took a few moments for Gaia to even find the door, which gave a desultory jingle when she opened it. Inside, the gloom was interrupted only by the dust that seemed to have collected in every corner. The dropped ceiling featured broken asbestos tiles and fluorescent tube lights, most of which were either completely dim or flickering faintly. Four industrial-size desks sat facing the center of the room, like a cloverleaf, and Gaia noted that the file cabinets were exactly where they were supposed to be according to Dmitri's e-mail. She was able to match the room around her to the map in her head perfectly.

Only one of the desks was occupied, by a woman who seemed to be the exact color of the grayish linoleum. "Can I help you?" she asked uncertainly, as if a customer were a rare bird she hadn't sighted in several years.

"Yeah, I go to NYU, and I intern down the street," Gaia told her, using her well-crafted cover story. "I was on my way to work when I noticed you're a travel agency. I wanted to know if you had any ideas for where I could go on my winter break."

"Oh. . . I don't know," the woman said, staring down at the brochures piled on her desk as if they would crumble to dust if she tried to open them. "We mostly do corporate travel."

"But look right here!" Gaia pressed a finger onto the top brochure. "It says 'student travel specials.' Those look good—can I find out more about them?"

"Oh," the woman said. "I forgot about that. Well, you can look through it if you want. But you know, I'm not sure if we can help you. I'm not used to booking individual trips."

"I have to go home, anyway, and check out the choices with my suite mates," Gaia told her. "Will you be open late tonight?"

"We stay open till seven," she said.

The phone on her desk gave a bleating ring, and the woman stared at it in alarm.

"Excuse me," she said to Gaia, who was pretending to leaf through the brochure as she took in the rest of the office.

"Yes. Yes. No, not really. Yes. No. Okay," she said into the phone. "Not now. I am! Okay. Yes. Sure." Then she hung up and peered at Gaia.

"I'm sorry, I have to close up the shop right now," the woman told Gaia.

"I thought you said you were open till seven!" Gaia said in her best complainy-student voice. Inside, she was beaming: Dmitri was right. This place was such a front, it might as well have had NOT A TRAVEL AGENCY, KEEP WALKING emblazoned on its sign outside.

"Normally we are, but that was my boss, and he said he wants the place closed up for some reason."

"Man, this sucks," Gaia said, still in her college-girl persona. "How am I going to book my trip?"

"Try Orbitz," the woman told her.

Gaia gave an exasperated sigh and left the agency. Just before she exited the door, she looked back: The woman, who just moments before had been so distracted she couldn't even focus on Gaia's request was suddenly going through the contents of her desk with well-organized speed. The soft bafflement of her features had been replaced with a razor-sharp grimace of concentration. `Oh, man, was this place a front!` In essence, a file bank for the Organization. Gaia couldn't wait to come back. All she had to do was wait for this weird chick to clear out and the place was all hers. Better than a playground. And educational, too.

In the meantime Gaia was glad to take a breather from the place. Something about it gave her the willies. The travel posters were all too enthusiastic— and about places where nobody in their right mind would really go on vacation. Clearly they had been fashioned by people with nothing but disdain for the common sense of the average customer. It was as if the Organization were subtly making fun of every unsuspecting civilian who walked through the door. Like they were playing games with people's lives and it was all the more fun for them that those people didn't know about it.

She couldn't wait to rip these jackasses off.

Are you tired of traveling to the same well-worn destinations?

Experience the land of bleak mountains and turbulent rivers. Unite with nature in a sparsely populated region nearly untouched by civilized man. Come face-to-face with the Snow Man——and barely live to tell the tale! Come to beautiful Siberia!

To: shred@alloymail.com
From: gaia13@alloymail.com
Re: Hope you are OK

   I feel really bad about how things ended
between us and I just wanted to say I hope we can
be friends at some point. I wish I could explain
why I snuck around and what was going on. But I
can't because slkdfjsghsoioiffdkslf THIS SOUNDS
SO STUPID.

<DELETED>

To: shred@alloymail.com
From: gaia13@alloymail.com
Re: Wish things had been different

   I hate the way things ended between us, but it
just has to be this way for now. I have some
crazy stuff going on and I'm just not going to be
a good girlfriend, and it's not fair to you. I
just wish you had trusted me more. Not that I
really gave you much reason to. OH, SCREW THIS.

<DELETED>

To: shred@alloymail.com
From: gaia13@alloymail.com
Re: Hi

   You were my best friend and I'll never forget
that. Thank you for the time we spent together.
It really was the best.

       <STORED ON HARD DRIVE—UNSENT>

The pungent
odor of
gasoline
hit her
nostrils
just as she **the**
realized **flame**
what was
happening.

IT TOOK EXACTLY TWENTY MINUTES

for Gaia to walk across the street, order one of the best falafels she'd ever had, and chew it slowly at a window table. The whole time, she kept her eyes on the travel-agency-slash-Organization-front. The woman from the desk left almost immediately, but Gaia knew not to count on that. She wanted to make sure the woman didn't come back—either to catch her or to get something she'd forgotten. But as Gaia wadded up the aluminum foil and wiped the last of the tahini sauce from the corners of her lips, the coast seemed as clear as it was going to get. It was time to make her move.

The first thing she noticed when she walked into the building next door was that the elevator shaft connected the two buildings. That was good news: If she could get in there, she'd have a strong chance of breaking through to the travel agency without alerting anyone on the street.

The trouble was, she had to get into that elevator shaft.

"Can I help you?" a voice came from behind her. Gaia turned to see a tall, hefty guy in coveralls. Earl, his name tag read in embroidered script. Standing between her and the elevator.

"Is this where Casa del Carpets is?" she asked, putting a hand on her hip and letting Earl get a good long look at her. She was wearing a tank top—it was almost guaranteed Earl wasn't going to remember her face.

"No, it's not," he said to her chest. "Casa del Carpets is down the street."

"Ohmigod, sorry to bother you. Thanks," Gaia said, and left the building.

Oh, great. That was one of the dumbest moves she'd ever made. Walked right into a security guard, or elevator operator, or whatever he was. She had to get past that guy and into the elevator—and there was no guaranteeing she'd get through the shaft even if she did get in there. Damn it, Gaia could *feel* time slipping away.

As if on cue, a huge dump truck, trundling down the street, stopped a few feet away. The driver got out and ran into a deli. Gaia could see him directing the guy behind the counter to pour him some coffee. This was her shot, and she took it.

In a flash she was up in the cab of the truck, faced with the dashboard. Mostly it looked like the usual car controls, but below the stereo, on the floor, there was a huge black box with an extra set of buttons. If she could just figure out which one. . .

CLANG!

That was it! The back of the truck began rising, lifted by the huge hydraulic cylinders that unfolded from its belly. Gaia pulled back on the lever that made it rise faster. If she was right about her calculations, the pile of garbage in the dump bed was too heavy to stand for much of a—

THUD!

Gaia felt the truck pitch backward as its dump bed hit the asphalt behind it, pulling the front wheels right off the ground. She gave a nervous laugh: It felt like an earthquake, the way the concrete buckled under the truck, and the huge load of ash created a choking cloud that gave Gaia just the cover she needed. She whisked out of the passenger door of the truck before the driver could get out of the deli and was safely in a crowd on the sidewalk by the time he ran up to the cab of his truck, frantically tugged at the controls, and waved his arms, as though that were going to undo what Gaia had done. The truck was a mess and would be completely unmovable until all the a s h was cleared away. More important, everyone on the street was awestruck by the colossal mess.

Including Earl.

With the elevator guy gaping openmouthed and watching as police cars sped onto the scene, Gaia had the opening she needed. She slipped into the building, stepped into the old-school elevator, and yanked a huge metal lever back so that the doors closed.

"Hmmm," she said. The walls of the elevator enclosed her, but she wasn't moving. A huge old crank stood to her right. She turned it and the elevator lurched upward. She rode it too fast up two floors, then brought it gently down so that she was between one and two. Then she yanked open the doors again, exposing the dank shaft in all its concrete-and-metal glory.

Layers and layers of filth, going back half a century or so, caked the walls. The only things that looked well used were the gears and cables, slick with oil, that kept the thing in motion. Gaia peered down into the shaft. She thought she could shimmy through the narrow hole into the open area below her. But once down there, she had to hope there was some way out. Because if the elevator went into motion, she'd be crushed like a bloody, bony pancake.

Still, it was her best option. She thought she saw a ventilation shaft opening down there. There was only one way to find out if she was right: She squeezed her legs into the narrow opening between the door of the elevator and the wall of the shaft, then shifted her hips so they hitched through the tiny space.

"Ow," she muttered, feeling the uneven edge of the elevator's lip scrape the button of her jeans. Then the cold metal grated against her chest, and for an awful moment she thought the life was being squeezed out of her as her lungs fought for air. Then she was through, hanging in the dim light of the elevator shaft, peering across to see if she was right about the way through to the other building—the one where the travel agency was.

There it was. A ventilation hole. She had to make it across the bottom of the elevator somehow. The ventilation system went along the ceiling of the room below, and if she plopped to the ground, she'd have a hell of a time getting back up.

She hoped the grease of the cables hadn't pervaded the metal bottom of the elevator car. It hadn't—but the grime was so thick, it was almost as slippery. She had one chance to get across, and it hinged on one metal pipe attached to the elevator. She reached out and grabbed for the pipe.

The dust made her hand slip right off. Her hand slid out into space, and she felt her left shoulder socket wrench with the effort of keeping her from falling.

"Huugh," she gasped, more from the pain and surprise than from any real concern that she'd fall. She had this under control. She just had to make it happen. And fast.

"Hello? What the hell is going on in here?"

Uh-oh. Really fast. Earl was back on the scene, and if he started up that elevator. . .

Gaia wiped the thick layer of dust off her hand and onto her jeans and reached for the pipe again. Not a great grip, but it was all she had, and as she swung across the bottom of the elevator, she felt herself slipping slightly.

"Easy," she told herself. No need to grab too hard.

Gaia swung her legs across and tested the metal

door of the ventilation hole. It was as old as the building—older than her father, probably—and it didn't want to give.

Gaia heard Earl come out of the landing on the second floor. He'd obviously taken the stairs up and was looking down into the empty elevator.

"Hello? Damn kids! Who's down there?"

She heard him swear a blue streak as he kicked at the elevator. It shuddered above her, making her already tenuous grasp feel even less secure.

"Damn it," she hissed.

"What? Is somebody down there?"

This was getting ridiculous. Gaia tightened her grip on the pipe. She heard Earl's feet hit the floor of the elevator just above her, and it shuddered again. Earl was not light. The elevator shifted at least two inches lower and began to rock. She had to get into that ventilation crawl space—*now*.

Gaia lifted her legs and kicked. Once. Twice. Three times. And then—"Jaah!" she yelled, feeling the metal door give as she gave it one last kick. The elevator shuddered again as she heard the machinery start up, high above her. With no time to waste she kicked the door out of the way and shoved her legs into the dark, musty tube. She pulled herself all the way in just as the elevator dropped past. A hunk of her hair got yanked along with it, and she grabbed at it, forcing it to break rather than pull her along its deadly track. Then she just breathed, feeling her racing heart, pumped full of adrenaline, try to return to normal.

She assessed her surroundings. She could feel that she had just inches of steel through which she had to shimmy backward to reach anything close to the travel agency. Behind her she could hear the alarmed skittering steps of water bugs and maybe even a rat or two. Gross. Gross, but not life-threatening. She began her slow journey backward. "I must look really pretty right now," she said to herself, feeling dust coat her skin as she pulled herself through it. But once she got started, she found herself making good progress— below her, through the slatted openings, she could see a hallway, and then, a few minutes later, the dim interior of the travel agency.

Bingo.

She held her face close to the thin opening, trying to see what was on the various desks below her. Ugh, it was no use. She jimmied her fingers under the edge of the covering and yanked it up. The place was empty; she didn't care about the noise. She remembered how dank the place had smelled when she'd walked in before—funny how after ten minutes in an elevator shaft, it smelled as fresh as a springtime meadow.

Now she could see. But she needed to be down there, going through the desks, finding the files that Dmitri needed.

Dropping to the floor, Gaia wasted no time. The gate covering the front window was down, so she had to work in near darkness. She had two things to find: the travel folder, which had an exact location, and the file on her father, which had only an approximate location. She knew that no matter what her emotional priorities were, she had to look for the one she was assured of finding first. She went to desk FF and yanked open the drawers on the right side until she found a yellow file folder labeled *Places of Interest*.

Seeing that folder fired her impatience. Adrenaline shot through her veins, and some unholy combination of joy and vindication filled her heart—she had the right place; the directions were correct. Now all she had to do was find the Moorestown folder and she'd be on her way out.

She shoved the yellow folder down the back of her pants for safekeeping and turned to file cabinet A. A quick search of the drawers revealed a lot of cardboard accordion folders wrapped with thick brown string— but none of them had a red label marked with anything akin to *Moore, Moorestown,* or *Moore*—anything.

Okay. No problem. Gaia set her jaw and turned to the next file cabinet, moving systematically through the drawers in search of the Tom Moore folder. Then she moved to the next one. With each failure and each opening of a new drawer, her movements became slightly more agitated. In her experience, if something wasn't where it was supposed to be, the chances of finding it were pretty much nil. But she had to try. Dmitri had warned her that the location was approximate.

She had worked her way through most of the file cabinets, yanking and slamming through them like a secretary on steroids, when something made her freeze and stand in absolute silence. A sound. The sound of someone opening the door of the agency even though the gate was down. There was no time to wonder how the hell that could happen. With lightning speed she leapt up to the top of one of the file cabinets and climbed back into the ventilation system, peering out to see what would happen next.

The woman who'd been behind the desk came into the room, along with two men. All of the woman's spacey disorganization was completely gone. She even looked different—she moved with athletic agility as she went to her desk and cleared a few things out of the top drawer.

The two men with her were of average height but were also powerfully compact. One sported a mustache, the other wore a baseball cap, and all three moved silently to separate desks. They were almost choreographed, their moves were so organized, like they had trained for this moment.

"I don't know how this happened," Gray Lady muttered in irritation. "This location has been under the radar for so long. I don't know how our secrecy got compromised."

"It lasted longer than it was supposed to," Mustache Guy said, moving a heavy object—Gaia couldn't see what—to the center of the room from just outside the door.

"It's just part of the deal," Mr. Hat said. "I hate when this happens, though. It gives me the creeps. I feel like someone's watching me right now. Let's get the stuff we're supposed to save and get the hell out of here."

"Keep your shirt on," Gray Lady said. "Okay, I'm ready."

Before she even completed the sentence, Gaia heard something being poured methodically around the room, and the pungent odor of gasoline hit her nostrils just as she realized what was happening. These Organization operatives were destroying this front as part of a random cleanup operation. In other words, the place was about to go up in smoke. She had to get out of there!

The agents left through the door, letting themselves out whichever way they had come, and Gaia heard the *whup* of the fire as the gasoline flamed under the match they dropped.

Tubes in and out of my body. An upside-down bag hung next to my bed. Faces of women. Concern. Where am I?

I think I hear sobbing. Is it real or in my head? Television. I hear a television. Canned laughter rolling in waves. Over and over again. New jokes, old laughs. Hahaha.

Someone's finger moves. I see a ring finger flick upward in a sort of spasm. Is that on purpose? It's mine. That's my finger. This is my body. I'm in a. . .

Everything is so streamlined. My vision is dim. Is it a spaceship?

I can't move. Even my eyes—I can't seem to move my eyes around the room. They stare out from beneath drooping eyelids, neither open nor closed. They blink automatically. My throat swallows at regular intervals. The nurses come and go.

Nurses. I'm in a hospital. I'm in a hospital and I hear nurses. They sound like they are at a great distance.

Everything is at a great distance.

I see my brother, Tom. I see his beautiful girlfriend sitting with me on the steps of Low Library. There is a place we go to eat, the West End.

Katia. Her face is so sad, as if she knows something that is going to happen to me. As if she knows what has happened to me.

I seem to be in a coma. I can't make sense of any of this. Who is Gaia? Why does her name float around and around in my mind like a mantra?

I become tired easily. I make an effort to speak. I feel like I am shouting, but nobody hears me because my lips stubbornly refuse to move, my vocal cords frozen, cut off from the words my mind screams out.

Some of the nurses are kind. They treat me like a beloved houseplant. I'm not.

I'm Oliver Moore. I want to wake up, and I can't.

Maybe he was
surprised
just to see **failed**
her without
a body **mission**
bag and
toe tag.

DESPITE THE YELLOW FOLDER IN HER

Steamy Bathroom

lap, Gaia sat on the subway as it lurched through the tunnels, feeling like the lowest form of life. She'd been given an assignment and had only completed half of it. Worse, the assignment had been integral to her finding her father; she had totally failed him already, and her search had just begun. She tried not to let it get her down—even Babe Ruth didn't always hit a home run, right?—but it was no use. Maybe if she'd searched the drawers quicker, or started from the other end, or stopped to think logically about where else it could have been. . .

She knew where it was now. In a pile of water-logged, smoking ashes being shoveled out of a busted-up storefront by the NYFD. Fat lot of good it was going to do her.

As her train pulled into the Grand Street stop, she began to worry. She was angry at Dmitri for not giving her more detailed information. How could he have been so right and specific about the Places of Interest folder—and so grossly wrong about the Tom Moore folder? What was it about the travel folder that was so important? And where was he getting his information?

But she squelched her questions. The fact was, she

didn't have what she had set out to get, and he could easily be angry with her for not finding the folder, with or without his directions. She was in a knot of worry and tension over her failed mission. It was all she could think about as she made her way to Dmitri's building on Forsyth Street.

As she lifted her hand to press the buzzer on Dmitri's door, Gaia realized that she had made a terrible mistake. She couldn't go up to Dmitri's. What if Sam was there? She couldn't face him. Not after he'd tried to kill her.

She buzzed again.

"Yes?" Dmitri sounded impatient.

"I need to know that you're alone," she said. "I want to know that nobody is up there with you. Nobody."

"I sent Sam for a walk," Dmitri answered, as if he'd known she'd ask for privacy. She sighed with relief. *Good old guy,* she thought. *Smart old guy.* He buzzed again, and this time she pushed through the door and ran up the four flights of stairs.

Dmitri's door was unlocked and open. Gaia walked through it and shoved it closed behind her, flicking the dead bolt. The old man was in the green-walled kitchen, dipping a tea bag up and down in a tall glass, clinking it against the spoon that stood in its darkening depths.

"Here's your folder," she said, plopping it on the table. Dmitri didn't look up.

"You are as skilled and powerful as they said you were." He sighed, shaking his head. "I knew you could do this, my dear girl. Please sit, and I will make you a nice hot tea."

"I don't want a nice hot anything," Gaia told him. "I've had enough heat for one day. The Organization destroyed their front before I could finish the job. They set it on fire."

That woke Dmitri from his meditative tea making. "What? My child, are you all right?" He looked up, and his face took on an expression of concern. For the first time he noticed what a mess she was, and Gaia saw herself reflected in his reaction. Her hair torn and matted. Her skin caked with dust and muck. Her jeans gray and her sneakers half melted. Ugh. No wonder people had kept their distance on the subway. She either looked like a crazy person or an extra from the newest Christina Aguilera video.

"Oh, my dear, I had no idea—how could I have let you go?" Dmitri asked, squeezing her upper arms and patting her face with concern. "I would never have sent you if I had known they were planning such an action."

"I don't know who you got your information from, but whoever it is might be trying to set you up," Gaia told him. "Not only were they planning on destroying the place. . . there was another problem, too."

"What?"

Gaia forced herself to spit out the bad news. "The dossier on my father wasn't where it was supposed to be," she said. "I found the right file cabinet, and there were files in there similar to the one you said I'd find, but none was labeled *Moorestown*, and none contained information about him. I was in the process of checking out the rest of the file cabinets when the Organization operatives came back to destroy the place." She paused. "I'm sorry."

The old man's face fell as she relayed the story. He shook his head and sank into a chair, looking even older than he had when they'd found him.

"Dmitri, are you okay?" He was looking distinctly ashen. Gaia thought he might be having a stroke or something.

"I feel terrible," he said. "I put you in danger for an empty reason. Perhaps you are right—I am too feeble-minded to help you find your father."

Gaia sat next to him at the table. "Here, drink your tea," she told him. He gave her a sad stare, and she pushed the tea closer to him. He took a sip, grimaced, then took a sugar cube out of a tin on the table and put it between his front teeth, then sipped again, and then a few more times. His color seemed to return a little bit.

Frail as he was, he was Gaia's best hope of finding her father: Even if fifty percent of his information were flawed, it was more than she was going to find anywhere else. Whether or not she trusted this guy, she had to keep the information coming.

"Don't worry about it," she said. "My dad used to tell me that was part of any kind of information gathering. You have to know that a lot of it is going to come up short. You get what you can and don't give up if it's not what you expect." She genuinely felt bad for Dmitri. She hated to see him blame himself, even though she'd been blaming him just a short while earlier. Funny how that happened. She was relieved to see him nod in response.

"That is true," he said. "I know it is true, but I wish I had not endangered your life for such a slim chance at finding what we need."

"It's okay. Does this folder have to do with my father?" she asked, tapping the yellow folder.

"Only indirectly," Dmitri said. "I need to go through the information and decode what is there. It is possible that there will be locations of other prisons and cells, and from there I can investigate to see if there has been movement recently that might indicate his arrival in one of them. But it is working backward. The other file would have led us directly to him."

Gaia felt a pang of regret. Once again, the crappy option had won. But there was nothing she could do about it now.

"Please, I would like you to clean up," Dmitri told her. "You must have a shower and let me wash your clothes. This apartment has a small washing machine and dryer."

"This place?" Gaia looked around.

"It was outfitted so that operatives like myself could stay inside for long periods of time." He shrugged. "I believe the addition of females to our ranks encouraged some creature comforts."

"Huh." Gaia had to admit, a shower sounded good. But she really didn't want to run into Sam. "No, I've got to go," she said.

"I insist," Dmitri said firmly. "Sam will not be back for a long time. I don't know why you wouldn't want to see him, but it's obvious that you don't. Please, don't let that stand in the way of your taking care of yourself."

Jeez, this guy was such a mother hen. "All right," Gaia relented. "I'll take a quick shower. I'd probably attract too much attention on the street looking like this, anyway."

"I'll turn on the hot water now," Dmitri said. "It takes a long time to warm up."

A few minutes later Gaia stood in the steamy bathroom, inspecting the damage to herself. She looked like absolute hell. There was an old brush sitting on the sink, and she tried to yank it through her hair. Giving up, she stepped into the warm stream of water and let the heat sink into her muscles. It burned where the fire had gotten too close. But it felt too good to stop. Forgetting herself, she relaxed and stood with her eyes closed for a long, long time.

Hidden Masses

SAM SAT IN THE PUBLIC LIBRARY, reading through the newspapers from the time that he'd been gone and trying to catch up on what he'd missed. He was tired of being a shadow in this world. And though he knew he had to hide—well, that was one of the things about New York that could be either great or horrible, depending on how depressed you were. You could be hidden in plain sight. The city was full of people who might as well be invisible. Old people with no way to fill their empty hours, young people with no direction or desire, displaced people waiting for the next adventure or catastrophe—they filled the public places, the parks and atriums and subways, and even this library.

And Sam fit right in with the hidden masses.

He just wanted to know what was going on. Paging through recent papers and magazines and flicking through microfilm was sort of soothing and reassuring. He followed the case of a city scandal about misdirected funds and the dog pound. Totally boring to most, but it was one more thread pulling Sam's consciousness together. He followed a celebrity divorce from bitter feud to conciliatory appearance on the red carpet. Another thread. He skimmed the top choices of a daytime show's book club. Whatever he could get his hands on, anything that could tell him what had happened in the world during his confinement, Sam gobbled up with greed. He couldn't explain why he had such a craving for information. The only reason he could think of was that he just wanted to make up for lost time. To re-create the world as it rolled on without him so he wouldn't have this massive blank spot in his worldview.

All that reading made Sam tired. He was still physically drained from his injuries—and the stress on his body wasn't helping his diabetes, either. He marveled at the fact that his captors had treated him so badly—neglected his every need—but had managed to get him the insulin he needed to survive. As if they wanted him to live, but with a broken spirit. Well, today's research mission had taken him a long way toward repairing that spirit.

But damn, his body still needed some mending.

As he hopped on the subway and headed back

down to Chinatown, Sam noticed with a rush that he hadn't thought about Gaia in hours. Not that she wasn't there—but she hadn't been in the forefront of his mind. She was starting to shrink from the massive icon in his mind into regular old Gaia Moore, high school girl who had stolen his heart.

Funny thing, though. His heart still tightened at the thought of her. His temperature still spiked when he pictured the way her hands brushed across his chest. He still had the most massive feelings for her. Even shrunk down to normal size, Gaia still ruled Sam's heart.

And damn it, between misplacing his cell phone, Dmitri's Internet habit, and the lack of working public phones in this city, he hadn't been able to get in touch with her all morning. Couldn't even comfort her—as a friend—after her fight with Ed. It drove him crazy. But that was the way it was.

The last thing he expected, as he exited the train and walked up to Dmitri's apartment, was to see the object of his desire, obsessive or otherwise, wrapped in a terry cloth robe with her hair swathed in a turbaned towel. Even in his fantasies, he hadn't thought he'd walk into the dingy apartment to find Gaia Moore dripping wet and basically naked. In fact, a postshower Gaia was the last thing Sam Moon had expected to find as he opened the door to Dmitri's apartment and trudged toward his room.

"OH! GOD!" GAIA YELPED AS SHE came out of the bathroom to ask Dmitri what he'd done with her clothes. *Stupid, stupid, STUPID,* she thought. Her heart felt like it had just exploded inside her chest, leaving pulsating bits of arterial matter splattered all over her lungs and stomach. All the

End of Story

warm relaxation of the hot shower drained from her body as she came face-to-face with Sam Moon.

Sam, the guy she still had lingering feelings for. Sam, the guy who had apparently arranged for her murder the night before. Part of her still bloomed with happiness at the sight of that handsome face; the rest of her wilted with disgust at the guy who'd set her up to be whacked. With all the breaking and entering and arson of the afternoon, she had forgotten her resolution to get out of Dmitri's apartment before Sam got back.

Because this was more than she could stand to think about right now.

"Gaia! Are you all right?" Sam seemed surprised and thrilled to see her—tried to hug her, in fact. Maybe he was checking for the bullet holes that were supposed to be there. Maybe he was surprised just to see her without a body bag and toe tag. Or maybe she was wrong and he hadn't set her up.

Click. Her mind turned off and her instincts

switched on. Gaia had to get out of this claustrophobic apartment, and pronto.

"Sam, you are back early," Dmitri said with dismay, appearing behind him with Gaia's clothes, cleaned and folded.

"I thought nobody would be here," Gaia said to him. "I thought our discussion was top secret."

"It is," Dmitri told her. "He only just walked in. Why are you so upset?"

"I'm not upset," Gaia snapped, taking her clothes and vanishing back into the bathroom. "I'm just mad that I hung out this long," she called out through the door as she frantically shoved her still damp legs into her jeans. *Mmm, that's a pretty feeling: wet denim is just sooo comfortable,* she noted distractedly. She did not care. She had to get out of there.

Of all the idiotic moves, she scolded herself. *Getting sidetracked by a shower. Running into Sam when you have to stay focused on your dad. Some reliable daughter you are.* She barely noticed how melted her sneakers were as she shoved her feet into them and twisted her hair into a waterlogged knot on top of her head.

She left the bathroom in a rush, heading straight for the front door as if she were a racehorse with blinders on. "Let me know what you found in that file," she called out to Dmitri.

"Gaia," Sam said uncertainly.

"Yeah?" She paused at the door, her hand on the

knob. She felt her heart take a swan dive into her small intestine, bouncing on her pancreas, liver, and stomach on its way down. Sam's presence loomed like a planet behind her.

"Are—are you okay?" he asked. "The last time I saw you, you were fighting with Ed. I just wanted to make sure things worked out."

Are you kidding me? Gaia shrieked inside her head. *Ed's not exactly primo in my mind right now, Mister Killing-Me-Not-So-Softly.* But she didn't want to let on that she suspected him. *Let him wonder why I'm not dead for a while,* she decided. *Confront him later, when you've got more evidence.*

"Everything's fine," she said stonily, glaring at the doorknob. "Can't you see for yourself? I'm in one piece."

With that parting shot, she yanked open the door and left the apartment. *Ha,* she thought. *Let him chew on that for a while.* She felt a certain satisfaction that her thinly veiled insult might dig into his double-crossing soul and show him that he couldn't eliminate her so easily.

Of course, it was hard to ignore the fact that the look on his face had been more baffled and hurt than insulted and evil.

But ignore it she did. He'd sent the message that brought her to the church. And in that church she'd been shot at and very nearly killed. End of story.

Right?

Right. *Right!*

Even in the life of Gaia, this was a **stark contrast** weird one.

CROSSING THROUGH THE PARK AGAIN,

Gaia felt her head reeling from the potent cocktail of Sam-induced hormones, dad-inspired guilt, and Dmitri-assisted annoyance. She just wanted to wiggle out of her skin like a snake and leave her old self behind. *Everything is such a mess,* she thought. *All I want to do is find my dad, and the harder I try, the more everything in my life gets more screwed up.*

Shoop—Shoop

Calling it a park was generous. Let's get real: To get to the subway, all Gaia had to get through was a half-block-wide strip of grass between two avenues at the base of the Manhattan Bridge. There wasn't much room for a lanky, athletic girl loping along in a blind fury. Predictably, Gaia collided with one of a group of geriatric Chinese people practicing t'ai chi.

"I'm sorry," she blurted out. Expecting to see an elderly Chinese lady glaring up at her, she was both relieved and confused when the victim of her klutziness turned out to be Jake.

"What the hell are you doing here?" she asked.

Jake lay on his back, looking just as startled and confused. "Gaia? Did you just try to mug me?"

Gaia let out an exasperated breath. "Yeah, I was trying to mug you," she spat. "Times are tough, you know. A girl needs her lunch money." Then she stepped over his prone frame and stomped up the street. What a day she was having. Even in the life of Gaia, this was a weird one.

"Gaia!" Jake stood and chased after her, dusting himself off as he went. "I was just kidding. Would you stop?"

"What do you want?" she snapped.

"I was just—jeez! Come on, Gaia, don't you think it's kind of funny that you literally ran into me in a totally different part of town?"

Gaia stood for a moment, glaring at him.

"Ha ha," she finally said. "Can I leave now?"

"No!" Jake scratched his head and looked at her curiously. "Are you okay? I mean, you're not exactly the friendliest person on a normal day, but you're acting really weird."

"Why, because I don't want to sit and chat with you?"

"No. Because you literally just knocked me over and you didn't even say excuse me. You're such a weirdo!"

Jake was still laughing, and it was making Gaia feel strange. Besides, the word *weirdo* was echoing in her head in a way it never had before. Ed's fault. He'd made that crack about how she couldn't be part of anything. Okay, so he hadn't actually made that crack; Gaia had just inferred it from the way he was looking at her. But it still snowballed with Jake's current crack enough to make Gaia stop herself from storming off.

"Sorry," she said. "I was in a hurry."

"Well, will you slow down?" he asked. "At least long

enough so I can save face with Mrs. Ong and her lady friends?"

Gaia looked over and saw the small crowd of still gently swaying t'ai chi people. A few of them, though they still had expressions of serene distraction, were peeking over between moves. Jake waved at them, like he was trying to be a little less embarrassed.

"You're friends with these old people?" Gaia blurted out.

"Well, I come down here sometimes just to watch them do their thing," he said. "Karate isn't the only stuff I do. The guy who teaches me said I should be familiar with yoga, t'ai chi, and whatever else I can scare up." He looked back at the swaying figures. "I keep wanting to join in, but I feel funny."

"Yeah, so would I," Gaia told him. "You'd kind of stick out. You're about two feet taller than any of them, for one thing."

"But they keep saying I should join in. I think if I had a partner, I'd feel a little better." He peered at her. She glared back.

"No," she said.

"I didn't ask yet," he objected.

"Fine, ask."

"Will you come do some t'ai chi with me and the old people so I won't feel so self-conscious?"

"*No.*"

"Gaia!" Jake shook his head.

Is this guy just relentlessly amused by every stupid thing that happens on the planet? Gaia wondered. *Just what is so goddamn funny?*

"Come on. Have you ever tried it?"

"When I was a kid," Gaia admitted. "And I did some yoga, too. But karate's more my style. I'm not really into deep inner calm."

"Trust me, neither is Mrs. Ong," Jake said. "The first time I met her, she was throwing a fish at someone."

Gaia laughed in spite of herself. She had to admit, the willowy movements of the serene oldsters looked very cool. Plus they all seemed to be absolutely free of the kind of anger and frustration that was turning her stomach into a bucket of acid.

"I suppose it could make me a better fighter," she admitted.

"Sure. Focus and whatnot," Jake agreed. "Help you stay cool in a hot situation, reducing that panic response most people get in the middle of a fight. Fear's a killer, you know."

"I've heard that," Gaia said.

"Come on," Jake wheedled, dropping his messenger bag at his feet. "I've always wanted to try this. We're so far from school, nobody will spot us."

People from school weren't the issue. Gaia peered up at Dmitri's building. His apartment was on the other side; she wasn't likely to be spotted by him or by

Sam. And it wasn't like she was in a hurry to get back to her Tatiana-infested apartment. This day had her totally frazzled. She hated to admit it, but Jake could be right: Something calming might be just what she needed to grab hold of herself and refocus her attention on the search for her dad.

"All right, I'll try it," Gaia said. "But the minute I start feeling stupid, I'm out of here."

"It's a deal," Jake said.

They joined the group in the middle of the park, imitating the poses of the people in front of them as they moved through a slow-motion series of stances that went back thousands and thousands of years. A lot of them were similar to the ones Gaia knew from martial arts training, but holding them and moving through them at superslow speed made her feel weirdly calm. Her muscles seemed to really enjoy it, and she felt the whirling gyroscope of her brain begin to slow to a comfortable hum. After a few minutes the two of them stopped, stepped out from the huddle of people, and walked slowly up the street.

Gaia didn't really feel like talking. She didn't want to break the silence in her head. She remembered this feeling from scuba diving: After coming up to the surface, even the biggest motormouths tended to just sit in a blissful daze. The shoop-shoop breathing sounds of the deep lulled everyone into a waking sleep. She felt that way now, too.

Apparently Jake felt the same way. He was just strolling along, eyes cast downward, in as meditative a silence as she was. He looked up and smiled, still not speaking. Gaia didn't go so far as to smile back, but she didn't feel the need to scowl at him and look away, either.

Well. This was nice. No accusations, no arguing, no betrayal, no weirdness. *Maybe all I needed was to get away from everyone,* Gaia mused. *Everyone I'm usually around, anyway.*

"So where did you learn to fight?" Jake asked her as they walked toward the F train.

"Oh. . . I don't know."

"Come on. Of course you know," Jake pressed.

Gaia shrugged. "It was just something I got really into when I was a kid," she told him.

"Uh, no." Jake shook his head. "If it was just a hobby, you wouldn't have such professional-level skills. What are you really? One of those circus kids? Like Jackie Chan? Did a traveling martial arts circus take you away from your parents at the age of three and mold you into a killer?"

Gaia laughed. That made twice in one day, she noted. "It wasn't quite that dramatic," she nonanswered, sidestepping the question. "What about you?"

"Oh, I got interested the way every other red-blooded American does," he told her. "By seeing a Bruce Lee movie with my older brother at an impressionable age. After that, I had to do it. I guess I was kind of a weird kid because I never got tired of it, never gave it up, even when we got Nintendo."

"Wow, you stuck with it even in the face of impending Sonic the Hedgehog," Gaia said dryly. "Who knew anyone could resist temptation like that?"

"Damn, you're harsh!" Jake laughed. Gaia shot him a withering look. "You're so different from everyone else at school," he added, almost as an afterthought.

You don't know the half of it, Gaia thought. "I do seem to stand out," she mumbled.

"Look, I know you think I'm a meathead or something," Jake said, stopping in the middle of the Houston Street sidewalk. "Or maybe you haven't given me much thought at all. All I know is, you absolutely refuse to respond to my friendly advances, which no one has ever done before."

Gaia smirked. "You're very fond of yourself, aren't you?" she asked.

"Not really," Jake answered. "I just want to hang out some more. I think you're very. . . interesting. It seems like you have a lot more going on here than you let on," he added, putting his hand on his heart when he said the word *here*.

What was he suggesting? That under Gaia's tough demeanor was some fragile waif waiting for someone to unlock her heart? Was he for real?

"Look, that's very touching and all, but I really don't have a whole lot going on *here*," she said as she put her own hand on her heart, mocking his previous gesture.

"Oh, I think you do," Jake said, this time putting his hand on *her* heart. "I can feel it," he said.

Now he was way out of line. Simply put, Jake was playing to the wrong audience.

"Hey—careful with the merchandise," Gaia said, swatted his hand away.

"Okay, sorry. I didn't mean to upset you," Jake said. "I won't do it again."

Gaia wasn't exactly sure what was going on in Jake's head. Was he flirting with her, or was he just trying to reach out and fix someone? Either way, Gaia was in no position to add any more names to the already too long list of people in her life.

"Look, I have to go," Gaia said.

Jake looked hurt and bewildered. "Gaia, don't leave. I promise not to come near you again."

"It's not that," Gaia said. "I just have to be somewhere."

Gaia hurried away from Jake, taking long strides down the sidewalk and feeling just as agitated as ever. God! She should never have done t'ai chi. It had relaxed her so much, she'd let down her defenses and opened herself up to yet another attack—of sorts. Right now she didn't need to be introspective or calm or serene. And she certainly didn't need to open her heart. She needed to stay on her guard, listen for bullets whistling past her head, and get things done.

103

What things, she didn't know. But she had to get things done.

BY THE TIME SHE GOT BACK TO THE

Upper East Side, Gaia had calmed down somewhat, but she was still in no mood to be messed with. She was glad she had been able to avoid a confrontation with Sam. She felt like an idiot over Jake. And she felt sad about Ed. All in all, her emotions were still a complete jumble, but at least she was blocks and blocks away from anyone who could—

Squeezed and Crushed

"Gaia."

Oh.

That voice drizzled over Gaia's heart like honey over a piece of toast. She turned around.

"Didn't I just leave you downtown, Sam?" she asked, trying not to look up at him. She had to keep herself safe. And noticing how rumpled and handsome he was—that was about as unsafe as it got. *He tried to kill you,* she reminded herself. That helped. A little.

"Well, yeah." He stood in her way, not moving.

"You did. But I couldn't let you walk away like that. Gaia, what is going on?"

"Nothing's going on," she mumbled. She tried to walk past him, but he wasn't budging.

"The last time I saw you was right here," he pointed out. "Right in front of your building. You were arguing with Ed. And I think it's partially my fault. I've been pushing myself on you and taking up your time. I hope he wasn't too angry at you."

"We broke up," she told him.

"Oh, Gaia. I'm so sorry." Sam made a move to hug her. Gaia stepped back. She was starting to get really steamed. It was painful, seeing how Sam could lie to her face like this. *He tried to kill you,* she reminded herself again. But this time it didn't help her feel better. It fueled her anger.

"It's okay," she said. "I mean, it was a long time coming. It's not your fault. Not anyone's fault. You should go back to Dmitri's."

"Look, what is your deal?" Sam was getting angry. "I'm just trying to be a friend, and you've put up the Great Wall of Gaia. Is something bigger going on? Is it something with your dad or—all this other stuff that's happening?"

"I can't believe you!" Gaia finally exploded. Her anger rose like vomit into the back of her throat. "How dare you talk to me like you give a crap about my well-being? Why don't you get the hell out of my life?"

105

Sam's face seemed to melt, from confusion to horrified incredulity. "Wha-what are you talking about?" he stammered. The old habit came out when he was under stress. Gaia was amazed he could fake it like that.

"You set me up, Sam. You tried to have me killed. Did you think I was too stupid to put two and two together? Here's a hint: When you've been that sloppy, you've got to finish the job or the girl you're trying to murder's going to be *really mad*." The words rolled out of Gaia's mouth. Not even his expression of complete and utter noncomprehension could stop her.

"Set you up? Have you killed? Gaia, I don't—"

Gaia whipped out her cell phone and shoved it in his face. "I've still got the text message you sent me," she pointed out, scrolling it up on the screen. "From your cell phone to mine, courtesy of Smith and Wesson."

Sam took the phone out of her hands and looked at the screen.

Don't be sad. Just received some new information. Meet me at the Ukrainian church on Eleventh Street. Tomorrow. 8:00 A.M.

"Oh my God. Gaia, I did not send this to you." The words tumbled out of Sam, who was staring at the cell phone with horrified shock. "I couldn't have. My cell phone has been missing since I left your apartment."

"Yeah, right," Gaia said. "I got the message like five seconds. . . after you left," she said, finishing her sentence in a self-doubting whisper.

No. No more doubt, she told herself. *You can't trust him. You can't trust anyone.*

"You're just saying that because I busted you," she insisted, snatching the phone back. "I know you tried to kill me, Sam. Now you want to talk your way out of it, and you can't. Just leave me alone." She pushed past him, feeling doubt nagging at her, tugging on her sleeve like an insistent child.

"Gaia—"

"I'm serious." She whipped around. "Just—leave me alone. I have to find my dad. I'll deal with you later."

Gaia blocked out the memory of Sam's confused, pained expression the minute she turned her back on him and went into her building. Her feelings for Sam were as intense as ever. But she couldn't ignore the message and its aftermath. She felt like a palm tree getting thrown around by a hurricane. *You bend this way, you bend that way, but that doesn't mean you can't break,* she thought. The confusion and emotion inside her were like a tourniquet around her heart. She felt squeezed and crushed. The pain was physical, and it was intense.

She took a moment in the elevator to shut her eyes and focus. Sam was not her problem. Finding her father was. She breathed deeply, forcing her heart to slow and her temperature to drop. By the time she entered the apartment, she had managed to push Sam to the back of her mind. She thought she'd lie down and try to figure out what to do next or just wait for Dmitri's next word.

Hearing a noise, she walked warily to the living room. There was Natasha, sitting on the bloodred velvet couch, folding laundry in a huge wicker basket.

"Natasha!" Gaia said, surprised. She had to admit, it was a relief to see someone familiar. Natasha was as close as she could get to her dad, after all. "I didn't think I'd find you here."

"Well, I do live here," the older woman responded.

"But you've been gone. Where were you?" Gaia sat next to her, thinking of the way Tatiana sat next to her mother, trying to imitate the same ease.

"Terribly busy," she said. "There has been much to do in searching for your father."

"You look tired," Gaia told her. It was true. Natasha's willowy, elegant frame looked as young as ever, but her face had a completely different cast to it than it had just a few days before. Gaia felt a swell of affection for her. It hadn't been easy, getting used to having a stepmother. But she believed her dad really loved this woman. The brief moment that they'd all been a family had already taken on the golden glow of nostalgia.

"Well, I guess I have been worried," Natasha admitted, putting down the socks she'd been rolling and resting her long, white fingers against her eyes, the red nails at her fingertips standing out in stark contrast to her pale skin.

"What did you find out?" Gaia asked.

"You know I cannot tell you that," Natasha told her sternly.

"Of course you can. You have to," Gaia insisted. "He's my father."

"I know, but there are professionals handling this. You have to have faith that we know what we are doing."

"Faith?" Gaia gave a frustrated roar. "Look, no offense, but it was you people who thought George Niven would keep me safe, and I almost got iced by him and his trashy wife."

"I know, I know," Natasha said. "That was regrettable, but I am telling you, the search for your father is being handled."

"Don't you get updates? I mean, aren't you his fiancée? Should I contact them directly? As a blood relative, I mean. Maybe I'll get more out of them."

"They hate that." Natasha shook her head. "No, we are supposed to be good soldiers and hold our positions until we get different orders. I am sure they have everything under control."

"Natasha! Will you stop saying that?" Gaia took a pair of socks from Natasha's hands and threw them on the floor. "My father almost choked and died. I'd say there's a pretty good chance he was poisoned. He was taken to a hospital, where he just. . . vanished. And all you want to do is sit here waiting for orders? I thought you *loved* him."

"I do love him," Natasha said firmly, fixing Gaia with a sharp glare. She stared at her for a long time, with an odd expression that Gaia couldn't quite read.

"Please," Gaia said. "Tell me whatever you know."

Natasha dropped her eyes. "The truth is, I am being stonewalled, too," she finally admitted. "I cannot. . ." She seemed to wrench the words out of herself. "I cannot seem to get a straight answer from our superiors. They tell me that he is alive but that he is being kept in a remote location."

"Which is where?"

"I do not know. They say the less I know, the safer I will be." She raised her eyes to look into Gaia's. "The same is true for you, Gaia. Obviously something terribly dangerous—more dangerous than anything we've faced before—is going on. We must be in danger. I think it is best to keep a low profile for now."

Gaia sat still, trying to take all of this in. Natasha was a trusted operative—and her own organization wouldn't tell her where her fiancé was?

"This is okay with you?" Gaia said. "I don't understand why you'd accept that answer. Didn't you press it?"

"I pressed. And I got nowhere."

Gaia sat back on the couch, deflated.

"Your father is in good hands—I am sure of it," Natasha told her. "If he comes back—I mean, when he comes back"—Natasha gave Gaia an apologetic shake of her head—"he will appreciate that we did not endanger our own lives to find him. He wants you safe, Gaia. Even if it means there's one less person searching for him."

Gaia scowled. "I don't think I can just sit here," she said. "And I'm trying to understand how you can." She stood and started to leave the living room.

"Gaia."

She stopped but didn't turn around.

"I know that Tatiana threw a party here last night. She should not have done that, and I have spoken to her about it. Especially when we are all so worried about your father. I think perhaps the stress is getting to her. Perhaps she is not being the most responsible person right now. I hope you will not be too impatient with her."

Gaia nodded, then kept walking. Stress. Stress had made Tatiana get totally drunk and blab about her friendship with Sam to Ed? *If I dealt with stress that badly, I'd never have made it this far,* Gaia thought. But she didn't want to start another conversation with Natasha. This one had made her too sad and confused.

She went to her bedroom. Before she even hit the door, she could hear tapping at the computer keyboard. She steeled herself to see Tatiana and hoped she wouldn't be—

Ed.

Ed was sitting at the desk, not Tatiana.

"What are you doing here?" she asked, standing uncomfortably by the door.

Ed looked up and seemed thoroughly resigned to the fact that he and Gaia were within ten feet of each other.

"Sorry," he said. "I had to do some stuff for Tatiana, and I didn't think you'd come home. I'll be out of here soon."

"No, it's okay," Gaia said. "I'll just go. I was heading back out, anyway."

"Wait."

A pause. "What?"

"I just—I mean, why don't you just hang out? I'll be done soon." He met her eyes for about half a millisecond. "There's no reason we shouldn't be able to hang out in the same room, Gaia."

She thought about that one. There were a few reasons. The totally harsh way he'd spoken to her, for one thing. The fact that he used to be the safest person in the world to her and that they had just broken up about ten seconds before. And she didn't know how to act around him. Because she couldn't even blame him for being mad at her, because she hadn't exactly been forthcoming or truthful with him. There were a lot of reasons why they couldn't really hang out.

Then again, he was Ed. What was she scared of? He was just Ed. Gaia sat on the edge of her bed farthest from her ex-boyfriend, ex–best friend, ex-everything.

"So what are you doing?" she asked.

"Tatiana asked me to burn some CDs for her, so I figured I'd Limewire some extra stuff and make her a mix."

"Hm."

Another pause. These pauses were getting really annoying. What had once been a comfortable silence now seemed like a screaming chasm of unspoken words.

"What?" Ed asked.

"Nothing."

"No, you said, 'Hm.'"

"Yeah, I mean, hm, so you're making some CDs, that's nice. Whatever."

"Whatever?"

"Yeah, whatever."

Ed poked a couple of keys to set the CD burner running and put his hands in his lap.

"Look, I know what you're thinking," he said.

"Really? Mind reading is quite a talent. Maybe you should go on *Letterman*," Gaia tried to joke.

"I'm serious. I know you feel weird about me and Tatiana, and I just. . ."

What, Ed? You just want me to know you're considering getting close to my roommate and almost stepsister? You just want to put my weird feelings out in the open so I can feel even weirder? Gaia wondered.

"I just—I'm not planning on going out with her," he finally said. "We're just friends."

"I don't care, Ed. I mean, it's fine. We're not together, so I can't tell you what to do."

"Well, if you don't care," Ed said, rolling his eyes to the ceiling. "I mean, I think you do."

"But it doesn't matter." The words came out more forcefully than Gaia intended. She was telling herself as much as she was telling Ed. And neither one of them was really buying it. So she said it again. "It doesn't matter," she said. "Tatiana's got her eye on you. Things didn't work out between us. If she's being a good friend, then why should I object?"

"I just don't know why you couldn't be—I don't know, more like she is," Ed blurted out. Gaia's eyes widened as she felt a wiggle of misery worming its way around her heart.

"I don't mean not to be yourself, but it's frustrating," he clarified. "I mean, you and I were best friends for, like, ever, but when I look back on all the time we spent together, I can count on one hand the number of times you just up and did something unexpected just because you were thinking of me."

"That's not true. I thought of you a lot," Gaia objected. "I just had other stuff going on. Some of the time. Okay, I mean, a lot of the time."

"*All* of the time." Ed shook his head, checked on the CD, and turned toward Gaia. "I'm not saying this to piss you off, but man, you might want to think about it for next time."

Next time what? Next time I have a boyfriend? Always-thinkin'-ahead Ed. "And you and I were great friends, but just look at all the stuff Tatiana does for me. I just mentioned in passing that I like cannolis, and voilà, today she brings me a cannoli from this place." He dropped a half-empty bag from Veniero's, a well-known pastry shop in the East Village, on the bed. "And look, this goofy bobble-head dog from Pearl River Trading."

"I mean, Ed."

"What?"

"The dog is kind of dorky. It's just a five-dollar trinket from Chinatown."

"I know!" Ed threw his hands in the air. "But it's nice! It's nice to have someone think about me for a change instead of me always wondering about—about you, and whether you like me or why you're ignoring me or when we're going to hang out again. Tatiana went all the way down to Eleventh Street, for no reason other than to be nice."

Ugh! Every word he said felt like a hornet in Gaia's heart. She *did* care about him! She wanted to yell it out loud. *I thought about you!* she yelled inside. *All I did was think about you. You and your safety were more important to me than I was to myself. You think it was easy avoiding you all that time and making you hate me? It was pure torture, but I did it because I love you.*

She couldn't say any of that. It was too embarrassing to admit, even to Ed. It left her too exposed. And anyway, what was the point? He was finished with her.

"Well, so that's great," she said. "You've got what you wanted."

"Gaia." Ed leaned back and stared at the wall. The complete and utter aggravation of trying to get his point across to Gaia was starting to exhaust him completely.

"It's what I wanted, but it's not who I wanted it from," he said. "I wanted it from. . . Gaia?"

He finally managed to look over, wanting to meet Gaia's eyes as he admitted how he really felt. But all he saw was an empty white wall next to an open door. The front door slammed. Gaia was gone.

This is just weird. I don't—it doesn't make sense. Veniero's on Eleventh Street—that's right across the avenue from the Ukranian church where I almost got my head shot off. Pearl River? That's in Chinatown—by Dmitri's apartment. By Sam's apartment. The cell phone. The last time I saw it, it was here, and Tatiana was standing three feet away. Drunk as a skunk, but still. . .

Or was she? I remember a story about Nikita Kruschev, the prime minister of the Soviet Union during the Cold War. He was at a big diplomatic party, and he was getting drunker and drunker. Then someone smelled his drink, and it turned out he wasn't drinking straight vodka, as he'd claimed. It was just water, and he was trying to catch everyone off their guard. Thinking they'd give away government secrets if they thought he was too drunk to notice. A sneaky little trick.

Could Tatiana have heard the

same story? Was she pretending to be drunk so that she could steal the cell phone?

Bigger picture: Is this loving mother-daughter team nothing more than a couple of double agents setting me up to get killed?

That was my first instinct about them. When I met them, I just didn't trust them. But they hung in there with me. They really did. And besides, my dad trusts Natasha. Enough to fall in love with her. Enough to leave me in her care. That's the bottom line, right? He taught me everything I know. He did something unbeliev- ably difficult—disappeared from my life—just because he thought it would keep me safe. Even though it made me hate him. Even though he had to fight to get me to under- stand. And that guy, the one who did all that—he trusts Natasha. So I should, too, shouldn't I?

These signs—these tiny clues and these little voices from deep in my subconscious—they have to be wrong. I have to be wrong when

I think there's something weird
going on with them.

It's impossible. I'm being
paranoid. This life is just making me totally paranoid, and I'm
letting the fact that my dad is
missing throw all my instincts
off. This is textbook psychologi-
cal crap: I can't figure out the
answer I need, so I'm finding bad
guys everywhere.

Get a grip, Gaia.

Natasha—I mean, okay, she's
not being as active in her inves-
tigation as I think she should
be. That doesn't mean she's double crossing me and my dad. Or
that she's somehow behind his
disappearance. That's just crazy!

And so what if Tatiana ratted
out Sam and me to Ed—that's more
about her being so desperately in
love with Ed, right?

Ugh.

I'm trying to believe my own
pep talk. But these weird little
details keep popping up, and I
feel like pieces of a jigsaw puz-
zle are putting themselves

together, and I hate the picture
that's starting to appear.

   If Natasha and Tatiana turn
out to be bad. . . I don't know
what I'll do. I don't think I'll
ever be able to trust anyone,
ever again. Not even Dad.

   Not even myself.

Interesting. Very

interesting. Apparently the word
cannoli has secret powers I would
never have predicted. Apparently
it can make a tall blond high
school girl vanish without a
trace. Maybe I should notify
someone.

Like who? Most people would
like to make a statuesque blond
appear, not disappear.

I'm the only one trying to get
the hell away from one. From the
moment I met Gaia, my world has
been a constant chaotic mess. My
feelings have gotten twisted, wrung
out, and stomped on. My friends
have gotten hurt. I've gotten hurt.
I really think the best thing is to
keep away from her and clear my
head. I need some space.

But I feel really bad. . . .
It's not like I want to hurt her
feelings. And that's just what I
did. That talk could not have gone
worse. I was just trying to say,
Come on, Gaia, you can act this
way, you can make me feel like I'm

wanted if you really try. If I *am*
really wanted. But every time I
opened my mouth, jeez, the wrong
thing kept coming out. I felt like
Adam Sandler. The eternal schmuck.
I think I made her think I'm going
to start dating Tatiana. That the
things Tatiana does for me make me
like her.

I mean, they do. I do like
Tatiana, but I don't LIKE her,
like her. Not the way I like
Gaia. I—I mean, I love Gaia. Even
if I can't be her boyfriend—even
if I can't really trust her—I'm
always going to care about her.

And if she ever decided to
start treating me the way Tatiana
does? I think I'd forgive her for
everything.

But I guess that's one of the
raving ironies of this world.
Someone you kind of like treats
you like the king of hearts, while
the one you'd lie down and die for
treats you like the joker.

Guess I'm not going to get
what I want in this hand. I'm not
even sure what I want, anyway, so

it's just as well. But no matter
what, the cards are stacked
against me.

Royal flush. Bad deal. Go
fish. Insert bad playing-card
metaphor here, indicating that Ed
Fargo is one confused dude.

Whatever. I fold. Gaia Moore,
you're too rich for my blood.

If she
could
prove
herself
wrong,
she'd be
really,
really
happy.

oh.
shit.

A FEW MINUTES AFTER GAIA LEFT

The Suckiest

Natasha poked her head into the room and caught Ed in a complete zone-out, staring at the wall, inwardly muttering about Gaia.

"Ed," she said.

He looked up with a start. "Oh, sorry," he said. "I'm all done here."

"I know she has not been kind to you," Natasha said, stepping into the room and leaning against the doorjamb.

"Tatiana's great."

"I mean Gaia. I am afraid I heard your conversation, and I know she is not being easy to get along with."

"Oh. That's Gaia, I guess," he said. "It's no big deal. We were friends for a long time; that's the only thing that's a drag about it."

"Well, I want you to know that I think you are a very nice boy, and if she cannot see that, then you are better off with someone else."

Ed felt his face flush with confusion. This was a speech he might expect from his own mom—if his mom was the mom from *Seventh Heaven*—but from Gaia's own almost stepmother? It seemed weird. Then again, Gaia was weird, too. Maybe Natasha just wanted her daughter to be dating him, the Nice Guy. That was a nauseating thought.

"Well, thanks," he said.

"I am glad you and Tatiana are friends," she said.

"Forget about your troubles and try to have a good time, okay? You are young; you shouldn't be tied up in knots and talking to a wall."

Ed laughed. "You weren't supposed to see that," he said.

"Do not worry. I have a houseplant that could collect a fee for being my therapist. I am going out now—don't feel that you have to run out. Finish what you are doing. And I will see you later, Ed."

Ed nodded, and Natasha left the room and the apartment. The silence of the big old place hummed in his ears. Turning back to the computer, he noticed that the last CD was finished. He slowly unhooked all the wires and packed away his equipment.

On the way downtown in the subway Ed cycled through the songs on his MP3 player, watching idly as the titles flipped past his eyes on the little screen. Some of them were most definitely Gaia-and-Ed songs.

All right. Do I delete these? he wondered. *We're getting space, we're broken up, and I don't think we're getting back together. But if we do, I'll have to download them again, and that's a pain.* Ed felt like he could have used a handbook to help him figure out the rituals of breakups. When did a break become a breakup? Who deleted what, and when was the most acceptable time to do that? Ed was getting dizzy just thinking about it.

The more he thought about it, the more he wished he could transfer his feelings for Gaia over to Tatiana.

Just *fwoop!*—move them over there. Create a hybrid female who liked him the way Tatiana did and who made him feel comfortable and excited and interested all the time the way Gaia did. Minus all the drama and all the anxiety. Now that would be the perfect girl.

Too bad she was entirely fictional.

A wave of Gaia anger broke over Ed's head. He was so frustrated. She was being such a jerk: Why couldn't she just act like a regular person? In a frenzy he deleted every single song that had any connection to her at all, including any song that started with the letter *G*. Out. Gone. Delete. *Yes, I'm sure,* he told the little blue screen. The train rattled through the tunnel as he looked down at it.

Now he felt bad.

He wanted the songs back.

Breakups were the suckiest events ever invented. And this one had to be the suckiest in all of human history.

GAIA SAT ON HER PERCH ON THE

Nice Guy

roof of her building. Technically she wasn't supposed to be up here, but she wanted to cool off and think—and she wanted to get back into the apartment when it was empty so she could look around. She didn't like her new theory—that Natasha and Tatiana were involved in a plot to kill her—but she couldn't afford to stick her head in the sand. Not on this one. Besides, she was sure her theory was wrong—and if she could prove herself wrong, she'd be really, really happy.

Despite the clues she had put together, it was a fact: She wanted to believe in Natasha and Tatiana.

Being alone was just too hard. Always having to depend on herself was unfair. Most of the girls she went to school with couldn't commit to a pair of shoes without asking the opinions of at least twenty people. Why did she have to make major life-and-death decisions with no help?

She watched Natasha exit the building, wearing a long red coat. Her white legs in high black pumps stood out against the dull concrete. Her dark hair tumbled down her back, so shiny Gaia could admire it from ten stories up. She looked like a perfume ad. Gaia could see why Tom loved her. She ached for her father, feeling his absence like a heavy, itchy army blanket.

A few minutes later Ed trudged out the front door, walking the same path Natasha had, toward the subway. He carried his skateboard loosely under one arm. Gaia squelched the pang she felt for him. Or tried to, anyway.

The apartment was empty; that was the important

128

thing. She went back inside the building and let herself into the silent rooms. She'd been living here for weeks and had made it her business to look over the whole place the minute she'd moved in. She hadn't found anything suspicious or incriminating back then. But this time she had much more serious evidence against them.

She could only hope it was false evidence.

TATIANA WAS PLAYING INTRAMURAL

Body racquetball, and Ed wanted to catch her performance. Since their high school didn't have a court, Ed joined a throng of students at a nearby gym. It was a gym designed especially for the tragically hip, and it looked like a disco. It even had a name—Smash. He passed the aerobics studio on the way downstairs—or tried to, anyway. Suddenly Ed understood why racquetball was drawing such a healthy crowd, especially of male students. The aerobics studio had tall silver poles in it, and women in workout gear were climbing up and down them, writhing like oversexed snakes as club music pounded and purple lights flashed around the room. He eyeballed the sign: Strip-aerobics. Clearly the VS administration had neglected to check out the Smash class schedules.

"Nice," he said.

"I love our school," a redheaded freshman kid stated with complete conviction. "It's worth every penny my parents pay."

"Come on, stud," Ed said, clamping a hand on the kid's shoulder and walking him down the hallway toward the racquetball courts.

"Oh, man," the kid groaned. "Just five more minutes?"

"I think you've seen enough to keep you going till your prom," Ed told him. "Anyway, if you time it right, you can leave during hip-hop class."

"I am so glad I didn't get into Stuyvesant."

Downstairs, students stood on the benches and sat on the floor to get the best view of the glassed-in racquetball court. Inside, Tatiana was fighting her third opponent of the day. Her stamina was unbelievable. So was her muscular body. Ed didn't like to think of himself as someone who objectified women, but looking at Tatiana clad only in a tank top–sports bra and bike shorts, he had to give in to his inner red-blooded American male. Her hair was pulled back in a sleek ponytail, and even her eye-protection goggles looked hot. But really, the most amazing thing about her was the determination and focus she displayed on the court.

Spinning her racquet, glaring at the ball, and springing into action when her opponent slammed the little blue orb against one of the white walls,

Tatiana was like a superhuman sportsbot, leaping around the cube-shaped room at a speed that made everything else look like slow motion. She managed to anticipate the angles the ball would travel along and a few times seemed to hit it without even looking toward it. Everyone broke into applause when she actually ran up the wall and flipped backward to make a shot. Nobody had a chance against Tatiana.

Ed was amazed. He'd known Tatiana had athletic ability, but he'd had no idea she was such a monster. Something about her seemed oddly familiar to him. She was so strong, powerful, focused, she was almost like. . . *Gaia! Ack!*

Tatiana's got nothing to do with Gaia, Ed told himself. *You just happen to like strong women—you're not attracted to Tatiana just because she reminds you of Gaia.*

Wait a minute. Attracted?

Before he could question that little voice inside him about what, exactly, it meant by "attracted," Tatiana won her last match and exited the court to more cheers and whistles. She was greeted by a gaggle of girlfriends and had to give a dozen high fives to admiring students. But the minute she pulled her goggles up on top of her head, her eyes searched out Ed. She came across the room to him, laughing and wiping the sweat off her face with a white towel.

"You won!" he told her.

"It looks that way. Would you like a hug?"

"Absolutely not!"

Tatiana gave a breathless laugh. "I am going to take a shower. After that, would you come and eat a giant mountain of pasta with me?"

"Sure, good plan," Ed said. "And I've got your CDs."

"How did I get so lucky? You are a good pal," she told him before she vanished into the locker room.

I am a good pal, Ed told himself. *A good pal. See? She's over that trying-to-kiss-you phase.* He was relieved to be out of the potential boyfriend slot. His feelings over Gaia were still too jumbled to add a new love interest to the mix. He wanted to just hang out, enjoy the attention, and fill the time he used to spend with Gaia.

Tatiana joined him in front of Smash in record time, freshly showered and dressed in jeans and a sweater. Ed watched as she inspected her cell phone for messages—then inspected a second one, too.

"What's with the two phones?" He laughed. "You need one for each ear or what?"

"Oh—one is my mom's," she explained quickly. "We were shopping and she left it in my bag by accident, and I just can't help seeing who might be calling her. Aren't I a terrible daughter?"

The story tumbled out in a rush, almost as if she had thought it through carefully in case anyone asked. Ed thought that was kind of weird. But it didn't really warrant thinking about. Especially when she looked up and gave him a dazzling smile of the you're-the-only-person-on-earth variety. That pretty much wiped any question from his mind. Stuck on Gaia or not, he liked being in the company of this very pretty girl.

"Okay, how did you get ready so fast?" he asked. "It takes my sister half an hour just to brush her hair. And that's right after she's had it blow-dried at the salon."

"I am magical," she said, hooking an arm into his. "And I am also starving."

"We can to go to Cucina in the East Village," Ed told her. "They serve the food on platters the size of flatbed trucks. If you can finish what's on your plate, I'll be seriously impressed."

"I think I will finish my food and yours," Tatiana told him. "Now tell me, did you run into Gaia when you were at my apartment, or were you safe from her prickly words?"

"No, she showed up," he said. "It was weird. She thinks something's going on between you and me." *If Tatiana's really taken me out of the potential boyfriend slot, she'll think that's funny,* Ed thought.

"Oh. Really?" Tatiana asked, peering at the cracks in the sidewalk.

Oops. Damn. Time to clarify things, Fargo.

"Yeah. She was asking how close we are, and I was trying to tell her that we're just really good friends, so I pointed out the cannolis and the bobble-head dog you got me and she just, like, left."

"She left?"

"Yeah. She looked at the bag and muttered something about Eleventh Street and Chinatown, and when I looked up, she'd left the room."

Tatiana didn't say anything. Her arm was still hooked through Ed's, but her hand gripped his anxiously as her steps slowed and she stared off into space.

Ed felt a sinking feeling of déjà vu. Walking down the street with a girl who seemed completely occupied with a mysterious, secret question. For the second time that day Tatiana was acting like Gaia.

"Tatiana?" he said.

"Yes," she said. "Oh! I am sorry, Ed. I just remembered something, but I can take care of it tomorrow."

"Did you leave something at the gym? Want to go back?"

"No, it is nothing. I just realized that I might have been careless with some. . . I might have done something careless. But it is nothing I cannot put right." She shot him a cheerful smile, erasing the Gaia scowl he thought he'd seen on her face.

"You're sure?" he asked, hoping she wouldn't excuse herself and leave.

"I am positive! In fact, I am thinking maybe we should have Indian food instead of Italian. Would you like that, Ed?"

"I could go either way," he said. "As long as we're eating."

"Oh, we are eating, my friend." She giggled. "We are having an eating contest."

They walked together through the city as the air thickened into night around them, scrolling through purple to black as they moved across town. By the time the sun was gone and their vegetable samosas hit the table, Ed was feeling fine. Tatiana was cheerful, funny, and carefree. She was nothing like Gaia. Nothing, nothing at all. Ed had found himself a Gaia-free zone, and that was just what he needed to stop missing her. Maybe even to get her out of his mind entirely. For now, anyway. Gaia-free for a night. That's what he needed to be.

GAIA CLOSED THE DRAPES AS THE SKY

Evil Ice

outside darkened into evening. During the day she couldn't be seen through the window, but since she had to turn on the lights, anyone peeking in would be able to plainly see her systematic inspection of every inch of the apartment. It wasn't likely that someone would do such a thing. But unlikely things were pretty much central to her life, and she wasn't about to take any chances.

She had dismantled and reassembled almost every

room in the house, finally arriving at the bedroom she and Tatiana shared. So far she had found nothing but a lot of dust bunnies, three buttons, and $5.32 in change. Proof of nothing but some lax housekeeping. Hardly the kind of indictment she both dreaded and was searching for.

This room, though. Where could something be hidden here? After checking all the furniture for false bottoms and compartments, she moved to the walls, knocking on each bit of plaster to listen for a hollow sound, something that might indicate the presence of a safe.

There was nothing.

She inspected the floorboards next. Any looseness, any variation in color—all of it was suspect. Again her search turned up nothing. She gritted her teeth, frustrated. She refused to feel relieved. She sat with her back against the wall, glaring across the room at the old, nonworking fireplace. The hole in the middle of it seemed to stare back at her like a big, blank eye. A big, blank eye that went nowhere and. . .

`Oh. Shit.`

The fireplace.

Gaia sprang from her seat and inspected the marble structure. This was a standard feature of New York apartments—an ancient chimney that had been closed off when the building got steam heat. A lot of people kept the structure of the fireplace with a false front just because it looked nice. Some even went so far as to put a gas burner in there, with faux logs that glowed like a real fire. This one was just a piece of metal. A piece of heavy, decorated iron that moved with a deep, heavy sigh when Gaia pulled at it. She yanked it away from the wall and saw that a compartment had been built into the old chimney.

Well, that certainly went against city regulations.

So did the object in the hole.

A high-powered rifle. Sniper style.

Gaia sat back on her butt with a thump, staring at the firearm with heart-sinking resignation. She could hear the bullets flashing past her ears. Could feel their heat as they barely missed her head. She'd studied firearms technology. She'd even grabbed a shell casing from the Ukranian church. She pulled it out of her pocket now and held it next to the rifle, a nasty-looking bit of machinery that would probably feel more at home in a South American cartel than here on the Upper East Side.

Perfect match.

Without pausing to listen to the wailing in her heart, Gaia stood, replaced the metal, and gathered her essentials: some clothes and. . . well, that was it. She was used to traveling light. It all went into her messenger bag and she was out the door like a shot. She felt violated, disgusted, like she was crawling with mites. Like it had rained maggots on her. Like she'd been living in a pit of snakes. Beautiful, friendly snakes.

She had known that she couldn't trust Tatiana and Natasha, but she had done it, anyway.

She'd been off her guard for weeks, sharing a bedroom with a cold-blooded killer.

She had accused Sam of being the one after her—and now his injured expression was burned in her memory as that of a totally innocent bystander. Sam, who'd taken bullets and survived weeks and weeks of imprisonment without knowing why. And she'd turned on him.

She had left Ed, her buddy and her boyfriend, in the company of a rancid chick with evil ice in her veins. And no matter how much she wanted to warn him to stay away from her, she knew—after the way they'd been nonspeaking to each other—that he'd never believe it. He'd think it was petty jealousy, not pure protectiveness.

And worst of all, she had let Natasha and Tatiana into her heart. She'd given them something she never gave anyone: her respect and her trust. Knowing she had been so wrong made her feel like there was nothing beneath her feet but miles of blue sky.

Gaia Moore had really screwed up this time. But she couldn't do anything until she was sure of what she was doing. So far, since her father's disappearance, Gaia had been flying by the seat of her pants, stomping around the city and having temper tantrums, bouncing from one neighborhood to the next, having weird chance encounters that seemed to lead her somewhere and just turned her in circles again.

She had to get rid of this gun. And then she had to leave the city for a while. Natasha and Tatiana were sure to know, or at least suspect, that she had found the gun. And they'd know she knew the truth about them.

Oh God. Oh *God*! The truth about them! That this home that she'd made was fake, that every word they'd ever spoken to her was a lie! Gaia felt her throat tighten all over again. Her mind dipped dizzily into fury and sorrow.

It was impossible to think with all these feelings swirling around. She had to get out of there. She grabbed the gun, shoved it into her bag, and left as quickly as she could. The door slammed behind her with a thud that echoed a thousand times in her head. She wouldn't be back. From now on she had nowhere to stay.

Gaia had to get a grip. Find a way to focus and set out a plan. And to do that, she had to leave her own contaminated turf and lose herself somewhere else for a while. Anywhere, as long as it was far away.

It was like
Great
Adventure
after a
nuclear
apocalypse.

too
much
fun

THE TRAIN OUT TO BROOKLYN WAS

Cardboard Skeletons

almost empty. It was a great place to sit and think. Like having her own private office, Gaia thought, except it wasn't really private and most places of business didn't have floors covered in pee.

But the comforting rumble of the train as it took her downtown was soothing. She propped her feet up on the seat next to her and watched people get on and off.

Different stops had different personalities. Midtown was for tourists and businesspeople; downtown was where hair got brighter and noses and eyebrows bloomed with piercings. But by the time the train shot out of the underground tunnels for its trip outside on the Manhattan Bridge, the crowd was a complete mix of every kind of person, from suit-wearing guys with briefcases to exhausted-looking women in fast-food restaurant uniforms. Manhattan from this distance looked like Emerald City, magical and simple and clean. The tall, glam buildings cleverly hid the trouble and confusion that existed just beneath the surface.

Gaia looked the other way, toward Brooklyn, and saw fewer tall buildings and lots of smaller neighborhoods. The girls she went to school with acted like the outer boroughs were no-man's-land, but Gaia thought that probably spoke well of the non-Manhattan sections of New York City. She had a sketchy knowledge of what was where. Brooklyn seemed like just the place to disappear for a while.

The crowd on the train thinned out as Gaia hurtled farther and farther from Manhattan. By the time she pulled into the last stop, Coney Island, Gaia was one of six people stepping out onto the outdoor platform, where the night air closed in around her. The entire station had been built with Astroland in mind—a permanent seaside carnival that hadn't been fancy since about 1907. It was like Great Adventure after a nuclear apocalypse: ancient, seedy, and busted up but charming and nostalgic at the same time.

Gaia walked through the amusement park. The fog that had closed in around her during the hour-and-a-half ride out of Manhattan—the haze of confusion, anger, and heartsick betrayal—began to lift just a little as she walked aimlessly around the park. She had to clear her head and figure out what to do next. Slowly she felt her consciousness begin to click into place, pushing her emotional miasma back into the box she had to keep it in, allowing Gaia to think clearly and logically.

As she looked around, she was amazed that anyone was there, but sure enough, a few families still straggled around the desolate rides. This place was a perma-holiday for the damned. An ancient roller coaster with wooden slats whipped people up and down a course of turns that Gaia thought couldn't be scarier than the 4 train at rush hour. The "haunted house" was a couple of dismal carts that rolled through a small structure decorated with truly terrifying cardboard skeletons. Go-karts buzzed around a figure-eight track, looking like they'd been constructed of leftover parts from a demolition derby. The place was like an old couch, one part comfy and two parts gross. Gaia loved it.

She stopped at a huge Ferris wheel that was the most obvious feature looming up out of the dark beachside neighborhood. Lights on the side of it spelled out *Wonder Wheel*. Gaia figured it was called that because everyone wondered why it didn't pop off its casters and roll over the boardwalk into the nearby surf. It had two kinds of cars: big white ones that sailed placidly in a neat circle and smaller ones in red, blue, and green that seemed just as placid until they got about halfway up. That was where they lurched sickeningly and rolled to the center of the wheel, sliding violently back and forth before speeding back out to the outer edge of the wheel. Those cars really looked like they wanted to pop off and sail over into the carousel. Gaia could hear thin, high screams drifting down from the lurching cars. They did the same thing on the way down; when they came back around to the entrance, the doors to one of them opened, revealing a small family in a hurry to get out.

The mom and dad of the family getting out of the

Wonder Wheel were laughing, and a big brother looked a little embarrassed as a girl, about ten years old, wailed at the top of her lungs. She was shaking as her mother put her arms around her, stroking her wavy brown hair and trying to shush her.

"She'll be okay," the operator told them, and the mom said, "I know."

The dad leaned down and spoke to the girl. "LuAnne, look, you don't have to be scared," he said. "You're safe on the wheel; it just feels scary, but you're okay."

"I don't like that ride," the girl wailed.

"Come on, it's not scary," her older brother insisted, waving a hand derisively.

"Don't let him fool you—he cried, too, the first time he went up," the mom said. The little girl looked up at her, amazed. "Ask him," the man said.

"You got scared?" the girl asked her brother. He rolled his eyes, stood back for a moment, and then laughed.

"Yeah, I was scared," he admitted, and his sister laughed, too. He pulled her back a bit and pointed to the huge wheel stretching above them in the sky. "This thing has been up there for like a hundred years," he told her. "Look at how they made it—those things never fall off. It's strong, see? It feels bad, but you're safe in there. Probably safer than when *Papi's* driving."

"Hey," the dad growled. The girl looked dubious.

"I don't like the way it feels," she said.

144

"That's 'cause you're a wuss," her brother told her, and she gave him a punch and started chasing him through the park, away from their parents, who yelled at them to slow down as they strolled to the next ride.

Something about the scene made Gaia feel like her stomach was made of lead. Was she pissed at the parents for taking the kid on the ride? No. Gaia realized she was sick with envy. Jealous of a child who'd thought her world had spun out of control but then found out everything was okay—because her family wouldn't let her get into anything really dangerous.

As opposed to me, Gaia thought. *In my case, there's no safety inspector making sure I'm rolling on my track. No one to catch me when I fall. In fact, there are monkeys loosening the bolts on my car, and when I feel like I'm falling, I really am.*

It was enough to make a girl need some cotton candy.

Gaia bought a bag of pink flax and broke off a piece, letting it melt in her mouth as she walked slowly out of the park and onto the boardwalk. A long pier stretched out into the darkness, lights twinkling at the end of it, just barely visible.

She walked all the way down. Here the wind was stronger, colder. She hunched her shoulders, feeling almost like she could be blown into the black waves at any moment. When she got to the end, she leaned against the wooden railing and pulled the rifle out of her bag, one handed. Never even put down her cotton candy. She saw the metal glint for just a second in the moonlight, then dropped it unceremoniously into the deep, cold, salty water.

She didn't look at it, didn't make a snappy comment about a watery grave, didn't even pause to reflect on the fact that it had almost been the agent of her death.

It was gone, and that was that.

There's only one thing to do, she thought as she gazed down into the inky blackness below her. *I've got to watch my own back. Check my own bolts. Run my own Ferris wheel. I've been doing it since I was twelve. Just because I thought for a moment that I didn't have to anymore doesn't mean I can't learn to do it again.*

She followed the pier back down to the boardwalk and turned right, walking along the strip of boardwalk between the beach and the amusement park, toward the tall towers of the residential buildings of Brighton Beach. After ten minutes she was totally out of range of the bright lights and well into dangerous territory. But she wasn't too worried. She could take care of herself. Unlike most people.

Unlike the woman wrestling with a couple of muggers about fifty yards away.

What kind of woman in her right mind would walk this boardwalk alone at night? Gaia wondered. A homeless person, maybe. Someone from out of town or someone who was lost. But now was not the time for profiling.

Gaia dropped her cotton candy and thundered down the boardwalk toward the attack in progress. The most likely result would be that the bullies would want to avoid any kind of confrontation and would drop their task and run at the first sign of interference. But Gaia kind of hoped they wouldn't do that. She could use a good ass-kicking right now. Anger still whirled in her head, and this could be just the stress-reducing workout she needed.

Yahoo! The muggers didn't even acknowledge her approach. An ass-kicking was just what was required. And Gaia was ready for it. She kicked forward, hard, making contact with someone's chest. The two guys dropped the woman, who ran shrieking toward the lights of the tall projects at the end of the boardwalk. Now it was just Gaia and her new friends. Fists rained on her from either side, and the second guy grabbed her from behind, an arm across her windpipe, trying to cut off her air supply.

Gaia grabbed at the arm across her throat instinctively, then put her training into action, turning her head to the side and shoving briskly upward with her hands. Your average girl would have had no effect on the oversized arm encircling Gaia's throat. But your average girl was not Gaia Moore.

Her choke-hold attacker fell forward, then grabbed at the air in confusion as Gaia stepped back and took a fighting stance. She gave a whirling roundhouse kick

147

that caught one of the guys in the nuts; he tried to grab at her foot, but it was obvious that his only training was as a street fighter, and he was too uncoordinated to disable her. She shoved the heel of her hand into his face and felt his nose break, blinding him with blood and tears. She didn't know how many other guys were on the shadowy dark boardwalk with her and didn't want to stick around to find out; Gaia took off running, sprinting down the boardwalk toward a streetlight, hoping there would be an exit back to the street there. She wasn't sure how many of these guys she could disable before they overpowered her.

Behind her she heard their footsteps thundering and realized she had really pissed someone off. She'd robbed these guys of an easy mark, and now they wanted revenge.

Gaia needed to turn the tables. Stepping into an alley, she leapt up onto a fire escape and waited a moment. She heard their footsteps approach and leapt quickly down with her full weight onto the last of the goons—there were three now, she could see that—and punched at his face from above. Gaia had both gravity and surprise on her side. The guy tumbled to the sidewalk and gave a shocked yell as she stomped her foot on his face. The other two stopped to look back. In that brief moment under the streetlight Gaia could see the damage she'd done to one of their noses. She gave a battle yell and ran at them like a crazy person, swinging a crowbar she'd found on the fire escape. She felt a thud as it made contact with some part of one of the two guys; that was all they needed. She almost laughed as she saw them start running again—in the opposite direction.

Now she had a taste for the fight. Though she knew logically she should quit while she was ahead, some ancient, instinctive voice from the deep recesses of her brain told her she was having too much fun. Her legs agreed and took off after them, racing to catch up and cause more damage. Attack a defenseless little female on the boardwalk, would they? She'd show them. Anger pumped through her veins along with adrenaline to keep her going at top speed.

But the goons knew this neighborhood, and she didn't. As they approached an avenue, they split off in two different directions. Gaia looked wildly up and down, through the sparsely populated street under the elevated train. One man hopped into a sedan that sped off; the other crossed in front of a bus and disappeared down a side street. She tried to run after that one, but a bus lurched in front of her, stopping her with a deafening honk as she felt the warm air of its exhaust hit her in the face. By the time it passed, the guy had melted into the night. Gaia's chase was over.

She stood for a long moment. She knew what would come next. After any ass-kicking there was a price to pay, and it came upon her from behind now with the force of an explosion: total exhaustion, turning her limbs to rubber and her guts to lead. She heard it in her ears, saw the world fade to black, and felt her back hit the sidewalk as she tumbled to the ground, unconscious.

HER EYES OPENED AND GAIA SAW. . .
uh. . . what?

Lights. Tons and tons of lights. Gold frescoes in arches. And a bear. A huge brown bear wearing a leather harness and standing in a ring of people. What the hell?

Her vision cleared a little. The bear was nothing but acrylic paint. Part of a mural on a vaulted ceiling. She blinked twice and faces came into view, ringed around the edge of her vision and looking down at her with varying expressions of worry, concern, and bemusement.

Carb- Loaded Coma

"She's awake!" someone said, and several voices gave a cheer.

Gaia tried to sit, and a soft pair of hands helped pull her up.

"You're passing out in front of my restaurant!" The hands and the voice belonged to a stout woman wearing

150

heavy sky blue eye shadow under short, bleached blond hair.

"I'm so sorry," Gaia said. "I'll go."

"Seeet!" the woman said, shoving Gaia right back down. Her arms were the size of huge legs of lamb, and their slack skin quivered as she sat Gaia on a high stool with surprising strength. "You are drunk?" she asked suspiciously.

"No," Gaia said. The woman smelled her breath, seemed satisfied, and clapped.

"Then you are hungry," she announced. She rattled off a series of orders in Russian and slapped the bar next to Gaia.

Gaia looked around her. This place looked like a palace—well, kind of. A palace built of plastic and mirrors instead of stone and tapestry. Everything around Gaia was shiny, reflective, and marbled. The bar stools were tall chairs with white pleather seats and shiny gold backs; the bar was cool black Formica with a gold pattern of flecks and veins twisting through it. Behind it, bottles gleamed in front of a mirror that wrapped all the way around an already huge room, making this restaurant look like a vast cavern of festive tables. Wherever she was, Gaia had a feeling there was a party here nightly.

"My name is Luda," the woman told her. "You?"

"Gaia," she told her. The woman's forehead wrinkled in dismay. "Guy-a," she repeated.

Luda shrugged and squeezed Gaia's knee. The man behind the bar, a huge bear of a man who looked as big as the creature in the mural over their heads, said, "You need strength. Good vodka wake you up, make you feel powerful."

"No, no, that's all right," Gaia told him.

"Don' be stupid," Luda yelled, smacking the man on his huge forearm with a resounding slap. "She needs food." As if on cue, three heaping plates of food rattled onto the counter, brought by a beefy man in a stained apron holding a cigar in the corner of his mouth.

"Stuffed cabbage," Luda told her, pronouncing it *"cebbedge,"* the way Natasha and Tatiana did. For a moment Gaia felt a cold shudder run through her. Were these people friends of her newest enemies? Was she about to be ambushed? But as she looked around the room, she saw nothing to make her feel nervous or suspicious. Besides, Natasha was so tasteful and vain; she'd never be caught dead in a place this tacky. Gaia relaxed as much as she ever did and tried a piece of the cabbage.

It was rich and flavorful—one cabbage roll felt like it could satisfy her for a month. And it just kept coming: bow-tie pasta with barley in a thick gravy, blintzes buried in thick sour cream. . . the kind of food that was designed to get you through a cold Russian winter.

A distant memory flamed up in Gaia's consciousness. Her mother. A fragrant kitchen. Snow outside but bright, yellow warmth inside. And these flavors. This fantastic food, served by her mother. It made her want to sob with the familiar comfort of it.

She couldn't believe how confused she felt. On the one hand, being here with these Russians reminded her of the way Natasha and Tatiana had tried to kill her. The horrible betrayal of it all. On the other hand, it brought back everything about her long gone, long dead mother—even the feel of her sweater against her skin, the warmth of her arms around a much younger Gaia. She had to get out of here. This outer-borough experience was making her feel confused and disoriented.

Gaia lost her appetite. She pushed her plate away, forcing herself to smile at Luda.

"That is delicious," she said. "Thank you."

"You eat more," Luda ordered. "You're skinny, like a stick. You pass out again if you don't finish food."

"I'm really okay," she said, standing up. "My parents will worry if I don't get home soon. How much do I owe you for the food?"

Luda waved off that ridiculous suggestion. "Where you going? I'll have Vahe drive you," she insisted. "He's got a Town Car."

"I'll get on the subway. It's really okay," Gaia said, giving her a hug. "You've already done too much—I'm embarrassed."

"You come back," Luda told her. "Come back and I feed you until you strong like me."

Gaia smiled and left the restaurant. God, what a homey place. Warm, safe, and caring. How come total strangers treated her like a queen and the people she'd been living with for weeks wanted her dead?

Just dumb luck, she supposed. She wished she could run back inside and eat brown bread slathered with thick butter until she went into a carb-loaded coma. But while she'd been sitting there, chowing down and making new friends, she'd realized how much she didn't belong there. While she was stuffing her face, her dad was suffering somewhere, and she was his only hope. And the only way she could find him was to spy on the spies she was living with.

The job seemed impossible. She dreaded the task ahead of her. But there was no other answer. She had to return to Seventy-second Street, act like she hadn't found anything out, and live in seeming ignorance, pretending to get along with Natasha and Tatiana while waiting for clues.

She had to climb back into the snake pit. Sit among the snakes. Let them slither over her. And listen for the secrets that their whispering hisses might reveal.

Putting the warmth of the restaurant behind her, Gaia faced the night chill and dragged herself reluctantly to the nearest subway.

ED SAT BACK AND LET OUT AN EXHAUSTED

Giggly puff of air. "I don't think I've ever eaten that much in my life," he said, blinking helplessly at the exactly one mouthful of saag motor ponir sitting in the silver dish in front of him.

"I will take that," Tatiana said, scooping it up with her fork.

"That's unbelievable! Where are you putting it all, in your backpack?" he asked, peeking under the table to make sure she wasn't. "You know, a lot of girls are afraid to eat in front of guys."

"I am not a lot of girls," Tatiana said.

"Well, you eat like you're about seven of them."

"Hey, you guys!"

Ed looked up to see Megan and three other girls from school.

"Oh, you found us!" Tatiana cheered. "I didn't know if you got my message!"

"You left them a message?" The question just popped out of Ed's mouth. He hadn't meant to ask it. He was surprised to find himself feeling disappointed that he wouldn't have Tatiana all to himself. Despite all the times he had told her—and himself—that his romantic feelings were only for Gaia, he thought—this twinge of regret told him—he might have a little crush on Tatiana, too.

"Oh, did you think you were going to have her all

155

to yourself?" Megan cooed, as if she'd read his mind.

"No," Ed mumbled. This was an annoying development. He didn't want his feelings to get even more messy and jumbled. Besides, this was a boisterous bunch—even though there were only a few of them, they were so giggly and chatty that they filled the tiny, train-car-size restaurant with their presence. People at other tables kept glancing over. Megan's book bag boinked a lady sitting across the aisle.

"Well, we definitely need to adjourn to another location," Megan announced as the lady glared at her and tried to protect her food from any further unintended book bag onslaughts.

"Sounds good to me," Tatiana said. "We should go to Blue and Gold and play pool."

"Very badly? Can we play very badly?" Melanie begged.

"Well, you can," Megan told her. "I think I'm getting better at it. I'll kick your ass, anyway."

"I hope you don't mind," Tatiana whispered across the table as she gathered up her things.

"Of course I don't," Ed said. "I might go home, though."

"No! You have to come!" Tatiana grabbed his arm affectionately. "I want you to come, too. Please?"

Ed shrugged. The fact was, he was glad this giggly posse had shown up. They'd stop another awkward confrontation from happening—like when Tatiana had tried to kiss him. If he was developing feelings for her, then he had to keep a comfortable distance. But he really wanted to be out. What was at home? Nothing but thoughts of Gaia.

"Okay, I'll come." He nodded. They went to the divey bar a block away and took over the back room, writing their names on the little blackboard so their mini–pool tournament could proceed. Then the girls started knocking the balls around on the green felt. They clearly had no clue how to play.

Ed couldn't resist. "You might want to hold it like this," he told Megan. "Look, between your knuckles so the cue actually goes where you're aiming it. Hit this one over here," he added, pointing out the sweet spot on the seven ball.

"Ohmigod, it went in!" Megan yelped. "Yay, I'm a pool player!"

Soon he was giving a miniclinic to the assembled girls. "This should have been your intramural activity, not skateboarding," Tatiana teased.

"You're probably right," he said. "Especially since there's a definite irony in my teaching skateboarding after what I did to myself. I should have handed out wheelchairs to everyone who took it."

Tatiana laughed. "Ed, you're terrible!" she scolded.

Someone handed him a Sam Adams, and Ed took it. It was fun playing pool, but if he'd been given his choice of activities this evening, hanging out with these girls would not have been one of them. As the novelty of the pool lesson wore off, there was more chatting and less ball-hitting. Ed noticed there was a distinctly catty turn to the conversation.

"I mean, I don't know who told her Burberry was still in style, but she was wearing that pukey plaid with no shame whatsoever."

"Wait, maybe she was being funny."

"No, she was not. She was just wearing it. I don't know why she didn't pair the skirt with a pair of Y2K commemorative sunglasses and some dot-com stocks. She looked so ninth grade."

"Maybe tomorrow she will wear the Ralph Lauren puppy sweater," Tatiana added to the conversation, pronouncing Ralph Lauren with the correct non-French accent and indicating not only a knowledge of but an interest in both fashion and bitchery. Ed wilted slightly. This wasn't a surprise, but it was a side of Tatiana that wasn't his favorite.

"I heard her father lost a bundle on that merger that never happened," someone else added. "But if she's scrounging, she's better off wearing no name than old names."

"She's better off staying home if she's going to let her ass get that big," Tatiana said. "Did anyone notice that the stripes looked like ocean waves?"

Everybody busted up laughing. Ed had no idea who they were talking about, but something about the conversation was making him kind of sick. Yeah, it was mean, but there was something else, too. He took a long swig of Sam Adams and suddenly felt dismally tired. He put down his cue and went to sit on one of the banquettes.

I should be happy, he thought. *Here I am, out with the hottest girls in school, and I'm the only guy in sight. Isn't this like the plot of some teen movie? I should be having the time of my life.*

Woo-hoo. The trouble was, something about this scene—the bitchy girls, the fashion report cards, the endless chatter—was awfully familiar. Was he just having a random case of déjà vu or. . .

Ugh. He knew exactly what this reminded him of.

Way back in the far reaches of his memory, he had a vision of himself—young, nervous, and eager to impress his new girlfriend, Heather. He'd fallen for her because of the way she was when she was just with him. But a major flaw in their relationship was the way she became in these packs of females. He had spent too much time hanging out with her in places like this. Listening to her yak with her girlfriends. Struggling to keep up with their cleverer-than-thou bitchfests. Years later, after all he'd been through, he was ending up in the same circle of girls, doing the same shit. Only this time the queen bee was. . .

"Ed, don't be so mopey," Tatiana complained, coming over and yanking at his arm. "Everybody's having fun. What are you, a lightweight?"

Tatiana. She had somehow turned into the new Heather. And she wasn't the queen bee. She was acting like the queen bee-yotch. All of a sudden Ed felt like he'd been yanked back into Casa Heatherosa.

"I want to see someone doing a shot," she announced, like a demented cruise director. "Who is first?"

Maybe he was overreacting, Ed thought. Maybe Tatiana just had a couple of drinks in her and was acting obnoxious. But even if that were true, it made him like her less.

But that wasn't the worst part. The worst part was that this was the second time in twelve hours that Tatiana had reminded him of someone else. An ex-girlfriend, no less.

Am I so predictable that I'm going to spend the rest of my life dating the same two girls over and over again? he wondered. *Or is Tatiana somehow doing this on purpose?*

He had no idea which—if either—was true. He took a closer look at Tatiana. She had seemed like her old self when he went to her match, but now he was replaying it. There was something in her eyes, some kind of bitterness that hadn't been there before. Almost like she had experienced some great personal letdown, a betrayal so huge, it had changed her outlook on life.

But she hadn't said anything about having problems. They were friends, weren't they? Ed would have known if something huge had gone down. Maybe she was worried about applying to college? Ed's sister had

160

turned into an obsessed monster before she'd even ordered her applications, and every meeting with her adviser had thrown her into a deeper funk over how she'd never get into Bennington or Bard. Or something with her dad? Ed had never heard a full explanation of who he was or why he wasn't around. Most of his friends had an almost fetishistic interest in their absent parents. The more he thought about it, the more he realized something was off with Tatiana, and try as he might, he couldn't figure out what it could be. She did well in her classes, and she had tons of friends.

Oh, jeez, it's not me, is it? he wondered. *What if she's upset because she's hung up on me?* The idea seemed impossibly self-absorbed, but Ed couldn't dismiss it as a possibility. Given how messed up he'd been feeling over Gaia, he now had ample evidence that a sick heart could ruin every aspect of someone's life. And knowing he might be having that effect on Tatiana just made him feel even worse, and weirder, and less like a party animal. This night was getting really unfun.

Ed shook his head and took another swig of beer. It wasn't having the desired effect. His mind wasn't clearer, it was more clouded, and he was starting to feel like Heather, Gaia, and Tatiana were three freaky personality-switching sprites. Heather went from bitchy to nice. Gaia was so hot and cold, she was practically a split personality. And now Tatiana had gone from *Pleasantville* to *Cruel Intentions*.

Ed watched Tatiana from his spot on the banquette. This was just so confusing. The balls on the pool table made sense: You hit them and they rolled into each other. But Tatiana was one giant curveball, a cue ball that wiggled off in bizarre directions. Come to think of it, all girls were like crazy cue balls.

It was enough to make Ed seriously consider some sort of skateboarding monastery.

I think I have a few things pieced together. I know certain things. I know that I am Oliver Moore. I know that my brother, Tom, has a wife, Katia, and that I think about her more than I should. I still don't know who Gaia is. But she's somehow connected to my brother and. . . damn. Whenever I try to force my mind to tell me what that name means, I hit a brick wall of incomprehension. She's like a blind spot in my mind. Maybe she's my wife? Could I have a wife who I don't even remember? Gaia. No. I don't think she's my wife. It's more complicated than that. With time. With more time, perhaps I'll remember.

I still have no way out of my body. My eyes blink, my fingers will sometimes make spasmodic movements, but basically I am trapped in a flesh prison. It's like a diabolical form of torture. It's all I can do not to go mad, with nothing but the

nurses' gossip and the nattering
of daytime soap operas to fill my
head. I force myself into disci-
plined mind exercises. First,
when I was still very, very
bewildered, it was all I could do
to get through the multiplication
tables. I would recite them to
myself like a third grader learn-
ing them by rote all over again.
Then I found the numbers came
more easily. Like old friends. So
I moved on to the periodic table,
the elements. . . though something tells me there are a few
new ones that have been added
since I went into this vegetative
state. I try to remember sonnets
and speeches from Shakespeare.
Poetry is more difficult than
numbers, though. More variables.
Less logic. But my mind needs all
the challenges it can get.

Lord knows, my daily dose of
Family Feud will not stretch my
intellect at all.

Sometimes I lose hope. All
this thinking, all this repeti-
tion of memorization, and for

what? To lie here inside a body
that ignores me? Legs that lie
like far-flung lumps, arms that
splay out to his sides attached
by tubes to watery bags filled
with food and medication—I don't
blame the doctors for ignoring
me. I see them poke their heads
in, whenever they feel they
absolutely must, and they hurry
away as quickly as possible. They
must hate to be reminded that
they can do nothing about me.
They think I'm dead inside this
flesh; they'd like to fill me
with morphine and free up my
hospital bed.

Sometimes I feel so hopeless,
I wish they would. Sometimes I
wonder why I'm still alive if I'm
just going to lie here for the
next forty years. I just hope
that if my mind gets stronger, my
body will follow suit.

Six times twelve. The square
root of 6,561. Aluminum, boron,
and cadmium. "My mistress' eyes
are nothing like the sun." These
are the twisted helices that I

hope will help me evolve back into myself. If I can just hold on to my sanity long enough to get there. I'm Oliver Moore. I'm Oliver Moore, and I want to wake up. How long have I been like this? Am I getting better or just fooling myself? Why isn't my brother here?

Can't anyone hear me?

Nurse's Report, New York Hospital
2:30 A.M.

   Checked on patient Oliver Moore. No change in
demeanor or physical presentation of symptoms. No
response to queries or attempted stimulation.
Some movement of fingers. Determined to be random. Patient still assumed to be in a persistent
vegetative state.

And that
would be
the end of
that.

gun

AS SOON AS GAIA'S TRAIN HIT

Blushing Brick Red

Manhattan, she was struck with a sudden, urgent need to set things right with Sam. The thought was clear and crystallized in her mind, like a diamond on black velvet—either it was the adrenaline of the ass-kicking, the hearty food, or just getting away from it all that snapped her mind into focus. Or a combination of the three. Whatever the reason, Gaia was shocked and ashamed that she hadn't thought of it before. The gun in Tatiana's bedroom proved that Sam wasn't the shooter. Her suspicions of him had been totally unfounded. Whether or not she was unsure of her feelings for him—romantically, hormonally, or whatever—she'd been one billion percent wrong when she accused him of setting her up.

Tatiana might even have his cell phone now. It wasn't hidden with the gun, but Gaia had to assume, even if she wasn't one hundred percent sure, that either Natasha or Tatiana had sent her that text message.

Ugh! He had even told her the cell phone was lost, and she hadn't believed him! The memory of that washed over her in a whole new wave of shame that left her blushing brick red. Apologies weren't her strong suit, anyway; this one was making her squirm beyond belief.

169

Before she went home to play ignorant-innocent with Natasha and Tatiana—pumping them for information while she pretended she hadn't found the gun—she wanted to tell Sam how wrong she'd been. She replayed the scene from earlier in the day in her head. She saw Sam's surprise, his concern, and his hurt when she'd turned on him. Over and over again. It drove her up a wall. Okay, so given the information she'd had—that the text message had come from Sam's phone—she had been entirely justified in suspecting him. But she should have been able to weigh that evidence against what she knew about Sam: that he was the most soulful, kindhearted person she'd ever met and that unlike the embittered, world-weary people she usually had to deal with, he was incapable of hurting her. Gaia had been pissed at Ed for not trusting her—and that was exactly how Sam felt. She should have trusted him. She needed to say that to him, and she needed to do it now.

Never mind that she really didn't want to go back to Seventy-second Street. Never mind that she was hoping for something, anything, to make her feel good before she steeled herself for that snake pit. All that aside, she still wanted to apologize, and now was as good a time as any.

She got off the train downtown and ran east, from the chichi galleries of SoHo to the place where the Lower East Side met Chinatown. The t'ai chi park was empty now; nobody was out but a few homeless people and the occasional person obviously hurrying home to a family or friends. Gaia hoped there were friendly faces waiting for her, too.

She buzzed and was quickly let up. Dmitri answered the door. This time she wasn't in a huff over almost getting barbecued in a fire. She couldn't believe how much he had improved since they'd found him in the prison.

"Wow, you look great," she said. He did. Getting rid of his ratty long hair and putting food in his belly had given the old man a complete transformation. His blue eyes sparkled with intelligence.

"Did you find anything out about my dad?" she asked.

"Not yet, no," he said. "But I think you are not here to speak to me."

"No, I'm not. Is Sam around?"

"I'm right here," Sam said, and Gaia whirled around to face him. But now that she was here, she didn't know how to say anything.

"I wanted to—Dmitri, could we?"

"I'm going now," he said, padding off to the kitchen.

"I have to tell you something," she said to Sam, grabbing him by the arm and pulling him over to the window for the illusion of more privacy. As she looked at him, her heart gave a disconcerting little wobble. Here was the first guy she'd ever fallen in love with, the guy who'd made her see that there was more to the world than being pissed and playing chess in the park. He was thinner, more tired, badly injured. . . and all of it just made him look more handsome. Not in a movie-star way. `In a real-person way.` The way his brownish red hair fell onto his forehead, that same brown jacket that had hung in his NYU dorm room—she felt so much affection for him. She didn't know if it was like, or love, or what, but she didn't want this person to hurt because of her.

"I was horribly, horribly wrong this afternoon when I got mad at you," she said.

"Yeah." He wasn't being helpful.

"I'm serious," she said, grabbing his arm. "I accused you of setting me up. And it's not even like that was the first time I said something like that to you. I've been suspicious of you ever since you came back, and that must have felt horrible."

Sam shifted his weight and leaned against the wall behind him. He wasn't able to meet Gaia's eyes. "Yeah. It did," he admitted.

"Well, I found out some things today, and they all point to someone else setting me up—I know for a fact it was someone else. It wasn't you. I know that now, and I'm so, so sorry."

"You have proof?" Sam still wouldn't look at her. He was staring uncomfortably out the window, at the moon, just about anywhere but at Gaia. And the way he asked—he was almost sarcastic.

"Yeah. I found some pretty damning evidence."

"Well, I'm so glad that this *evidence* made you believe it wasn't me, Gaia." Sam sighed, finally turning his eyes to meet hers. They looked like sad brown puddles. "I just wish you had known that from the start."

"Sam, I'm sorry—I've had to watch my back for so long, it's just instinct," she tried to explain. "If you knew how many people have turned on me—"

"I know that," he said. "Look, I understand you're involved in something huge and weird. But it's turned you into someone I don't know how to deal with."

"I'm not asking you to deal with anything," Gaia said, finally putting a hand on his forearms, which were still crossed protectively across his chest. He didn't pull away—a tiny slice of relief. "I'm just trying to admit I was wrong and to apologize for the fact that you got caught in the cross fire," she went on, glancing down at his chest where his bullet wounds were still healing. "I'm not asking anything else from you."

As soon as she said the words, Gaia realized with a thud of her heart that it wasn't quite true. She might not be asking for more, but she *wanted* more. A lot more. Maybe not love and romance, but at least affection, friendship, a warm hug to get her through the next few days. Forgiveness. A friend.

"All right. Good." Sam stood, no longer leaning against the wall, and Gaia's hands dropped to her waist. She looked up at him helplessly. The ball was in his court.

"I understand what you're saying," he said. "I mean, I accept your apology. But I'm glad you're not asking anything else of me. I'm not sure I've got much left to give." His eyes flicked toward hers, but it seemed almost painful to him. He went back to studying the wooden slats of the floor. "We'll talk later, okay? I'll see you."

"Okay, bye," she said, though he had left the room by the time she got the words out. She felt like a total schmuck. And lonely. She felt weirdly lonely. She turned and saw Dmitri standing in the doorway.

"I'm sorry you had to overhear the latest episode of *Dawson's Creek*," she said.

"I am sorry you are having a difficult time with Sam," Dmitri said. "But perhaps you will feel better when I tell you what I have now found out."

"I have information, too," Gaia said. "It's horrible news. Because of it I may be killed if I go back to the apartment on Seventy-second Street."

"What?" Dmitri was incredulous. "Something about the women you live with? Natasha and. . ." His voice trailed off as he searched for the other name.

"Tatiana. Yes," Gaia said. "They're dangerous— more dangerous than I ever imagined. But if you can help me figure out how to handle them, we can get back to finding my dad."

She followed Dmitri into the kitchen. They both heard the front door of the apartment close with a slam. Sam was gone. Dmitri gave Gaia a sympathetic look. It wasn't much, but to her, it was the most affection she'd had in forever, and she accepted it gladly. She felt a wave of fondness for the old guy. Then she steeled her mind for the task ahead and sat down at the kitchen table to discuss what was going to happen next.

Okay, so that was everything I wanted from Gaia. She admitted that it was totally wrong to accuse me and even agreed she should have trusted me.

So why couldn't I do what I wanted most? Why couldn't I gather her up into my arms and give her a crushing hug? She was so close, I could feel the warmth of her body. Her hands were on my arms. I was so close, but something wouldn't let me do it. . . .

I'm just angry. I'm really still angry. I don't understand how I could love someone so much and she would still suspect me. Of trying to kill her, for chrissake! It's such a deep, huge thing to think I could do. She just doesn't know me at all, and that feels so weird.

I feel like now it's me who can't trust Gaia. It was just so crazy, the way she accused me, the way she looked at me with so much hate, with bullet-proof glass in her eyes. There was

SAM

nothing I could do to get through
to her. No way I could make her
believe me. That was a cold, cold
feeling. It hurt like hell.

Gaia, I'm sorry. I wish I
could have reached out to you
like you were reaching out to me.
But it came a little too late for
the wholehearted response you
wanted. I have to test my heart
and see if it can still reach out
to you. If I still have the nerve
to get close to you. Whatever we
are to each other, it all has to
be on hold.

Sorry again.

Maybe tomorrow. Maybe someday.

But not now.

AT THE BAR ED WAS STRUGGLING TO

stay interested in the evening going on around him. He was planning to leave as soon as he could. The trouble was, every time he tried to make an excuse, Tatiana begged him to stay, and for some reason he wasn't telling her no.

Glowing Green Screen

What's going on here, Fargo? he asked himself. *Are you trying to make Gaia jealous? It's not like she's here to see this. Or are you seriously whipped—by a girl who's not even your girlfriend?*

He was sitting next to Tatiana when she reached into her pocketbook and pulled out a strange cell phone. It wasn't the one she'd been using that morning. She studied it as if she were checking for an incoming call she might have missed, then put it back in her bag. Ed remembered the two cell phones she'd pulled out after her racquetball game. Now it struck him as weird all over again.

"What is with that thing?" he asked. "You've been checking it all night."

"It's a cell phone, silly."

"Yeah, but it's your mom's cell phone."

"So?"

"So why are you so worried about it?"

Tatiana turned to him, turning up the heat in her

eyes with a teasing wink. "Oh my, so many questions," she said. "Do you really want to know what is going on with my mother's messages?"

"No!" Ed gave an I-surrender wave. "Forget I asked. Whatever."

"Such an inquisition," Tatiana went on. "For someone who says he wants to be just friends, you do show an unusual amount of interest."

"Jeez, Tatiana," he began, but he was cut off by a strange ring. It was the mysterious cell phone. Tatiana took it out of her bag and stared at the glowing green screen.

"Aren't you going to answer it?"

She didn't even answer. Just stared at the ringing phone for three. . . four. . . five. . . six rings, until it stopped. Then she waited, still staring, breathing slowly, until a small envelope popped up. It beeped once, announcing that there was a voice mail message. She put it back in her bag.

"I am exhausted," she announced to no one in particular. "I am getting in a cab and going home."

"Nooooo!" Megan said, hugging her like a long-lost relative. "You can't go!"

"I must go. I just realized what time it is. My mother is so angry about the party I threw, and if I am not home tonight, she will send me to one of those boot camps for unruly teens."

"That was a quick switch," Ed commented.

"Oh, look who is trying to tempt me to stay out," Tatiana sang, totally missing (or pretending to miss) Ed's jab. First she'd begged him to stay out—and now that he'd stayed, she was making her exit faster than Cinderella at 11:59? It didn't make sense. But he didn't have a chance to ask her what was up. She was out the door before he could say a word, and by the time he got through the crush of girls between him and the door, she had slammed the door of her yellow cab. Through the window he could see her pull out the phone and hit one of the buttons to check the voice mail message. Then the cab sped away from the curb with a squeal, and she was gone.

He knew there were men who liked women with a little mystery. But right about now, Ed Fargo would have loved to meet someone ridiculously predictable.

Amazing. This apartment
is completely empty of people.
But full of whispers and ghosts,
phantoms of the past, crowding me
out of each room. I've been wandering from the kitchen to the
living room to my bedroom, in
search of peace each time but
each time finding some new memory
that pushed me away from comfort.
Is it the apartment that's
haunted? Or is it me?

It makes me laugh. Even when I
make a home for myself, I am
still a wandering nomad.

Look at this room, now. The
room that is home to my daughter
and Gaia. Tatiana was such a brilliant child. Even when she was
tiny, running around on her sturdy
legs and laughing in that charming, tinkling way that she had, I
knew she was special. I watched
her get what she wanted with charm
and, when charm didn't work, with
a well-placed chubby fist. I used
to pretend to chide her, but
underneath, I knew the two skills

would complement each other perfectly to take my daughter wherever she wanted in the world.

And I have done whatever I had
to do so that Tatiana could have
the most opportunities. Some very
distasteful things. And then,
some that were more pleasurable.
But it was all done for Tatiana.
So that she would never have to
live the way I lived.

Yet here, in the small twin
bed next to my precious daughter,
there has been an interloper.
Someone who wanted to usurp
Tatiana's birthright. I have been
forced to care for this ill-mannered creature, who did nothing
but resent me and spit in my face
in return for the care she was
given. And the worst part was, I
had actually begun to care for
this Gaia. For a brief period
things seemed calm, almost normal, almost homey.

Until I found out that this
mediocre child wanted the power
that Tatiana deserved.

That was entirely too much.

Just looking at their beds, you can see which belongs to the superior child. One, with fresh bedding neatly arranged, as pretty as a picture. The other, strewn with crumpled sheets, the pillow slumped on the floor like a defeated marshmallow. Who would live so disgustingly? The heiress to power? Or an annoying creature who must be eliminated?

Not many things really make me laugh. But there is no other response to this. To the idea that Gaia could ever be given such power when she so clearly doesn't deserve it. When power is exactly what Tatiana so richly deserves.

Not Gaia.

Tatiana.

And I will make that happen any way I can.

NATASHA FLUFFED HER DAUGHTER'S
pillow, stepped on Gaia's, and went over to
the false-backed fireplace to look at the gun.
She hoped to have an opportunity to use it
again soon. And this time she wouldn't
miss.

Gone

She moved the heavy piece of metal and peered
into the dim chamber, reaching for the instrument of
her revenge. Her hand closed on nothing.

Natasha gasped as if she had been bitten and
yanked her arm back out. She stepped back and looked
up at the wall, wildly thinking that maybe there were
two holes and she'd reached into the wrong one. But
there was just the one. It was supposed to hold the
beautiful gun. And it did not. It held nothing.

With a cry of fury she reached back into the dusty
chamber and flapped her arm desperately, trying to
locate the gun somewhere, anywhere inside. But all
she hit was bare walls and dirt. The gun was gone.

The gun was gone.

Had Tatiana taken it? Was she trying to act alone?
The thought hit Natasha like a cold fist clenching her
heart. Could she be so foolhardy? She would get herself
killed! She had picked up the phone to call her daughter when the real explanation blossomed in her mind.

Of course. It had to be.

Gaia had somehow found the gun and
taken it.

That little monster. Now Natasha wanted her dead more than ever.

The phone rang, startling Natasha from her reverie. She stepped into the kitchen and picked it up.

"She is going to Greenpoint. To the water towers near the docks."

It was Tatiana, sounding calm but excited. This was the chance they had both been waiting for. What they had failed at yesterday, they would now complete.

"My darling," Natasha said. "You're all right?"

"Of course. Why would you ask such a thing?"

"Just humor me," she said. "You don't have. . . anything you're not supposed to, do you?"

"What are you talking about? Of course not. Mother, are you all right?"

"It's nothing. Excuse me," Natasha said, relief flooding her veins. She composed herself quickly. "How did you find out about this odd location?"

"She called to tell Sam," Tatiana told her. She gave a lilting laugh. "She begged him to meet her—gave careful directions—said she had to be sure they would be alone. She says she has reason to be very paranoid. But she loves him and she must see him tonight."

"Oh, I'm sure she'll be just fine," Natasha said. "But we'll make sure, eh?"

"Do you know where these water towers are?"

"I will find out. You're coming home now?"

"I'm in the cab. I'm almost there."

"Good. By the time you get here, I'll be ready to go."

"I have to change. I'm dressed for a night out with those stupid girls."

"Yes."

Tatiana clicked off the line, and Natasha stood, holding the receiver as her daughter sped uptown toward her in a yellow cab. She caressed the telephone in her hand, as if her warm, loving hand would reach through to her daughter. No, Tatiana would never do something so foolish and ill-mannered. Only Gaia would take something that didn't belong to her. It made her dangerous, but now that Natasha knew where she would be, she'd be able to neutralize the troublesome girl, and that would be the end of that. It would be a little more difficult this way. She'd have to get close to her to end her life. But maybe that was the way it should be. Up close and personal. A final embrace for the girl who had almost been her stepdaughter.

She sat back in a plastic chair in the white-tiled kitchen. She was absolutely still. It was so quiet, she could hear the buzzing of the fluorescent light fixture above her head. She no longer felt the need to wander from room to room. Everything was ready to go. She simply waited for her daughter to come home.

A sharp
smell of
river
water **deserted**
pervaded
the air
out here.

NATASHA WAS GLAD SHE HAD USE OF the sleek black sedan that took her and her daughter across the Fifty-ninth Street Bridge. She found the red-and-white water towers easily— **Zagged** they were the only shapes rising out of the gloom of the warehouses surrounding them. A sharp smell of river water pervaded the air out here. And there was another scent: the scent of victory close at hand.

"So she is coming here to meet Sam," Natasha reiterated.

"Yes, I suppose she thinks this is a nice, romantic spot," Tatiana told her. "Yech."

"It is strange," Natasha said. "But she is such a strange girl. Nothing surprises me anymore."

"We should be careful. Maybe she will have the gun with her," Tatiana suggested.

"Not to meet her boyfriend. But of course you are right—we should always be careful, anyway." Natasha turned off her headlights for the final approach and put the car in neutral, slipping silently down the last block as they came within hearing range of the water towers. Then she pulled up the parking brake.

They were quiet for a moment. Both with an unspoken understanding that this moment of meditative silence would focus them for the task ahead. Full of anticipation, with a tiny bit of dread. But quiet and calm.

"Did you feel bad?" Tatiana asked.

"What?"

"Did you ever feel bad? About her father? And about her?"

Natasha turned to look at her daughter. So poised. So ready to take any action, with a maturity that set her completely apart from other girls her age. Yet Natasha could look into her eyes and see the pleading, unsure girl behind them. She took her hand.

"There are some sacrifices that must be made," she told Tatiana. "If it were easy, anyone would be able to do it. It is people like us, who have the bravery to make the difficult choices, who will always win. Remember, my *lapatchka*, we are soldiers first."

She was gratified to see the fear subside in Tatiana's eyes. But her gaze didn't waver.

"But you did not answer my question," she said.

Natasha looked away, out the windshield.

"Some sacrifices must be made," she repeated. "Now shush. Ready yourself. Tonight we must succeed."

Together she and Tatiana left the car and walked quietly out toward the looming towers. Everything seemed deserted, no sound but distant sirens and the quiet rustle of city life. In the bright moonlight they could see a figure with long blond hair standing uncertainly between the towers. Waiting for a boy who wasn't on his way. Because her phone call had come straight to Tatiana. It was too delicious.

The two women approached Gaia from two different directions, taking wide paths to the right and left of her so that they could complement each other's approaches and minimize the risk that she'd get away. From her vantage point Natasha couldn't even see Tatiana. But she could sense her presence, flitting like a bat in the dark shadows. When she was sure Tatiana was situated, she gave a loud whistle and began to run toward Gaia.

It was a bright night, and the open lot was lit by the moon. That was why they couldn't get too close without leaving the shadows. It meant Gaia had a good ten seconds before they could reach her. In that time she looked around, confused, and realized she was being ambushed. Quickly—so quickly Natasha almost had to admire it—Gaia turned and ran.

But she hadn't been expecting more than one attacker. She'd run away from the sound of the whistle and straight into Tatiana. Natasha's daughter clotheslined Gaia with a stiff-armed shot to the throat; Gaia ran right into the wrestling move and was knocked backward.

She stumbled, momentarily stunned, and then stepped backward a few paces. She zigged a few steps one way, then zagged in another direction, looking totally haphazard. This time it was Natasha who attacked her, grabbing her around the waist and slamming her into the metal wall of one of the water towers.

She heard the *thud* as Gaia hit the wall like a sack of wet sand. Then Tatiana arrived and grabbed her by the hair, snapping her head back and slamming it into the metal once, twice, three times in succession. Gaia let out little cries with each hit—but she didn't fall. Tatiana gave her one last angry shove and finally knocked her off balance. Gaia dropped to her knees and nearly fell to the ground, catching herself on her hands, instinctively pitching herself away from the two women.

"Wha—who—" she huffed. Natasha couldn't tell if she was asking or just gasping for air, but the damn girl was already running again, her feet moving one in front of the other as she flung her torso ahead of herself, doing an awkward, injured ballet in her effort to right herself.

Tatiana followed after her, grabbing for the waistband of her jeans. But Natasha could see Gaia twisting around, aiming a wild fist at Tatiana's head.

"No," she shouted, and Gaia turned, confused, before her fist could make contact.

"Natasha?" she asked. "What—what are you doing here?"

Damn. Cover blown. Oh well, it was bound to happen.

"Don't worry about why I'm here, Gaia," Natasha hissed. "Worry about whether you'll live long enough to leave."

"You found our little friend, eh?" Tatiana asked her. "Our third roommate. I wanted to use it to kill you. Now I have to find a different way."

"Oh my God—no," Gaia said. "Stay back. Stay away from me!"

191

This was too excellent. Natasha had never seen Gaia off balance before. The girl began running again, her blond hair looking blue as it flipped behind her in the moonlight, but Tatiana was right on her heels. Natasha saw her catch up to Gaia, shoving her, pushing her, tripping her until she fell to the ground. It was beautiful. Her daughter was perfect. She ran to join her in the wide, pebbly open space, surrounded only by looming warehouse buildings.

By the time she got there, Tatiana was on the ground, straddling Gaia, her hands in a choking stranglehold around her neck. Gaia's arms were flailing, smacking haphazardly at Tatiana's face, shoulders, anywhere, just trying to get a grip on her to defend herself. But it was useless. Natasha approached and placed a foot squarely in the center of Gaia's chest, making it impossible for Gaia to move. Tatiana let go of her throat and held her flailing arms to the ground.

"Natasha," she wheezed, unable to get a decent breath with a boot on her chest. "Why are you doing this?"

"Stop the charade," Natasha scolded her. "I think you were expecting to see us. Perhaps not tonight, in this place, but when you took our gun, you knew we would come after you."

"Yeah, it was a big surprise," Gaia answered from her prone position. "Finding out you were double crossing me and my father after all. So tell me—do you get paid well for being a whore?"

"Shut up, you bitch," Tatiana screeched. She spit in Gaia's face. Gaia flinched but couldn't turn away; her hair, stuck under her shoulders, kept her head pinned helplessly.

Natasha gave a deep, throaty laugh. "My daughter is very protective of me," she said. "It is the kind of trait you find in families. Oh, but you wouldn't know anything about that, would you, my little orphan?"

"I'm not an orphan," Gaia seethed. "I'm going to find my father."

Natasha's face darkened, and her smile turned to steel.

"The only place you'll find him is in hell, when I send you there," she said.

Gaia's eyes widened. Natasha could see her expression change even in the dim moonlight. She gave an incredulous stare.

"You're a liar," she said. "You're a bitch and a liar. My father's not dead."

"Oh, but he is," Natasha wheedled, in a parody of the soothing voice she used to use to comfort Gaia. "He is dead. I fed him poison at that dinner myself. I watched him choke and hoped he wouldn't make it to the hospital. And I worked with our agents to have him disappear from under the doctors' noses. He's gone, Gaia. Deep under the East River by now."

Gaia seemed paralyzed. She glared at Natasha, weighing the truth in this statement.

"It's terrible," Tatiana taunted her. "If anything happened to my mother, I would know immediately. And I certainly would find her and protect her if she was in danger. But you? You just let your father die. You did nothing."

Gaia roared and bucked her body backward. The convulsive movement caught Natasha off guard and she reeled backward, momentarily off balance. Gaia punched and kicked at her wildly, then turned and ran back toward the water towers, running toward the gap between them.

"Coward!" Natasha called after her. She gave chase, galloping after Gaia, Tatiana lagging behind. This was becoming tiring. Amusing as it was to tease this pathetic creature, Natasha wanted to silence her once and for all. Perhaps with a twist of the head to break her neck. Perhaps with the long, thin weapon she had tucked into her boot. But first she had to catch the stupid girl yet again. She saw her disappear around the right tower, but she was right behind. She rounded the tower and saw—

Ha!

A dizzying halogen light splashed into her vision. Her pupils ached as they tried to dilate in the sudden flash. But before she could figure out where it was coming from, arms grabbed her from every direction, knocking her backward, shoving her against the metal side of the tower.

Ambushed? Attacked?

194

Impossible!

Unless. . .

"Gaia!" she shrieked. "It's impossible. I'm supposed to kill you! What did you do? Who are these people?"

"CIA," she heard Gaia's voice tell her from somewhere in the gloom beyond the spotlight.

Natasha fought. With every fiber of her being she lashed out against the black-clad men who had her pinned from every angle. All her satisfaction, all her anticipation turned to horrified dread and the sickening realization that she'd been had.

"The phone call. You knew," she snarled. "Oh, you think you are so clever. You little bitch, I'm so glad I killed your father. Do you know he died begging to see you again?"

"Shut her up," Gaia's voice snapped. Natasha heard footsteps crunching away.

"You can't shut me up," Natasha screamed after her. "You'll hear me in your dreams, Gaia. You'll hear me and see me and you'll never forget how you loved me. Me, Gaia. The woman who killed Thomas Moore!"

Natasha felt her windpipe being squeezed by the leather-clad hand of a CIA operative. She gave a strangled shout and felt a flash of pain behind her eyes as she gasped for breath. A moment later she could breathe again as she was thrown bodily into the back of a paddy wagon. She struggled to stand and look out the back window. Then she began pounding on the doors.

Pounding. First slowly. Then quickly. Pounding in time with the wild beating of her heart. Fury ripping through her veins as she saw her prize snatched from her grasp with one stupid voice mail. She could kill herself for this. So anxious to close the deal, she hadn't seen the glaringly obvious fact that she was being set up.

"Gaia!" she screamed. "Gaia! GAAAIAAAA!"

TATIANA SAW THE BURST OF LIGHT

as Natasha was captured and stepped backward into the shadows. She watched her mother, her beautiful, proud mother, **Instincts** captured by thugs and treated like a common streetwalker. She nearly leapt into the light to join her mother in battling the attackers. But something stopped her. Almost like a hand, reaching out and pulling her back.

Stop. Something told her. Some*one.* It was her mother's voice, speaking from her heart.

What is the logical progression if I run to help her? that part of Tatiana asked.

I'll fight, but I'll get captured, too. There are too many of them, she answered inwardly.

Then run.

With the instincts Natasha had instilled in her, Tatiana cut her losses and turned her back on her mother. It was the most wrenching thing she had ever done. But that voice inside her had spoken the truth. What good was she to her mother from inside a prison cell?

Tatiana could hear the shouts of the government agents behind her. Looking for her. Clumsy men. Fools. If she hadn't been concentrating so hard on slipping, invisible, into the streets of Brooklyn, Tatiana would have laughed.

But there would be plenty of time for laughter after she crossed the water. She'd use whatever she had to use to get back to Manhattan and contact the people who would help her.

Then she'd laugh. And she'd wait. Wait to get her revenge on Gaia. For trapping her mother. For taking her place. And just—just for being Gaia.

Then Tatiana would laugh like hell.

Rivulets of Dread

"DMITRI," GAIA CALLED OUT AS SHE stormed away from Natasha. "Where's Dmitri?" she asked one of the big CIA guys. He ignored her. She caught another one by the arm.

"I'm looking for Dmitri," she said.

He barked into a walkie-talkie. "We need to find the daughter," he told someone. "Excuse me," he said to Gaia, shaking her off as he ran to round up Tatiana.

Gaia felt sick and desperate. And cold inside. She had to know. She'd been told her father was dead before, but this—coming from someone so close—Natasha really seemed to know. Rivulets of dread snaked through her heart as she made her way back to the caravan of cars and vans hidden behind a warehouse. A huge square light created daylight on the deserted street. It was like a movie set. Only this was real life, and Gaia had to find out the ending. Now.

Then she saw him. Dmitri. Standing off to the side, eerily still among all the activity. Dressed in black, his close-cropped gray-haired head pale in the light, he stared at her from across the street. She met his eyes and felt drawn toward him. She stopped running and walked, her stride even and purposeful, willing the space between them to shrink more quickly with each step.

"It's not true, right?" she asked, stopping a foot away from him.

He just gazed back at her, his eyes impossibly sad, the blue of them as open and endless as a noontime sky over a freshly dug grave.

"Dmitri. Is it true?"

He shook his head. "We don't know," he said. "There is no way we can be sure. Given what we know about Natasha, it's definitely possible."

Gaia knew Natasha could be lying. She'd seen her father rise from the dead more than once. But the possibility of it made her tired. Exhausted, in fact. Like her heart was made of granite. `If it were true, then she had totally failed him.` And if it weren't true? She wasn't any closer to finding him than she had been the night he disappeared. It was all too much.

She didn't know if she took the last step toward the old man or if he moved toward her, but Gaia felt his arms fold around her as she closed her eyes and stood trembling with confusion, allowing herself for one brief moment to feel the comfort of another human being. She'd searched so long for her father—wasted so many years hating him when she should have just been glad he was alive. Glad to share a planet with him. And when she was supposed to be watching out for him, she'd lived nose to nose with his wanna-be murderers, never lifting a finger to help him. Guilt turned her insides to custard. She thought she'd die of this feeling. The only thing that would ease the pain was her father. Her father. And she was farther away from him than ever.

And after all he'd done for her, she'd been so inept and useless—it was as bad as if she'd tried to murder him herself.

It was a touching sight, the young mournful girl in the old man's arms. Gaia barely noticed when Natasha's paddy wagon started up and drove past her and Dmitri down the artificially lit street. But

Natasha's face gazed dispassionately from the window. Watched Gaia as she pulled away. Receded as the truck gained speed. Soon she was nothing but a speck in a tiny rectangle of light, disappearing down the dark, desolate streets of Brooklyn.